ORCHARD BOOKS

First published in Great Britain in 2016 by The Watts Publishing Group

1 3 5 7 9 8 6 4 2

Text © Val Hudson, 2016

A CIP catalogue record for this book is available from the British Library.

ISBN 978 1 40833 740 0

Typeset in Helvetica Neue by Avon DataSet Ltd, Bidford-on-Avon, Warwickshire

Printed and bound in Great Britain by Clays Ltd, St Ives plc

The paper and board used in this book are made from wood
from responsible forests.

Orchard Books
An imprint of Hachette Children's Group
Part of The Watts Publishing Group Limited
Carmelite House
50 Victoria Embankment
London EC4Y 0DZ

An Hachette UK Company
www.hachette.co.uk

www.hachettechildrens.co.uk

BOYWATCHING... UP CLOSE

CHLOE BENNET

ORCHARD

Also by Chloe Bennet

Boywatching

My Enemy's Friend

'Don't look now,' said Sally, as she pulled me off the pavement and into a small puddle.

Of course I tried to look, past her bouncing head and her waving arms.

'Point the other way,' she said, now sounding almost hysterical even for Sally (who can be over-excitable at the best of times).

'What? Where? Why?' I said, noticing that Sally had gone rather pink as she waved her arms about in front of me – as if she could somehow block out all the view if she waved hard enough.

But there was no 'hard enough'. At that very moment I could see behind her. To the two figures who were walking ahead of us towards the entrance to the football ground. One was tall, dark and indisputably handsome even from behind. With floppy dark hair, tight jeans and shirtsleeves rolled up just the right amount to show off perfect tanned arms.

One of those arms was steering a short, high-heeled, long-haired, short-skirted girl, who was tripping along in a hideous sort of I'm-just-a-helpless-girl-and-you're-a-big-strong-man way. Just from the back of her head I could tell that she was gazing up at him with an expression of revolting sickliness.

Unbearable.

Unbearable to the power of nine hundred.

I looked at Sally, who was now slightly less pink, but looking back at me with such an expression of concern that I realised it showed. It showed that there was a pretty good chance that I might cry.

'But he said he wasn't coming back till tomorrow.' I could only just get the words out. 'He said he couldn't see me till after term started. He said he'd be jet-lagged. He said...' My voice trailed off.

We both looked towards the entrance. They were now nearly at the gate. At that moment the short girl was saying something, and the tall boy was looking down at her and laughing. They went into the gate and passed out of sight.

'I'm going home,' I said to Sally. 'Somehow the charm of buying a welcome-home present for

Mark has worn off.'

That was yesterday, and today's today. Which doesn't seem to be any better than yesterday. And why would it be, when it's only been a mere twenty-four hours since you've discovered that the love of your life has betrayed you with your very, *very* worst enemy?

I pulled the laptop towards me, unable to resist having one more look at his picture on the St Thomas's website. Only the sixty-fourth look that morning, but definitely, definitely this was the last time.

With one click there was Mark again, all laughing and dimply. With his dark floppy hair and his knowing but intelligent smile – gazing deep into my eyes as I gazed deep into his, wondering how someone so beautiful could be so treacherous.

He was absolutely perfect, except for a crooked collar. Yesterday I was enchanted by the crooked collar; after all, a hugely intelligent boy has better things to do with his time than make sure his collar's straight. Hasn't he? But now it just looks like a crooked collar.

Your looking @ him arent you?????

The sound of the Tardis signalled a text message from Sally. My BFF has an absolute fixation with Dr Who and everything to do with him, and occasionally an uncanny way of knowing what I'm thinking.

Also she has yet to learn the proper place for an apostrophe. There's never a wrong time to insert the right apostrophe. Even on a text message. Even if you're feeling the kind of pain that wouldn't be out of place in a Shakespearian tragedy. As my ultimate ambition is to be a prize-winning writer, I'm quite keen on proper punctuation. Although I realise this makes me a bit unusual.

I should explain, though, that I'm not really unusual in any other way. Like most people, I have a dysfunctional family (apart from my mum, who's lovely) – ghastly stepfather, greasy monosyllabic older brother; a challenging relationship with a lot of my teachers at school; all sorts of concerns about my friends; worry and misery about the boy who I thought was my boyfriend; and a fear of anyone noticing my badly plucked eyebrows.

Today is the last Friday of the summer holidays, and I'd never imagined it would be a day of aloneness and introspection and sadness. The aloneness and introspection is good because as a future award-winning writer I need to introspect a lot. But the sadness is not so good.

I am at home alone, as discussed, because Mum is out being a professional hairdresser, and my ghastly stepfather, Ghastly Ralph, is at the Jobcentre trying to get his job back. (He was caught doing some betting thing with the office central computer. You really, really shouldn't use the central computer in a Jobcentre to calculate betting odds and set up an online gambling company. It's not as if they didn't give him lots of Written Warnings...)

And then there's my brother Steve, who isn't here either. After his shock decision to join the army, he's been away on training. It's all very worrying for Mum, and for me too when I think about it. But I try not to think about it too much, especially as I reckon Steve's not at the moment in mortal danger just from practising press-ups.

'Sally?' I decided to use the voice-to-voice communication system that they've cleverly put into mobile phones.

'Chloe! It's you!' Sally sounded astonished. It actually doesn't take much to astonish Sally. I hope one day she'll grow out of it, because I'm sure it must be bad for you to live your life in a perpetual state of surprise.

'You *were* looking at him, weren't you?' she went on. 'I *knew* it. You mustn't make yourself sadder. If you go on being tragic like this you're going to waste away, like that girl in the book.'

I wondered which girl in which book she had in mind, but knew it would take a long time to work it out. Sally only has a very indirect relationship with reading.

'How can I help being tragic, as you put it?' I asked my BFF, who sometimes can be a bit obtuse. 'When we Skyped last week Mark said how much he was looking forward to getting home and seeing me. He said he missed me. And he wanted to put his arms round me and hug me for ages. I mean that's almost like saying we're properly together, isn't it? Isn't it? Isn't saying that at the very top of the chart?'

There was silence the other end. I wanted to think this was because Sally was trying to find the right wise and comforting words to say to me, but had a sneaking suspicion she was concentrating on looking at herself in the mirror and applying another layer of eyeliner.

The 'chart' was all part of our mastermind subject: the watching of boys. Our quest to understand the nature of the Boy of the Species.

I reckon we had Boy Watching down to a very fine

science. Or art, depending on how you looked at it. And we'd looked at it so long and so hard that we knew it had made a life-changing difference to our lives earlier that summer. At the end-of-term school dance – between our girls' school, Queen Mary's, and the boys' school, St Thomas's – I and my friends had had a bit of a boy triumph.

For me – and after all, this is all going to be pretty much quite a lot about me – it was a dream come true. Mark, who I think – thought – of as beautiful, wise and clever and sensitive and funny, two years older, and way out of my league turned out incredibly, INCREDIBLY, to like me. *Really* like me. I couldn't believe it, but he said so, at the dance and... He. Kissed. Me. And it was all that they say it is, and it was just as wonderful the next time, and I am – was – utterly, utterly bowled over, and would do – would have done – anything for him, and cannot CANNOT stop thinking about him.

But then he went to America for the summer holidays.

His grandfather is the conductor of a famous orchestra there, and he wanted his grandchildren to hear him conduct some important concert in New York. So his parents decided to make a holiday of it and took

Mark and his sister Georgie to America for SIX WEEKS! And that really does need capital letters and an exclamation mark. Six weeks is forty-two days. Or 60,480 minutes. Or 3,628,800 seconds. It was such a long time...and only texts and a handful of Skypes to keep me going. It was a wonder I *didn't* waste away like the girl in the book.

And now. Well, now everything has turned to dust. And not just any old dust. But a bitter and painful dust. Not just because he lied to me, not just because he hasn't contacted me, not just because he was going to a *football* match (me and football simply don't get on), but because he went with Maggie. Or Queen Beeyatch Maggie, as she's popularly known.

QBM is one of the most unpleasant girls you could wish not to meet. She is short, sly and manipulative. (OK, so the short thing isn't her fault, but everything else is.) She is a cruel little bully who manages to get most people on her side simply because the thought of being the target of her beeyatchery is too horrible to think of.

Yet she has a teasing little 'innocent' way with her that the Boys of the Species seem to find fetching. But Mark Anderson was always way too clever to be fooled by such an act.

12

Or so I had believed.

'How's the House of Pox?' I said to Sally, since I felt a sudden urge to change the subject. It was only four hours since Sally had been incarcerated at home with her two young twin brothers, Harris and Jock, and her mother, Liv. The twins were angry young nine-year-olds at the best of times, but being covered in itchy rashes had made them even more toxic than usual.

Sally and Liv had been advised to stay at home with them out of everyone's way, which would almost certainly make Sally bored and Liv more inclined than ever to dive into a bucket of chilled white wine. Metaphorically speaking.

Poor Sally. I guess being grounded at home not ill was almost as bad as being grounded at home ill. And at least if you're ill you've got something to do.

'Soooooo boring,' said Sally. 'Wish I could come over and cheer you up.'

I love Sally's optimism. I expect she really did think that listening to One Direction, eating ice cream and watching *Hunger Games* for the ninety-seventh time would extract someone from the darkest depths of utter despair. Though it would have helped a bit.

'I wish you could, too,' I said. 'Feel like I need my best friend more than ever.'

There was a silence the other end. I started to wonder if the voice-to-voice communication thing on my phone had unexpectedly packed up.

'Awwwwwwwwwwww,' said Sally eventually. And there really were that many w's. 'That's so sweet. You said "best friend". You hardly ever say that.'

Oh dear, Sally was going sentimental on me. 'Well, no,' I said in my best let's-move-on (though still friendly, obvs) voice. 'These things don't really need saying, do they?'

Perhaps I should explain, in case anyone should think I'm being a bit harsh.

Sally *is* my BFF, but I don't often say so, especially not in front of Amy and Gemma who are really, *really* good friends too.

Amy isn't around to comfort me, because at the moment she's busy running round Scotland. Not literally running round Scotland. She's there because she's a brilliant runner, like properly-brilliant-could-run-in-the-Olympics-one-day brilliant. So she often has to go to extreme ends of the country to do a lot of demanding and probably very uncomfortable training. (Personally, I've never seen the charm of running, unless it's to get away from something truly horrible or to chase something truly fantastic. And I've found

14

that in life generally you're not often faced with either extreme.)

Amy is completely lovely: the nicest, kindest girl in the class, if not the school, if not in the country. At the Snog Fest/school dance, she was firmly and totally joined at the hip (I think pretty much literally as well as metaphorically) with Charlie, who's very good-looking and very nice – our favourite combination. Plus he does seem to be a bit devoted to Amy, which in Boy Watching terms – our very subtle and scientific system of points and unpoints – scores him so many Compatibility and Suitability and Fit Points he's almost off the scale.

And then there's Gemma. Where to begin with Gemma? She looks like a model, walks like a model (but isn't one, or not yet anyway); she has a revolting father, an enigmatic, absent mother, who lives by the sea (which is where Gemma's been most of the holidays), and a bit of an obsession with a tall, skinny, Scottish boy called Jezza.

Generally the Boys of the Species are drawn to Gemma like iron filings to a fridge magnet, and she seems to get away with murder. The older generation would call her 'wayward', we would just call her 'cool'. But inside that tall, slim, beautifully straight-haired, confident outside is actually someone who I think is just as uncertain about life, the world, the universe and the whole thing as we are. I haven't tried to tell her this, because mostly we're all too busy trying to deal with life and the universe. And anyway I think she'd be cross.

Thankfully, I didn't have to expand on my theories of friendship this time, though, because we were interrupted by a loud and insistent barking coming from downstairs.

Albert.

Albert is a handsome terrier with a thoroughly misleading air of innocence. He and I have had our ups and downs. Mostly because, being a young and strong and badly educated dog, he gets himself into trouble on a regular basis. And usually it's me who has to get him out of it.

This is all the more awkward because Albert isn't actually ours. He lives in the flat downstairs with Mr Underwood, a horrible hairy man who's even more rude and slob-like than Ghastly Ralph, my stepfather. In an ideal world I would have nothing to do with Mr Underwood (I expect he feels the same way about me), but Albert and I have grown close and I know he appreciates the quality time we have together when I'm allowed to take him for a walk in the park.

'Gotta go,' I said to Sally. 'Good luck with the pox, and send my love to Harris and Jock. Not.'

I had heard our front door slam in a way that could only mean there was some kind of male on its way in. (I've found that females don't slam doors unless they're in their mid-teens and have a really strong point to make to their parents. Usually something to do with what time they're expected back home or whether their room needs tidying.)

I was right. It was Ghastly Ralph.

After the slam there was a loud burp. That's the other thing about the male of the species: they're full of wind, as Shakespeare once said. At least I think it was him.

I opened my door.

'That you, Chloe?' he shouted up the stairs, and gave another burp, just in case I might have thought he didn't mean the first one.

'No, it's the Duchess of Cambridge,' is what I didn't say. After all, that would just be facetious and childish. Though that *is* one of the things Ralph does – he brings out the facetious child in me.

'Yup,' I said heading towards the kitchen, where the burps were coming from now. 'I've got your laptop. Just doing some work on it.'

This wasn't strictly true, unless you counted checking out the St Thomas's website for photos of a certain Mark Anderson as work. But it was important to establish the principle of my free access to the ghastly one's laptop, and besides, it *was* true that I had a holiday project to do on the poets of the First World War.

'Your mother's coming home early,' said Ralph, not looking up as he rummaged around in the bottom of the fridge. 'Not feeling well.' With a sigh of satisfaction he brought out a can of his favourite extra-strength lager.

Still without looking round he padded out of the kitchen in the direction of the sitting room. He walked with the kind of rolling motion that a bowl of jelly might have if it were wearing outsize jeans.

I had an internal bet with myself that within forty-eight, or possibly forty-nine, seconds I would hear the sounds of football commentary coming out of the TV. (You can always find a game of football on some channel at any given time, I reckon. Or at least you can if you're Ralph.)

Sure enough, twenty-one seconds later: '...Brazil unlucky to have missed that pass,' said a voice against the background noise of a loud, shouty crowd.

You might get the impression that football and all that goes with it isn't a favourite thing of mine. Well, you would be sooo right. It's probably not the game's fault. As such. It's just what it does to the people watching it – and to the air quality in the sitting room. (I'm talking the pungent odour of stale beer, of things recently fried, and seemingly endless quantities of methane (qv wind).)

I shut the sitting room door on the whole sorry mess just as young Albert downstairs started up again. His barks were coming in such quick, excited succession that I began to fear for his vocal cords.

This time the front door opened quietly, and a moment or so later closed even more quietly.

Mum.

I was glad she wasn't doing a late night at the hairdressing salon; they always seemed to make her so tired. Besides, if there were two of us we might be able to wrestle the TV remote from Ghastly Ralph's sticky grasp.

As a gesture of solidarity, and with heart-warming daughterly devotion, I filled up the kettle to make her a cup of tea. For me, tea is right up there with football as a thing not to like. I have never seen the appeal of all that brown, bitter wetness. But still, mums tend to love the stuff, so if she wasn't feeling well, the least I could do was boil some water for her.

'There you are, love,' said Mum as I came into the kitchen. She looked rather pale. So I once again resisted the temptation to take her up on this habit of hers of stating the obvious.

'Sure am,' I said in what sounded a falsely hearty tone even to me. I didn't think now was the moment to burden her with talk about the unendurable tragedy that is my life. 'Thought you'd like some tea, Mum.'

I wrestled, for the thousandth time, with the curly lead that connected the kettle to the plug. It had a mind of its own, and it was not a helpful mind. With its unerring ability to tie knots in itself it had been enraging generations of Bennets for years. It was right up there with football and tea as a thing to hate.

'Thanks, love.' Mum was taking off her coat, which was the sort of safe brown colour that doesn't show the dirt. It had a threadbare bit on its left elbow which I could see she'd painstakingly and carefully patched up. For some reason this made me want to cry.

'They want someone to help around the salon for the next few days,' Mum was saying, unaware of the effect her coat was having. 'I thought you might like to give it a go. Earn you a few bob to spend before term starts.'

I didn't know quite what a bob was, but something to 'spend before term starts' had immediate appeal. There were lots of things I wanted to do – like go bowling, buy a particular pair of black boots, see a film, upgrade my phone – which all seemed to cost so much more money than I had.

'That'd be great, Mum,' I said, pouring the hot water into a mug. I carried it into the sitting room for her, and left her to debate the evening's TV channel with her other – but not remotely better – half.

I headed off to my room. I had some thinking to do.

Hairy Business

I shut my bedroom door with a thump.

This wasn't the thump of petulance (such a great word – unless it's applied to oneself, of course). It was just a necessary thump because all the doors in the house seem to have swollen over the years. (Probably due to all the male methane.) So I can only shut my door by swinging at it hard with my right hip. I expect one day I won't be able to get it open again. I'll be trapped, only to be found days later, a gibbering, dehydrated wreck writing the first page of my novel over and over again.

But for now I had better things to worry about.

Last night I had – in a fit of what might even be described as petulance – deleted every single message and picture of Mark I'd ever received or sent. It had taken me ages. I'd also blocked and then deleted all his contact numbers and unfriended and unfollowed him on every form of social media known to boy or girl.

Even if he tried to get in touch with me I wouldn't know.

It was OVER. The boy I'd fallen head over heels in love with didn't exist.

My life had to start all over again.

Amy and Gemma were coming home on Saturday, and I needed both of them to know what to expect before I saw them. As a future prize-winning author, I decided to put it all in writing in an agonised but painfully moving blog.

'On a scale of nought to five hundred trillion,' I wrote, 'my life is unbearable to the point of four hundred and ninety-nine trillion and...' At which point I realised I didn't know how big a trillion was, and rather lost heart in the whole enterprise.

Instead I just texted: Welcome back to Boringsville! Come and see me tomorrow. Can't wait! xxxxx Chloe

And with that I switched off and steeled myself to do some work and read a poem by Wilfred Owen.

No wonder I'd been putting it off, the First World War

poets were never going to end happily.

It was a rotten choice for a summer project.

Saturday morning started a lot earlier than Saturday mornings are meant to start. It was only half past seven when there was a cheery knock on my door.

'Time to get up, love,' said Mum. 'Don't want to be late on your first day.' She pulled the handle down, for all the world as if that meant she might actually be able to open the door.

'Oh dear,' I could hear her say. 'Stuck again.'

'Don't worry, Mum,' I said from under the duvet. 'I'm already up.'

Horrible, horrible business, getting up in the morning.

Ten minutes later and I'd eased open the door (must remember to tell Ralph that it was only a matter of time before the handle came off), and by holding my breath quite a lot, had managed to get through the business of using the bathroom. (Ghastly Ralph has a way of bringing the pungent smell of methane with him everywhere he goes. It is impossible not to know where he is, or where he has just been.)

Dressing was a bit trickier. The not very happily

named 'Happy Hairliners' where my mum worked was neither upmarket nor downmarket. I had no idea what you wear to work on your first day at a middle-market salon.

Nor what you should do with your hair.

In the end I put on my skinniest jeans and my second favourite crop top. And I piled my hair up on the top of my head in a sort of carefully managed but also wild-and-carefree manner. (When I first did this, Sally told me that I was being soooo predictable and on trend. I had to be quite sharp with her. After all, I said, just because some numpty YouTube video tells us to tie our hair in a ponytail it doesn't mean anyone who ties their hair in a ponytail is in thrall to the said numpty YouTube video. I feel quite strongly about this.)

As Mum and I set off towards the bus stop I felt rather pleased that I had the distraction of a sort-of job on Day Two of Utter Misery.

Of course I had told Mum about the moment when the bottom fell out of my world, but I don't think she really grasped the truly terrible nature of the feeling of abandonment and hurt I had.

'Are you sure it was him?' was her first response.

I gave her short shrift. And anyway, I said after the shrift, it wasn't just me who saw them.

And then the best she could come up with next was 'Are you sure it was her?' That got even shorter shrift.

I realise that Mum meant well. She had only met Mark once, when he came round to our house just before he went to America, and she just couldn't believe this paragon of wonderfulness that she's heard so much about could possibly betray me.

She and me both.

By half past ten I was ready to go back to bed. Who knew that standing around smiling and trying to look busy could be so utterly exhausting?

Mum and the other two stylists were rushing around and crimping and chatting and washing and snipping. But my only exciting moments came when there was a bit of chopped hair to sweep up, or someone needed some foil cut up.

The manager of the salon was a fearsome woman who had a brittle platinum helmet on her head. Presumably she had her hair 'done' pretty well every day to encourage her punters to do likewise.

'Towels!' she suddenly shouted at me, and pointed to a pile in the corner. I rushed to pick them up and went downstairs to put them in the washing machine. I was amazed at how excited I was by the change of scene.

When I got back upstairs, the scary helmeted manager had disappeared and the noise of chat and blower was nearly deafening. Sometime later, in the middle of all the noise, I could hear the phone ringing.

Excited again at the thought of having something to do, I went to pick it up. 'Happy Hairliners, can I help you?' I said in my best grown-up voice.

'Oh, hello there,' said a nice, quite old-sounding voice. 'I'm so sorry about this, but I've got to cancel my appointment for Monday morning. Our dog's just had multiple puppies. Early. And I can't leave the house for the moment.'

'Oh how brilliant!' I said, forgetting my grown-up voice, and really wanting to know about the puppies. 'Are they all right?'

'Yes, they're fine. But there are seven of them and they are very rambunctious,' she said, sounding nicer and nicer. Plus rambunctious is one of my favourite words, even though it's very hard to spell. 'But I'll have to ring you back next week to make another appointment. OK? The name's Anderson. Patricia Anderson.'

I felt like I was going to pass out. I hadn't actually met her, but I knew several things about Mark's mother. One, that she was kind and funny, two, that she was something big in television, three, that she was called Patricia.

'Thank you,' I just about managed to say. 'I'm sure that will be fine. Thank you.' And with a little more unnecessary thanking, I put the phone down.

Vaguely remembering that the way to stop yourself fainting was to put your head between your knees, I sat down at the reception desk, bent over and found myself looking closely at the floor.

In between feeling inexpressibly sad that I'd never get to know Mrs Anderson or the puppies, I examined the rubbish under the desk – piles of dust, hair, a penny, a bent paperclip, a playing card and a pencil sharpener. Perhaps someone somewhere was playing bridge with a 51-card deck and keeping score with a very blunt pencil.

Bathos, I thought to myself as I felt more and more blood rush to my upside-down head. That's what this is – the appearance of the commonplace in the midst of catastrophe. Here I am, feeling a deeply tragic sense of loss and confusion, and I'm analysing the sad little dusty things that never made it to the wastepaper basket.

Perhaps I am going mad.

'Chloe!' It was Helmet-Hair back from wherever she spent her two-hour lunch hour. 'What on *earth* are you doing?'

I sat up straight, trying to look alert despite the rushing of blood going the other way, 'Just going to sweep up the dirt here, Mrs Cadwallaby.' (Because, yes, that was her name. It's a name that just begs to be twisted into something highly appropriate and utterly hilarious, but for the life of me I can't think what that is.)

'Well, then, better get on with it,' she said in her usual clipped tones.

As I straightened up from sweeping up the floor, dustpan and brush in hand, I saw out of the corner of my eye two familiar figures approach the entrance to the salon. One was a sweet-looking girl, dressed in tracksuit and trainers, curly hair scraped back under a baseball cap, the other a tall, crinkly-eyed man with quite a lot of grey in his thick dark hair.

It was Amy, the super-swift runner, and her father, The Dad Who. (His full name is The Dad Who You'd Most Like If You Didn't Like Your Own, because he's absolutely that sort of dad. He teaches photography, truly seems to love the company of his daughter, and is always there with wise advice if you should ever need it. Which often we do.)

'Amy!' I couldn't help crying out, even though salon assistants are supposed to be seen but not heard. 'You're back!' There I go again, my mother's daughter when it comes to pointing out something that really doesn't need pointing out.

I rushed over and gave her a huge hug, unfortunately tipping out the contents of the dustpan all over her as I did so.

'Yay, Chloe!' said Amy as she brushed herself down. 'Lucky this tracksuit needs a wash.' There. What did I say about her being nice?

'Well, it certainly does now,' said The Dad Who, looking down at me quite tolerantly, and with a hint of real crinkle in his smile.

'We just came by to say hi,' said Amy. She and The Dad Who waved at Mum, who was in the middle of painting an elderly woman's hair. Mum, whose hands were full of pins and paint and cotton wool, couldn't do anything but smile back. 'Also to say we've just seen Gem, and she's said to come round this evening. Merv's out, so we could do pizzas or whatever.'

'Great,' I said, really meaning it. This was good news on all fronts.

Especially Merv being out. Merv, Gemma's dad, was tall and fat and always dressed like he was some kind of aging rock star; it was not a good look. He also managed to be both boring and sinister at the same time. His house was by far the richest and poshest of anyone's we knew. Nobody seemed quite sure where the money came from, supposedly some TV game-show format sold all over the world, but we were convinced something criminal was involved and his gains were ill-gotten.

But there was always a brilliant choice of pizzas in his state-of-the-art kitchen.

'Can I help you?' Helmet-Hair was heading our way. And sounding particularly acid-tongued, because clearly the servants having friends drop in was strictly not allowed.

'Thank you, but we were only making a very quick visit, because we haven't seen our friend here for ages,' said The Dad Who. 'So sorry to interrupt the work, we'll be on our way now.' And he gave such a charming smile that I could see Helmet-Hair melt before my very eyes.

I backed away from Helmet-Hair, knowing her

meltiness wouldn't last once The Dad Who had gone, and bent down to brush up the sad little dusty things again.

Happily there was by now a lot more hair to sweep up in the salon, and lots more bits of foil to cut up. I was able to spend the remainder of the day with something to do, and thinking about seeing my friends again.

As well as trying to forget about Patricia Anderson's puppies.

Weigh hay! Sally's text came through as Mum and I sat on the bus going home. Sometimes you have to read Sally's texts out loud to get the gist. No moor quaranteen!! Coming tonite!!xx

Great! I sent back, and I meant it. It would be good to have everyone there in my hour of need.

'Mrs Cadwallaby seemed pleased with you, love,' Mum was saying as we watched a massive traffic jam build up in front of us. 'At least, she wants you to come again on Monday. So that's good, isn't it?'

Mum was looking slightly anxiously at me as she said this. I think she knew as well as I did that 'pleased with me' and 'Mrs Cadwallaby' simply didn't go together. But I could feel the new notes and coins in my pocket, and was already imagining myself in that particular pair of black boots that had caught my eye on my favourite website.

'Yes, Mum,' I said, as I settled into my seat for what looked likely to be a very long time – this was a rush hour that had no element of rush in it at all – 'it's very good.'

She was looking paler than ever. I half thought of asking her what Patricia Anderson was like, but her eyelids were flickering, and I knew any second now she'd be dead to the world.

What seemed like *hours* later – it's amazing how time doesn't fly when you're stuck on a bus – we got back home.

Maybe it was the smell of the two of us, but something threw Albert into a frenzy of high-pitched barking as we came into the hall and passed his door.

With the sound of a bang and a curse, the door opened. Holding the dancing, yapping Albert by his collar was the hairy one, AKA Mr Underwood.

He looked at us angrily, as if it were us who were making all the noise.

'Oh,' he said gracelessly, 'it's you. You're meant to

be the plumber.'

I wanted to ask Mr Underwood exactly who had 'meant' us to be the plumber. And if I'd been even braver, I would have suggested that his pyjama bottoms were 'meant' to be worn in bed rather than when opening the front door. He was not a pretty sight.

'Oh dear, is something wrong?' said Mum. 'Is there anything we can do to help?' Mum has a bigger compassion gene than anyone else I've ever met. The slightest sign of someone in trouble and it didn't matter how horrible they were, she'd give you the (painstakingly darned) coat off her back.

'Not unless you're a fully qualified plumber, no,' said the unpleasant hairy one unpleasantly. 'There's water all over the kitchen floor, and someone needs to find out where it's coming from and stop it.'

I'm sure Mum was all set to wipe it up, but was fortunately interrupted by the arrival of a man dressed in a bright-blue boiler suit with the words 'Practically Perfect Plumbing' sewn on it.

'At last,' said Mr Underwood as gracelessly and charmlessly as ever. 'This way.' And he ushered the rather bewildered-looking plumber past the dancing Albert and into the kitchen at the back.

'I wonder,' I said to Mum as we climbed the stairs

to our flat, 'if it's a good idea to call yourselves "practically perfect". I mean, wouldn't you rather have an "absolutely perfect" plumber?'

'Perhaps they just want you to think of them as being very practical,' said Mum, amazingly entering into the spirit of my question.

I thought this was such an interesting point that at first I didn't notice that there were some strange noises coming from the bathroom. The door was shut, but you could still hear a rather low-key splashing and gurgling sound. A bit like a slowly draining basin, or a washing-up bowl filling up, or – I looked at Mum, and she looked at me.

'Ralph!' she cried and opened the bathroom door. Through the mists of steam and methane we could see the Ghastly One's head slumped back against the end of the bath as the water overflowed onto the floor where it was already starting to soak out of the door and onto the carpets on the landing.

As Mum darted forward to turn the taps off – happily shielding me from the prospect of seeing any more of my stepfather than was strictly necessary – she cried out again, 'Ralph!'

'Wha'? Wha's goin on?' Ghastly Ralph suddenly came to from what must have been a deep sleep, and with a rush of water leapt up in the bath and grabbed a towel.

Although still protected from the sight of too much Ralph, I looked down at the floor, where I could see how the water must have soaked into Albert and Mr Underwood's kitchen below.

'Put some clothes on and mop this lot up. For *goodness'* sake, just *look* at this mess,' said Mum with a sort of fury I'd never seen before.

'Not my fault, taps…' said Ralph, slurring his words.

It had been a scene that might have been one of great tragedy (don't people drown in the bath? Commit suicide in the bath?) but actually it was just one of farce. Too many extra-strength lagers and a man falling asleep.

I realised I knew just the word for it. *Bathos*.

Revenge is a Dish
Best Eaten With Friends

As I stood in the middle of my room, surrounded by my seven favourite outfits, trying to decide what to wear for our reunion at Gemma's, I thought that actually Fate was doing a neat job of distracting me from my broken heart.

Outside I could hear Mum swabbing and scrubbing and squeezing out water. She'd sent Ralph downstairs to explain everything to Mr Underwood and the practical plumber. He was still down there; if ever the expression Serve Him Right could come in useful, it would be now.

And in between taking off my blue top and putting the white one back on for the third time, I had another great thought: what a strange thing it is that the world depends on boys and girls being attracted to each other, and yet didn't provide for them turning out to be utterly long-term incompatible.

I mean the falling for each other bit is difficult enough. Qv above. But then there's the living together thing. Not that every grown-up man is as repellent as Ralph, or as kind and nice as The Dad Who. There were lots of in-between. But how can you tell if a Ralph might not grow into a Dad Who, and vice versa?

I decided we needed another category in our Boy Watching charts: a Long-Term Prognosis column. Or: what sort of Man do we think the Boy will be?

Selfishly leaving Mum to the joys of water management, I walked to the bus stop, warm in her furry boots. (On Mum they looked comfortable and practical, but on me – with my skinny jeans and high ponytail – they looked cool. I was almost completely sure I was right about that.)

Sally had sent another seven texts to tell me she was going to be late. She sounded a bit hysterical and said we'd know why as soon as we saw her.

Poor Sally. I wondered if you ever grow out of being accident-prone. And then I started wondering what our own Long-Term Prognoses might be. What sort of Women will we Girls turn into? Will Sally ever be highly organised with lots of little Sallys of her own? Or will she be forever getting into scrapes and need looking after? Will we all score points for being Kind to Children and Animals, even if we're Captains of Industry or Bestselling Authors?

I stopped thinking about the prognosis for Poor Sally as I got nearer to Gemma's house and recognised two people walking towards me from the other direction. One was Amy, now out of her dusty tracksuit and in her favourite red dress, and the other was Charlie.

With his arm round Amy, and his fluffy hair and friendly smile, he looked like what he was – kind and funny, and very fond of our friend. It's a measure of how great he is that I didn't feel:

a) irritation that he might somehow muscle in our Girls' Night In or

b) fear and loathing because the sight of him reminded me that his very good friend was one Mark Anderson.

They saw me just as I was starting to feel extra sad because there was now bound to be awkwardness between me and Charlie because of the inexplicably evil behaviour of his friend.

'Chloe!' Charlie cried out, and he waved in the super extra excited fashion that he has when he wanted to make a point. Clearly his point this time was that he was pleased to see me. How nice.

'How's it going? What you been up to over the holidays? Have you been good?' he called out. And when he got close enough he folded me up into a great big exuberant hug. That was nice too.

'Hi, Charlie,' I said. And then, because it was true, 'You smell lovely.'

'Shucks,' he said, 'You don't smell so bad yourself.'

'Cool boots,' said Amy, looking approvingly at my furry feet.

Result, I thought. But before I could get too pleased with myself and how nice I smelt and how cool my boots were –

'You and Mark coming to the Shedz gig with us next Saturday?' Charlie asked.

For a split second I thought how beautifully the words 'you and Mark' sounded, and then I realised that nobody apart from Sally knew there was anything wrong. Everyone else thought that all that had happened since the night of the magical moment at the Snog Fest was that Mark had been in America.

But I was saved from having to answer by Amy. 'Hey, we've no idea what's going on with Gemma and Jezza. Let's decide tomorrow, shall we?' she said to him. 'You've got to go now. Girls only this evening.'

And she looked lovingly up at him and started to put her arms round him. I looked away. I really didn't feel like watching The Long Goodbye. Good friends though they were, the thought of real, proper kissing only made me feel desperately sad.

I started to head towards the horrendously high and electric gate that Gemma's father had surrounded his house with. Heaven knows what kind of grisly secrets needed so much ironwork and electricity to protect them from prying eyes, but it was pretty obvious visitors were not meant to feel welcome.

As I could hear The Long Goodbye was still going on, I started to think about the Shedz gig.

Shedz were the band that the skinny Scottish Jezza played in, the very Jezza that Gemma had such an intense Thing with. But it was a very on-again-off-again Thing. One moment Jezza was cool and funny, and his badness (of which there was a lot) was just part of his charm, the next he was a selfish punk who she hated with a passion. Kind of fascinating, but a bit exhausting for the rest of us.

At last I could hear the Goodbye coming to its end, and I turned round and waved at Charlie, who headed off into the dark, whistling. As I texted Gemma to tell her to open the gate, I found time to think how attractive the male whistle can be when it's not coming from a lecherous builder.

Moments later there was a whirring and buzzing, red lights started flashing and all the gates started to move. Amy and I looked at each other apprehensively like people do in a movie to signal that there are some really impressive and scary CGI action sequences coming up.

Only this time it was just more whirring and creaks.

The huge gates were letting us into the land of gold-plated pizza, existential kitchen appliances – and a Girls' Night In.

The first thing that always strikes me about the kitchen in Merv's mansion is the scale and shininess of it all. Everything is huge, and so gleamy that you could check your eyeliner in pretty much any surface. Even the bar stools (because of course Merv had bar stools) are shiny.

And there are so many gleamy cupboards that it's a wonder Gemma can ever find anything anywhere.

Gemma herself was standing in the middle of all this, dressed in a brilliant blue dress, hair beyond shiny, and looking at her most bored and modelly. I don't think she was bored with us, in fact she'd given us such a rare and real smile when we arrived, and such a hard hug (my second of the evening – I like hugs) that I truly think she was very happy to see us.

No, she was doing her bored negative thing because Merv had just entered the room.

Merv was looking at his fattest and sleaziest. The little buttons on his black corduroy shirt were straining, and the seams on his jeans were bright white with the pressure of keeping themselves together. I couldn't help wondering what would happen if all the stitches gave way at the same time. And then I had to tell myself to think of something else.

'You can go out now, Merv. We don't need anything. Only to be left alone.' Gemma spoke to her father with such disdain that I wondered, not for the first time, who was in charge in this house.

'Well, you've got the takeaway number if you want anything extra, haven't you?' said Merv, pretending his was a normal household with a normal

43

balance of power.

Then he turned with an awkwardly grotesque grin to me and Amy. 'Help yourselves to whatever you fancy, girls. Saturday night's all right for eating, eh?' I had a feeling this might have been a reference to some Stone Age pop song, but wasn't about to ask. We just smiled weakly and hoped he'd go away.

Not getting any reactions to his comments, Merv looked around the room, picked up his man bag (because of course Merv had a man bag) and walked out of the kitchen.

He must have met Sally and let her in just as he was leaving the house, because moments later, there she was, standing in the kitchen.

The silence went on for a lot longer than it should have done.

Sally's face was covered in grey and red dots, and the bits in between the dots seemed to be a not very fetching shade of light yellow.

'Oh dear,' said Amy, because even sweet Amy couldn't disguise her horror. 'It's not the twins' pox, is it?'

'No,' said Sally miserably. 'The twins are nearly better now. No, this is my miracle home-made face pack. For a smooth, spotless skin. Who knew that a mixture of ripe bananas, tomatoes, yogurt, egg white and honey could do this to you?'

'You need to find out what bit of that you're allergic to,' said Gemma not very sympathetically. 'Although having put half a supermarket aisle on your face, it may take some time.'

'I knooooow,' wailed Sally. 'I thought if I put the cures for oily, acne and blackheads together then I'd save time, and I'll be perfect for when school starts and the Shedz gig.'

'Poor Sally,' said Amy, echoing my thoughts entirely. 'We'll just have to find you some anti-allergic or whatever make-up if it hasn't got better by Thursday.'

Thursday was back-to-school day, but I think the more important deadline was next Saturday and the Shedz gig.

'But it'll be all right in a week, won't it?' Sally was still wailing a bit. 'I'll be all right for Saturday, won't I? Rob'll be playing, so I'll see him again, it's been so long, I expect he's forgotten what I look like, although he mustn't see me like this, and the last time he texted he didn't put an x at the end, so I've got to see him, and maybe he'll let me come backstage and perhaps he'll let me have a go drumming again or he'll take me for a coffee first and then, or no, it would be better if he did that afterwards, don't you think?'

Sally was now properly out of breath, which wasn't really surprising given that when she got excited she punctuated her speech even less than her texts.

Rob was the drummer in Shedz, and had been the object of Sally's adoration ever since she'd seen him playing Frisbee with his little sister. This had scored him lots of Kind to Children and Animals points on the Boy Watching chart, and whenever Sally saw him play the drums she'd go into a sort of trance.

We think Rob likes Sally enough, and he's definitely a good guy, but he can be a bit dreamy. I don't think he THINKS. But then – as we've proved in so many of our Boy Watchings – THINKING isn't right up there at the top of the list when it comes to boy skills.

'I think,' I said, because it's something I reckon I'm quite good at, 'that it'll all be fine in a few days' time, and there's no point in worrying about it all just now.'

The others nodded in a sort of noncommittal way.

'OK,' said Sally in a slightly more cheerful voice. 'It's very difficult, all this, isn't it?' she went on, looking at me. I guess she was thinking about my 'difficulties' as well as hers.

And I did know precisely what she meant. It wouldn't exactly make for the title of a self-help bestseller – *All*

This Is Very Difficult, and Other Life Lessons wouldn't fill you with confidence – but still, 'it' *was* pretty difficult and maybe part of the point was realising that.

Before I could get pleased with myself for this thought, Sally said to me, 'So, have you told them?'

'Told us what?' said Gemma instantly, narrowing her eyes at me in a half suspicious, half worried way.

'It's Mark. It's over.' I felt my shoulders droop and the corners of my mouth go down in that rigid way that a mouth has when it's trying not to cry. 'We saw him on Thursday. Going to the football. Draped all over Maggie.'

Even Gemma gasped at that. Amy went completely still, everything about her face showing astonishment.

'We'd spoken over Skype last week,' I went on. 'He said he was looking forward to seeing me, but wouldn't be back till just before term started. He said…' And then I felt I was losing it again, and stopped.

I looked hard at the stony kitchen floor, half thinking it might be nice to lie down and beat my head on something so utterly hard and ungiving.

'Haven't you heard from him?' asked Amy, at the same time as Gemma said, 'What was the match?'

'No, not a thing, not a word. And just some sort of qualifying match thing,' I said. And I realised there was

47

not a crumb of hope. Even if he had bombarded me with handwritten letters because all electronic means of communication were blocked, even if the match had been the greatest cup final of cup finals, I still couldn't begin to imagine why he had returned to the country early and secretly gone out with my very worst enemy.

'It's going to play havoc with all the charts, isn't it?' said Sally. I gave her a steely look, which she didn't notice because she was busy fiddling with the yellow bits of her face. 'After all,' she went on, 'he ticked all the boxes and was top of everything. And now what? I mean it just goes to show, doesn't it?'

I must have looked as dangerous as I felt, because when she looked up and saw my expression she said, 'Sorry,' in a very little voice.

'I can't believe it, Chloe,' said Gemma, 'Of all the boys to turn out to be a…well, anyway. What can we do to cheer you up now? Help yourself to anything here, goes without saying, but what can we DO?'

'Nothing really, just be you,' I said, realising I was on dangerous and unfamiliar ground here saying this stuff out loud. 'Friends, you know. They're what matters.'

There was a bit of a silence.

'But let's talk about something else,' I said, not wanting our reunion to be all about bad things.

'How was training and Scotland, Amy? How's Gorgeous Gregory?' Normally Amy's coach was The Dad Who, but Gregory was her handsome new Scottish coach who was in charge of her long-distance training in the holidays.

'Well, he's not so gorgeous when he's drilling you in a field,' said Amy, who then looked a bit surprised when we giggled. I don't think Amy has been listening in her *double entendre* lessons.

'I mean it was such hard work. Who knew there were so many hills in Scotland?' she went on. Which made me wonder if geography lessons came in the same category.

'But you got the times you needed to get, did you?' I asked, because the one thing I did know about all this running is that it's all about how many minutes and seconds it all takes.

'Yup, Dad and Gregory reckon I'll make it to the championships next year,' said Amy, looking quite smiley and happy and full of health and successfulness.

As I say, Amy is a sweet person, and that's really lucky because otherwise you would just have to hate her.

'What about you, Gem?' I said. 'Have you left Cornwall full of more broken-hearted surfer boys?'

'No idea. Didn't ask them,' said Gemma, more than living up to her reputation for cool.

It had been a feature of our half-term holiday that handsome boys, and even not-handsome boys, looked Gemma's way whenever we went to the beach. Usually they tried to offer her surfing lessons, sometimes they tried to buy her coffee or a Coke, rarely did they get anywhere.

Except one, a Jack Harrington. Who was blonder and browner and taller and better looking than pretty well all of the others. Also, and quite coincidentally given that he lived in Cornwall, he'd been to junior school with Mark and Charlie. So not only did he score LOADS of points on all the Boy Watching charts, but under the guise of seeing his old school friends, he also had a really good excuse to come and see Gemma.

'But it turns out Jack's got an aunt who lives near here,' Gemma went on. 'He's threatening to come and visit next week.'

'That's good, isn't it?' said Sally, sounding quite excited. I think she's got a bit of a crush on Jack. Which was entirely understandable, because he really was incredibly cool and good-looking. (Plus when we first met he'd noticed I was reading *To Kill a Mockingbird*, and had told me what a good book he thought it was.

If ever anyone wanted to win my heart [note to The World] loving the same books I do is a great first step. But I digress. Massively.)

'So he comes here,' Sally was warming to her theme, 'Jezza sees you together and gets all jealous and falls even more in love with you because he's just soooo jealous, and then you go back to Jezza and then Jack needs someone to console him and that's where I come in!' She looked at everyone with an expression of triumph on her yellow, pink and grey face.

'What about Rob?' said Amy, slightly reproachfully. I think her happy-ever-after relationship with Charlie makes her think that everyone has A One and that's it. She wouldn't dream of fancying anyone other than Charlie, so she's got a rather Victorian novel/'Reader I married him' view of the whole thing.

'Oh,' said Sally, the yellow and grey going a bit crestfallen. 'Well, yes, of course, but once he sees me with Jack he'll know he's got to work SO HARD to keep me. Or get me properly in the first place, I suppose, now I come to think of it,' she finished, with a world-weary sigh.

'And now *we* come to think of it, this is all getting a bit silly,' said Gemma. 'Because, actually, if we're going to play that game then it's Chloe who Jack ought to go out with. She's the one who *really* has a reason to make someone jealous.'

Everyone looked at me. I knew I was still much too raw to play games, but they meant well, and – who knew – perhaps a bit of handsome distraction was just what I needed.

'Please let's not think about it for now,' I said, really meaning it.

Although the concept of Revenge had its appeal, all I really wanted was the warm cosy feeling of being with my friends again. And possibly the warm cosy feeling of Merv's gold-plated luxury pizza.

I turned to the giant, shiny, promising-looking Merv fridge, opened its door and starting selecting the very best comfort food it had to offer.

Dog Day

Sunday morning was brilliant and bright and warm.

It seems to have no truck with sadness, I thought, as I lay in bed looking at the sun's rays lighting up my bedroom. (Incredible how there could be so much dancing dust in the air which you couldn't know about until it's all lit up. Do we breathe it all in? And if so doesn't it clog us up?)

'Chloe?' Mum was knocking on the door. 'Breakfast is ready, and Mr Underwood wants to know if you'll take Albert for the day.'

And so life goes on. Even in the midst of abject misery, breakfast has to be eaten and dogs walked.

'Coming, and yes, OK,' I said, kicking the sheet off me.

I headed towards the bathroom, which was still on the puddly side after the Great Overflow of the night before. It smelt even more pungent than usual and there was a squelchy quality to the carpet outside. Yuck.

I took a deep breath and set to work on the weekend's goal of twenty plucks of the eyebrows. Somehow abject misery seemed to help with the pain, and I got to Pluck Twenty without much trouble. But I couldn't help thinking that extreme misery was a high price to pay for painless plucking.

As I got dressed I noticed that there was a loud silence coming from the kitchen. Usually a Sunday morning was filled with the noise of Ghastly Ralph ranting and raving as he read the papers. An illegal immigrant there, a greedy property company here, something European, something Russian, and – most terrible of all if you're a Ralph – a bit of Political Correctness Gone Mad. (A phrase that he seemed to think he'd only just invented. Every weekend.)

But today all was nothing and no noise. As I got nearer to the kitchen I realised why. Seated at the table, opposite a very quiet and stern-looking Mum, was a totally silent Ralph, looking a bit pale underneath his beardy and bloaty skin.

He was looking at his cup of tea as if it had done something a bit politically correct, and therefore needed him to hate it properly. There wasn't a sign of a sausage, or a piece of bacon, or a piece of deep-fried sliced white bread – the natural foodstuffs of a Ralph.

Clearly Ralph was a) in the doghouse and b) hungover.

Fully deserved on both counts, I thought.

'There you are, love,' said Mum, when she saw me in the doorway. (There will come a point when I won't notice her habit of stating the obvious, but it's not here yet.) 'Your stepfather is very sorry about what happened last night. I think he's got an apology to make.'

She looked across the table at her beloved. At least I assume there was a once-upon-a-time when this man was her beloved. When she – such a kind and soft and lovely person, who looked like what she was – actually fell for this blubbery, bloaty, goatee-beardy individual and saw love's young dream. Or love's middle-aged dream.

I know my father was her real love. I just know it. But that's another story.

'Yes,' said the bloaty one interrupting my thoughts. 'Sorry, Chloe. Fell asleep in the bath. Working too hard. Very tired. You know the sort of thing.'

Yup. Absolutely. Like I'd know about necking ten cans of lager and passing out in the bath. But I looked at Mum, who seemed as tired as she was angry, and I decided not to make a thing of it.

'OK,' I said, looking hard at the spice rack over the fridge. Anywhere but at Ralph. 'Have you heard anything from Steve?' I asked Mum, just to change the subject.

'Well, it's funny you should ask,' said Mum, suddenly looking much better and much more cheerful. 'He just wrote this morning to say he's got leave and he's going to come and see us next Sunday. And he's bringing a friend. Isn't that lovely?'

'Lovely' isn't really how I'd describe the prospect of seeing my pockmarked, monosyllabic older brother. He hadn't been far enough away for long enough for my heart to have grown fonder, and I was pretty sure he was still the same irritating individual that he'd always been.

'Oh. Yes. Lovely,' I said trying to sound like I meant it.

Mum had hated Steve going off to join the army. There'd been so much on TV lately about the First World War, that I think she'd immediately imagined him cowering in a trench, before climbing over the barbed wire and being shot at in no-man's-land. But I reckoned the greatest threat to him probably came from a shouty sergeant major sending him on five-mile runs.

I reached into the fridge for some fortifying OJ. One of the many benefits of being Without Steve was that you could open the fridge and it wouldn't be full of empty cartons. (What is it with boys and putting empty things back in the fridge?) Plus one of the benefits of Ghastly Ralph losing his appetite was that there was a plate of sausages lying in there unloved. I grabbed one, because I knew a small border terrier who'd appreciate it.

'I'm going to take Albert to see Sally,' I said as I poured myself a large glass of juice, just because I could.

Sally had put herself under house arrest again, due to the colour of her face. She had vowed not to let anyone outside the family see her until she'd gone back to normal. So I'd reckoned that a visit from me and Albert – we pretty much counted as family – would be just the thing to cheer us all up.

The merry sound of Albert barking his head off got louder and louder as I went downstairs.

It was almost as if he knew he was soon going to be allowed out and away from his horrible owner, crabby old Mr Underwood. (Although Mum told me he wasn't actually old – 'only' about fifty, she said – but he certainly seemed old to me. And definitely crabby.)

Mr Underwood opened the door just as I started to knock on it. Albert was bouncing around at his feet, looking up at me in a state of gratifyingly high excitement. Mr U was wearing his stained old tartan dressing gown, circa 1999, and had a piece of toast in his hand. I noticed the jam on his toast was starting to slide gently downwards.

'You're late,' he said to me, as the large lump of jam slid a little nearer the edge of his toast. I wasn't late, and would have said so had I not been mesmerised by the sliding jam.

'Here's his lead,' said the crabby one, handing me a piece of string that had been hanging on the back of the door. The extra movement gave the jam a little added momentum and it slid off the toast and landed on the carpet.

I'd decided to head off to the park and then take a bus to Sally's. That way Albert could get rid of some of his youthful energy and high spirits in the open, and he'd be all sleepy for the afternoon at Sally's. Which would mean that she and I could get on with the serious business of eating ice cream and watching movies without having to entertain him.

The park looked relatively empty when I got there. Just a few dogs going about their business – and each other's. (Extraordinary how much fascination the poo of another dog holds for the average dog.) So I decided to let Albert off his string.

He shot off with such speed that soon he was just a speck of fur in the distance. I started to wonder if I'd done the right thing. Albert had form when it came to running off and causing trouble.

But I could see that he'd soon found some friends. In the distance, a group of girls of about my age were crowding round him and obviously showing him a good time and a lot of admiration.

I only had about thirty seconds of feeling relieved and pleased, because as I got closer I could see that in the middle of the group of about seven or eight girls was one who was clearly the leader. Although she was shorter than any of the others you could just tell by the way that everyone else was pointing towards her – as if they were waiting to be told what to think – that she was the boss.

Of course she was the boss. And not just the

boss, but the biggest Queen Beeyatch boss of them all. Maggie.

Oh how do I hate thee, let me count the ways, I found myself thinking. I knew it was a quote from somewhere, but in the heat of the hate couldn't have said where.

I really didn't want QBM to see me. She'd only have something vile to say. She didn't know I'd seen her with Mark. She didn't know I knew she'd won. But if you're a professional Beeyatch, seeing someone on their own, when you're surrounded by your own cohorts of suckers-up (and QBM was always surrounded by cohorts), you can never resist having a go.

If I could just get Albert's attention, I thought, if I could just get him to come to me before they recognised me, then I might get away with it. If only—

'It's Chloe!' The QB's voice rang out. 'Look everyone, it's sad old Chloe! Lonely old Chloe! Out for a sad old, lonely old walk in the park old Chloe!'

Without pausing for breath, and while the others looked on with a smirk or an expression of outright relief that they weren't me, she went on, 'This your dog, Chloe? See how he wants to be with us, and not you! Poor little dog. Fancy having to go for a walk with Chloe.'

The others gave a snigger or a titter. Gleeful that they were on the winning side.

I had only one hope. Only one card to play. Reaching into my pocket I unwrapped the sausage and as I took it out called, 'Albert, come here,' with as much authority as I could possibly inject into my voice.

Whether it was the smell of desperation or sausage that drew him to me, something made him come hurtling in my direction. He leapt up at me, grabbed the sausage and bounced around at my heels as I turned away and walked as quickly as I possibly could in the opposite direction.

I could sense some muttering behind me, but nothing more. Not even the queenest of beeyatches could turn that moment into a victory.

As Albert and I headed off towards the bus stop, I felt such an overwhelming affection for my furry friend that we had to stop while I picked him up to give him a cuddle.

Not wanting to risk another encounter with the QB of QBs, I put him back on his piece of string for the rest of our walk. Albert didn't like this at all, and yapped and pulled all the way to the bus stop, obviously thinking it all a poor reward for his loyalty.

Almost everyone we saw in the park seemed to be

part of a couple being coupley. I guess it being a sunny Sunday, and us being in a park, and people being people, it wasn't so surprising that couples gathered together to do their thing. But – being so very single – I was noticing them all for the first time and finding it rather painful.

It seemed like Fate was making a point of showing me how good life could be...for other people.

Other People

What with one thing and another, by the time we got to Sally's house I was in urgent need of comfort in general and ice cream in particular.

'Thought you were never coming,' said my best friend, not at all comfortingly, when she opened the door. 'Harris and Jock are being a nightmare, and Mum's locked herself in her room.'

Her face was looking rather pink under its grey and yellow.

'Why? What do you mean? What's happened?' I said, already giving up on the idea of being comforted. Harris and Jock and the nightmare were predictable enough, especially after their recent pox, but Liv, Sally's mum, was a more alarming kettle of fish altogether.

'Mum had a phone call this morning. She didn't say who it was, or what they said, but she went all white.

63

And then she went out for a bit, and then she came back with like LOADS of bottles, and then she went to her room, and she hasn't come out even though Harris and Jock have been yelling and yelling at each other all morning.' Sally paused for breath. She looked at me slightly as if it was all my fault and slightly as if I might be able to help.

'What are the terrible twins doing now then? Why's it all so silent?' I said. Although it wasn't completely silent because Albert was snuffling and whining and generally wanting attention. I gave him a piece of the cheese that was sitting on the corner of the kitchen table. It looked rather strangely shaped and foreign, and perhaps not a favourite with border terriers, but it seemed to do the trick.

'They've gone to their room. I think if it's quiet that means they're beating each other up,' said Sally.

'Well, then that's one thing less to worry about; we can just wait for one or other to come out alive. What about your mum? Shall I go and knock on her door?' I made the offer a little nervously. It sounded to me like there was a bit of a grown-up problem here.

'Oh *would* you?' said Sally, looking relieved.

I went upstairs, with Sally walking so closely behind me she hit her nose on my elbow. I went quite slowly and slightly dreadingly.

'Liv,' I said as I tapped on her door. She'd always told us to call her 'Liv'. I think she liked to be thought of as one of the younger generation, and she often behaved like one, especially after a bottle or two of Pinot Grigio.

'Liv. Is everything all right?' I said.

There was a snuffling and whining noise from behind the door. For a moment I thought Albert had sneaked round the back of the house and got in through her bedroom window. Then the door was flung open with a theatrical bang.

'*Darling*,' said Liv, peering at me through half-closed eyes. Her grey dress was creased and her blonde hair all over the place. She had an empty glass in her hand, which she put slowly and carefully on the dresser when she saw me looking at it. 'I've had some news. Which takes a bit of getting used to, that's all. Nothing serious. Let's go and have lunch, shall we, darlings?'

She smiled with the air of someone who is enormously drunk but thinks they've got away with it.

Which I guess is not surprising because that's exactly what she was.

We headed down to the kitchen to find that Albert must have decided that he liked the foreign-looking cheese, because the cheese plate was on the floor and there wasn't any sign of it.

'Now, that,' said Liv rather slowly and carefully, 'is a naughty dog. I think he's had all my Brie. Hasn't he? Sally? Has that naughty dog had all my Brie?'

'I don't know, Mum,' said Sally a bit wearily. 'If you say so. I don't know what Brie is.'

Albert was curled up in the corner of the kitchen eyeing us all rather warily. The only things I knew about Brie was that it was French and rich and shouldn't be eaten if you're pregnant. Perhaps it shouldn't be eaten if you're a border terrier either. Albert looked a bit sick.

Hoping we could all move on from this rather extreme cheese and wine party, I offered to get lunch ready.

Except there wasn't much lunch to get ready. Liv's fridge looked a bit like ours when Steve was in residence: full of empty packaging. But I managed to find some lettuce, a bit of English-looking cheese and a large tub of ice cream.

And with these Sally and I headed off for some quiet time with her laptop. I thought a bit of YouTube nonsense would be the perfect thing to distract her from the Liv Drama.

'What do you think's happened?' I said to Sally as I

opened up her giant laptop. 'Is it something to do with your dad?' All we knew about Sally's father was that he was Scottish and he was something secret in the RAF. Or at least we'd always been told that the big photograph in the sitting room of a handsome man in an RAF uniform was her dad. It had been so long since Sally had seen him she could hardly remember him. 'Has he come back with another woman? Or is he a spy who's been captured? Or is he dying of a hideous disease on the other side of the world?' I felt sure there would turn out to be a good plot for a novel in all this.

'I dunno,' said Sally miserably, her odd complexion looking odder than ever. I felt a bit bad that I'd been mentally turning Sally's troubles into a bestselling novel. Perhaps it was time to find her some distraction.

With gritted teeth I found the latest from her favourite vlogger. Soon we were being told exactly how to paint our nails in two colours.

It is a measure of my friendship and support for my BFF that I resisted saying anything throughout this fantastically irritating broadcast.

Much later that day Albert and I set off on our journey back to our respective homes. I'd decided to avoid the park – you never knew when a QB might be lurking behind a bush – so we had a rather long drawn-out walk along the pavements instead. There seemed to be no end to the businesses that needed Albert's inspection, which made for rather jerky progress. In fact, by the time we got back to *chez* Underwood/ Bennet I had almost begun to go off Albert.

But then, as I undid his string outside the crabby one's door, Albert turned to me and jumped up at me and generally tried to lick me. All was forgiven. He could eat as much French cheese and sniff as much poo as he liked so far as I was concerned. He was my Albert, and at this rate would probably be the most reliable male in my life for ever.

Mr Underwood, still in his favourite tartan dressing gown, opened the door and let Albert in with his usual grunt.

I climbed upstairs wondering how Mum had got on after a whole day of having her horrible husband to herself. I determined to be polite to Ghastly Ralph, if only to make life a bit easier for Mum.

Anyway, it wouldn't have to last long, I thought, as I would have to have an early night, tomorrow being a

68

Happy Hairliners day. Lord. Something else to not look forward to.

As I unlocked the door, a blast of boiling hot air hit me in the face. It felt extremely humid and smelt incredibly rank.

'Hello, love,' said Mum, coming out of the kitchen, holding a half-peeled potato. 'We've had a hot old time of it while you've been out,' said Mum, sweat running down the sides of her face. 'But I think Ralph's got the carpets dry now.'

An industrial blower was belching out hot air from the corner of the landing. Underneath the belching noise, I could hear the sound of the TV – and the sound of a roaring crowd. Football.

All my good resolutions disappeared in a second. Ghastly Ralph was being as ghastly as ever. As if installing a heater made everything all right. No doubt he was sitting there with a tin or two of extra-strength lager as a reward for all his hard work.

I looked round the door into the sitting room to test my theory. Yup. Can of Stupid Juice on the table, feet up, remote fallen out of his nerveless fingers, head down, snoring.

Revolting to the power of revolting.

'I'm off to do some work, Mum,' I said, knowing that

69

if I had to talk to Ralph there'd be a nasty scene. 'I'll take Ralph's laptop as it looks like he won't be needing it.'

I grabbed it off the kitchen table, trying not to notice the disappointed look that Mum gave me. I knew she'd make peeling the potatoes last as long a time as possible, so she wouldn't have to go in the sitting room before she had to. It looked like the balance of power was back to its usual self.

Safely in my room I opened up the laptop. I couldn't resist checking Ghastly Ralph's search history. Already in trouble for his illegal spread betting syndicate, I half hoped there'd be evidence of some other dodgy dealings. Something only a bit illegal, but illegal enough to get him locked up. How nice it would be to have Ralph locked up.

There wasn't anything except football results and more football results. I deleted it all and thought that, before I got on to the torment of the First World War poets, I'd torment myself with updating our Boy Watching charts.

I felt rather sentimental as well as sorry for myself when I looked at the early stages of the charts. Right up at the top there was the almost complete project of Amy and Charlie. There were some early Suitability and

Compatibility points, and there were lots of Fit, Looks Good in Jeans, Kind to Children and Animals points. Later there were Good Chat-Up Techniques, more Compatibility points, and then lately lots of Sustainability points. Perhaps we also needed some Selfless Devotion points categories, because over the holidays Charlie had more than proved his devotion by following Amy up to some of her remote training grounds. No greater love hath boy than spending a weekend going somewhere in the middle of nowhere where nothing, but nothing, is going on except a lot of watching his girlfriend running.

Then there was Sally and her massive crush on Rob the Drummer. Ever since Rob scored untold numbers of Kind to Children and Animals points for being so sweet to his little sister, and then turning out to be a drummer just like Sally, I know Sally thinks they're meant for each other. There was a huge flurry of points at the end of the summer term, culminating in all sorts of Compatibility points after Rob let Sally play the drums with him at the Snog Fest. Which led to some cups of coffee together (additionally remarkable because I KNOW Sally hates coffee) on a few occasions over the holidays. But since then there's been a bit of a shortage of Sustainability points, mostly due to

71

Sally's not having heard from him much recently. I hoped all would be resolved at the Shedz gig on Saturday.

Then there was Gemma's chart. Although 'chart' didn't really describe the utterly all-over-the-place records we seem to have of Gemma and her Boy Watching activities. Most of the time there seemed to be her rather difficult relationship with the (very) difficult Jezza, who seemed to be wildly attractive to pretty well every girl (except me). And doesn't he know it. But then there was also the fact that everyone fell at Gemma's feet too. Especially when she was on holiday, on a beach, and in her red bikini. Most of the time it was quite difficult to put all this activity into Boy Watching language. Gemma has her own rules…

Oh, yes, and then there was me. I'd only ever had eyes for the one Boy. Mark, the most handsome and clever and funny and kind of them all. Perhaps I'd been just crazy to think that I could ever hope to be with someone so utterly perfect. But then he said things, and he did things, that showed that he does care. I know he does care. But why… Oh no, here I go again. How can he turn from someone so perfect and perfectly caring into someone so duplicitous? When he'd definitely and definitively said – before our very first kiss even – that he didn't care a hoot for Maggie, that she was only out for number one, it was me, *me*, he wanted to be with.

WHAT'S to become of *me*?

I decided that I'd better get on with a different sort of torment. I'd only made slow progress with Wilfred Owen and his fellow poets, and it was now only three days till back-to-school.

I turned back to the poems with new enthusiasm. Sort of.

So much hopelessness, and death, and destruction, surely it would put my own small misery into some sort of perspective?

Well, that worked.

Although after an hour or so of reading First World War poetry, I decided that poetry is actually quite difficult. And that's a good thing, because if you could really understand it on the first time of reading, it would give you nothing to work on. Also it would make you infinitely and immediately miserable.

...Which is a bit how I felt – in a very minor way of course – when I went into the kitchen to eat some of the potatoes Mum had so carefully peeled. The ghastly one was sitting there, looking sulky, and clutching the inevitable can. Mum bustled about with a pan full of some form of fried meat and some Brussels sprouts.

I was strangely cheered by the sprouts. I am unusual – in this respect as in a number of others – in that I love the Brussels sprout and think it a much-maligned vegetable. After all, it's just a small cabbage. What's not to like?

'God, I hate sprouts,' Ralph said suddenly, watching his wife drain a large number of them. 'And potatoes. Why can't we just have chips?'

'Well, I love them,' I said. 'Thanks, Mum,' I added as I helped myself to a good mound.

We sat and ate in silence. I would have said something, just to relieve the tension, but I was busy wondering which psycho film we reminded me of. Was it the one where the whole family murdered each other actually at the dinner table, or the one where it took them years to hunt each other down all over the world as they bumped each other off one by one?

I headed off to bed as soon as decently possible.

Life. It just keeps on giving, I thought, as I picked up my tweezers, ready to do battle with a bit of errant eyebrow. Which is just as well, I supposed as I gave a mighty pluck, because otherwise we'd all be dead. With which great thought I headed off to my room and my bed and welcome unconsciousness.

night... the Turning of Chargesd we'd all be dead. With a sigh I at thought dthly soffth off to the room and
I. At least We're coming through business

6

Tressful Times

I woke up incredibly early. Perhaps it was the torment, perhaps it was the industrial quantity of Brussels sprouts I'd eaten, but one way or another I was up and out of bed and ready to get on with the day.

My bedroom door opened without the handle falling off, the carpet had lost its squelch, and the bathroom window was open so the room was blissfully free of Eau-de-Methane. Perhaps the day was going to be a good one.

Four hours later, standing in the corner of Happy Hairliners and holding a piece of used foil, I felt like laughing out loud at my optimism. I didn't of course, because that would have made me look very silly, but I'd had four hours of either being bullied by Helmet-Hair or being so stiff with boredom and the effort of trying to look busy that I thought I was going to pass out.

'And you can take that look off your face, right now.' Helmet-Hair's rasping voice made me jump to attention and try to look interested, or whatever it was that I hadn't been looking before. 'There's some hair here needs sweeping,' she went on, pointing at a corner of the salon.

There wasn't, but I went off to get the broom anyway, because at least that meant I could go downstairs for a few moments. Mum had been properly busy all morning mixing up colours and treatments, but otherwise things were pretty quiet *chez* Helmet-Hair.

I was busy sweeping away at a perfectly clean floor, when I heard the ping of the door. Hurray, a new person, I thought, as I looked up to see who it was. In walked an elegant-looking lady – of a certain age I think you would say – in a long black coat with a high collar, and thick auburn curly hair. I wondered if one day Sally's might turn that sort of colour, and made a mental note to tell her what a good look auburn could be.

'Morning, Mrs Cadwallaby, how are you?' she said in a warm and rather nice voice.

I recognised it instantly. My future mother-in-law. Not.

Feeling an enormous blush coming on (*why* does that happen?), I turned round and headed towards the door to the basement. That way I could observe without being observed, or in desperation could simply disappear downstairs.

'*Missus* Anderson,' said Helmet-Hair in her best fawning, sucky-uppy voice. '*What* a lovely surprise. I didn't think we were going to have the pleasure of seeing you today. Is everything all right with the little puppies?' she asked with a sickly smile.

'Yes, they seem to be quite good at sleeping as it turns out. My son's very kindly offered to look after them, so I can have my hair done today after all,' Patricia Anderson went on, unaware of the fact that a few feet away a bright red teenager was on the verge of having hysterics at the mention of her son.

'Well, that's splendid,' said HH, sounding more and more nauseating. 'I'm sure we can roll out the red carpet treatment at short notice.'

Revolting.

But it got worse: HH turned in my direction and said, 'A gown for Mrs Anderson, straight away, if you please.'

Thank goodness she was one of those rude people who treat you like a servant without a name. I so wanted to be anonymous. It would be mortifying beyond belief if Mrs Anderson knew who I was...the silly girl who had fallen so deeply for her cruel (not 'kind' at all) and duplicitous son.

I went over to the gown cupboard and picked out an emerald green gown. I thought it would go well with Patricia Anderson's auburn hair.

'Thank you,' she said as I took the long black coat and gave her the gown. She held on to her coat for a fraction longer than she needed to, which made me look at her properly. 'I haven't seen you here before, have I? Are you new here?'

'Yes,' I said, looking down at my feet, furious with myself for feeling so shy, 'but only for the holidays. My mother works here,' I added, looking over towards Mum who was leaning over an elderly grey head and gently putting in curlers.

'Oh, Gill's daughter, that's nice. She's told me a lot about you.'

Crapola squared. Then she must know my name, I thought, and that I go to Queen Mary's school, and... Gawd.

'She said you want to be a writer,' said Mrs Anderson, who'd let go of her coat and was putting on the gown. I was right about the green being a good colour. 'I'm often working with young writers in workshops. People who want to write screenplays and novels. A lot of them aren't that much older than you. We must keep you posted about any opportunities that come up.' And with a smile she turned and followed Helmet-Hair, who was ushering her into prime position in the middle of the salon.

I was shooed down into the basement to collect various lotions and potions and more foil and a dustpan and brush. I took longer than I should have done, as I felt quite faint. To have had such an encounter with his *mother,* who was so, SO nice, and was so nice to *me.*

Life is weird.

The next couple of hours went by in a bit of a haze – a clump of hair there, some spilt dye there, and a lot of towel washing.

Helmet-Hair continued to treat Patricia Anderson as some kind of celebrity and seemed to want to keep her in the salon for ever. But eventually, after much faffing around with a mirror, HH deemed the auburn hair immaculate and Mrs Anderson was allowed to go.

She gave me another nice smile as she handed me back the gown, but it was actually a huge relief to watch her walk out of the door.

For now at least, the danger of her knowing about my inner secret turmoil had passed.

The bus that evening was late, as buses on a Monday evening so often are. Perhaps they're still tired after the weekend, perhaps they don't like Mondays any more than we do, but by the time we'd found a seat Mum was looking more exhausted than ever.

As I watched her lean her head against the window and close her eyes, I decided that grilling her about the celebrity visit of the day could wait and I turned my attention to some St Thomas's boys at the front of the bus. One should never miss the chance of a bit of Boy Watching, after all.

They were younger than the objects of our adoration, about my age, and even at a distance you could tell they were strangers to the concept of the shower. They were waving their phones around, and all shouting at once. And pretty much everything they were shouting would have to be bleeped out on pre-watershed television. Probably on post-watershed television too.

There were two boys from another school, also about their age, on the seats three rows in front of them. One was on the large side of fat, and the other wore glasses and had his nose buried in what looked suspiciously like a book.

I had a bad feeling about how things were going to go.

Sure enough, I saw the one I had reckoned to be the leader of the St Thomas's gang (proving my theory that you can always tell who is the boss in any given gang – whether they're boys, or girls, or bank robbers, or aliens) look their way.

'Hey,' he said to his hangers-on, 'check this out.' And he led them up to where the two boys were sitting.

'What you got there then?' he said to the boy reading the book. He grabbed it off him and starting waving it about in the air. The boy with glasses and his enlarged friend both tried to grab it back.

Which of course was exactly what they were meant to do. Within seconds, they were surrounded by all the other boys who started nudging and jabbing at them, laughing as they did so.

Other people on the bus were starting to look nervous as the nudging and the jabbing got more and more lively and the language more and more bleepy.

Then suddenly – oh, there is a god for bespectacled and/or fat boys after all – one of the smaller St Thomas's bullies yelled, 'This is it, we're here, quick!' And they all pushed their way to the door and jumped off the bus.

Almost instantly everything went quiet. The enlarged

boy and his friend sat down and tried to pretend they weren't upset. The older people on the bus were clearly relieved they weren't going to have to intervene to prevent child murder. And I was pleased to see that they seemed to have got the book back, because the bespectacled one was soon head down and buried deep in it again.

As I settled back to looking out of the window at the stationary traffic, I reckoned this was a potentially interesting sidebar for our Boy Watching charts. The Boy Bully vs the Girl Bully. The first physical and on impulse, the second psychological and the result of what I think they call in courtroom dramas 'Malice Aforethought'.

As I was dwelling on these great insights, I glanced at Mum. To my surprise she was awake and looking at me rather thoughtfully.

I'm not sure I like being looked at thoughtfully. I think I'd rather be the one having the thoughts and doing the looking.

'What's up, Mum?' I said.

'Nothing particularly, love,' she said. 'But I meant to tell you that you'll have to get the bus by yourself tomorrow morning as I've got a doctor's appointment.'

'OK. I mean that's OK, but why have you got to go

to the doctor?' I had an uneasy feeling about this, but was pretty sure that that was because I'd seen too many weepy movies where Doctor's Appointments are said in capital letters and usually mean Something Serious.

'Just a check-up. You know how doctors like to make a fuss. They're doing blood tests and that. Nothing much,' said Mum, fiddling with the buckle on her handbag.

'OK,' I said again, thinking that the buckle-fiddling wasn't a good sign. But then Mum *had* said there was nothing to worry about, so perhaps she was just tired and fed up with the journey.

We got off the bus several hundred hours later, both properly exhausted and – in my case at least – ready for nothing more than a quick plate of something, ten minutes of trying yet again to understand Wilfred Owen's poem 'Strange Meeting', and bed.

It wasn't quite to be. When we got in, there was the smell of deep-fat-frying coming from the kitchen, and the sound of crockery being moved about rather angrily.

As we came into the room what should we see but the table laid and Ghastly Ralph standing over a spitting frying pan.

'Special chip treat,' he said when he saw us. 'Reckoned you'd need building up before you go to see the doctor tomorrow.' And he came over to Mum and put his arms around her.

Mum's smile was a bit on the washed-out side, probably not unconnected with being up close and personal with Eau-de-Ralph, but you could tell she appreciated the nearest thing to a nice gesture she was going to get from a Ghastly Ralph.

We sat down and I watched in a mixture of wonder and slight revulsion as Ralph heaped chips and sausages on our plates.

As he heaped, he told us what a great day he'd had at the Jobcentre, how his colleagues had told him how good he was with the punters, and how soon he reckoned he'd be back on the payroll proper, all his past sins forgotten.

I found all this highly unlikely but I did have to hand it to Ralph that he was doing a good job of cheering Mum up. For most of all this time he completely ignored me, which was fine by me.

I got up to clear the plates. On the floor by the sink there was a letter addressed to 'Miss Chloe Bennet'.

'Ralph,' I said as I picked it up, 'when were you going to tell me that something had come in the post for me?'

'Oh, yes, there's a letter for you. Came today,' he said, barely looking up.

I wasn't sure whether I was more furious with him for practically throwing my letter away or alarmed at the thought of what on earth it could be.

An absurd number of theories floated through my head as I carefully opened the envelope. It was a nice envelope, and nice handwriting, and it didn't LOOK like a dull communication from school.

It was short.

Hi Chloe,

I don't seem to be able to get through to you on any of your numbers or anything. Hope you had a great holiday. Let's get together at the weekend? Saturday before the gig? I'm on the usual number – can't wait to see you!

Mark xxx

So there we had it. Almost normal. Almost like he's just been away, there's something wrong with the electronic communication systems, but we can still have a date, just a question of my calling him back, and there we are. Nothing wrong at all.

Almost normal.

I went straight to my room and tried to shut the door behind me. Typically it chose that moment not to shut properly, even after the right-hip swing that usually sorted it.

Which meant that very shortly after I lay down on my bed and got under the duvet – in the foetal position that's so comforting when you're traumatised – Mum came straight in.

'What's the matter, love? What was your letter? Has it upset you?' she said in her extra-specially kind voice.

'It was from him,' I said, pathetically unable to say the M word. 'He's just behaving as if nothing much has ever happened between us, never mind his betrayal and sneaking around with Maggie. Just suggesting a date. Like everything was normal. And not very important. Not very important at all.' My voice faded away. It was difficult saying stuff.

'I'm sure he doesn't think it's not important,' said Mum. 'He wouldn't have written you a letter if he didn't think it was important. Boys don't write letters very often these days, you know. The very fact that he did it means he realises it IS important.'

I stayed in the foetal position. It was nice being all curled up. Nothing can hurt you if you're all curled up.

I couldn't say anything though.

'Listen, love,' said Mum. 'He doesn't know you're cross with him because you saw him with that girl. You should tell him, you should talk to him. There may be something you don't know. Some reason... I don't know.'

Yup, when she came to think about it, even Mum couldn't come up with an explanation.

But all I wanted to do was wallow in the misery and pain that the letter had brought rushing back to the surface. I didn't and couldn't talk about it, and anyway I didn't want Mum to worry about it when she had other things to worry about.

'It's all right, Mum,' I said eventually, from the safety of the duvet. 'I'll ring him. You just go to bed. I'm all right. I'll see you in the morning.'

Mum got up off the bed, slowly and a bit sadly. But she headed off to bed. Where I really, really hoped she got to sleep.

It would be nice if one of us did.

Facing Reality

Mum had already left by the time I got up the next morning, so I had a fleeting moment of fear that without her getting me to the bus on time I was going to be late at the salon.

It was good to have something practical to worry about, I thought...when I got to the bus stop just as my bus was leaving it.

There wouldn't be another one for twenty minutes, so I decided to race the bus to the next stop. Luckily, it was a trainers day, so I was able to zip along at a pretty good speed. Plus, people seemed to see me coming and get out of the way.

All was going according to plan, and I was on track to beat the bus, when a paving stone jumped up and hit my toe, sending me flying into the gutter.

I lay there a bit stunned. I could feel that my jeans

were ripped and my knee was exposed to the elements, also that my arm was bent in a way it hadn't necessarily been designed to bend. But the worst bit was a feeling of soreness and rawness all down the side of my face.

The bus drew away just at that moment.

There seemed to be a sea of concerned faces hovering over me, and then I was being helped to my feet. Somehow the pain was nothing compared to the worry about my face. The mirror in my bag had smashed (how many years' bad luck was that supposed to mean? Probably enough to see me comfortably into my old age) so I had no means of knowing what the damage was. Other than the slightly appalled glances that people were throwing me.

Eventually the next bus came, and I finally arrived at the salon. Helmet-Hair looked at me with a disgust she made no attempt to disguise.

'You'd better go to the toilet and clean yourself up. And you're nearly an hour late. That will have to be deducted from your pay,' she said, turning away from me to direct one of her horrible false smiles at an old lady who'd come in after me.

I went to the toilet. And looked at myself in the mirror.

Fan-bloddy-tastic. The whole of my right cheek seemed to be scraped away, leaving deep red lines all down the side of my face. I shall be scarred for life, I thought. Or I shall spend a fortune on plastic surgery, and die on the operating table. Or there are bits of poisoned pavement in my face that will mean I'll develop a lethal form of blood poisoning. Or—

'Is anyone in there?' There was a hesitant tapping on the door. I opened it to find the old lady, looking rather nice despite being dressed in one of the salon's most unflattering black gowns.

She looked hard at me. 'Oh dear,' she said (too right), 'that looks rather nasty. Let's get you cleaned up. I've got some antiseptic cream in my bag.'

Moments later there was a stinging sensation all over my face as I was being wiped – surprisingly vigorously – by the old lady.

Looking in the mirror again I saw that half my face was now absolutely scarlet. But at least terminal blood poisoning was one less thing to worry about.

That morning at Happy Hairliners had very little to recommend it. As usual there was less to do than time to do it, but woe betide me if I ever looked un-busy. Most of the clients (I had been told to call them clients) were too busy looking at their own reflections to look at mine, but those that did would give a very slight recoil of horror that they'd then do their best to hide.

The first good thing that happened was that Helmet-Hair went out to lunch. The atmosphere in the salon lightened considerably.

The second good thing that happened was that I had a visitor. Or two visitors to be precise.

I was busy (for me) washing hairbrushes when the door pinged. And in came my glamorous friend, Gemma. She looked fantastic in a black dress and a half-length fake leather jacket. For a second I felt very proud of her, and then I clocked her expression of horror and concern as she looked at me. The concern was nice, but the horror not so. I couldn't help thinking that a good friend shouldn't look quite so absolutely disgusted when they look at the face of their friend.

Then I noticed that behind her was a tall, blond boy wearing a grey jacket, jeans and big black and silver cowboy boots. He looked great. They both looked great. I suddenly recognised him: Jack Harrington, the blond surfer boy who we'd met on holiday in Cornwall in the Easter holidays. He looked a bit different with clothes on. But he was the one who'd been at junior school with Charlie and...everyone.

'Chloe!' said Gemma. 'What have you done to your face? You haven't been experimenting with Sally's cosmetics, have you? Bit of DIY sandpaper exfoliation going on here?'

'Not remotely funny, but actually very painful,' I said stiffly, aware that Beautiful Jack was looking at me closely. 'Fell trying to catch the bus. Classic, really. It'll probably take several years to heal properly. If it ever does.'

'Well, we'll have to get some industrial strength concealer for you as well as for Sally then,' she said, I suppose not unkindly. 'We just came by to say hello. Jack's off to his aunt's this afternoon, but he's coming back on Saturday to come to the Shedz gig with us. Good plan? Remember?'

I nodded. I remembered all right. But I hoped that Jack didn't know that we all wanted to be his girlfriend for our own reasons. Still, he looked like he could take care of himself. Actually he looked like a million dollars, and you shouldn't ever have to feel sorry for people who look like a million dollars.

The door pinged again. This time not so happily – Helmet-Hair back early from lunch. She looked at

Gemma and Jack, seemed to decide immediately that they were of no use to her, and changed her expression from Fawning Customer-Greeting to Busy Employer Irritated by Time-Wasters.

'OK, then,' said Gemma, immediately getting the message. 'So don't forget to text me about Wilfred Owen, and I'll see you on Thursday.'

Yeah. So that was going to work. Pretending we were having a lunchtime seminar about First World War poets.

'No, seriously,' hissed Gemma on her way out. 'Tell me what to think about him – I have absolutely no idea!'

I went back to cleaning hairbrushes, trying not to notice the glares HH was giving me. If I could just keep my head down for the rest of the day, I could get off on time and see if Mum had a miracle cure for raw cheeks.

Mum. That made me remember what I was trying to forget. Should I be worrying? What a silly question to ask myself. I already was.

Buses on a Tuesday must be generally better rested and refreshed than their Monday friends, because mine positively raced along, and I was home in half the usual time. Plus I got a seat, didn't fall over, and didn't have to watch young boys be persecuted.

So I was feeling a bit better when I put my key in the lock.

I could hear Mum and Ghastly Ralph talking in the kitchen. And as I got nearer I could hear '...decide what to tell Chloe.'

Pointless to pretend I hadn't heard. 'What? Tell me what?' I said as I went into the kitchen.

Mum and Ralph were sitting at the table in front of cups of tea and the remains of a packet of biscuits. No extra-strength lager. It must be serious.

'Well, love,' said Mum looking up – and then she did a double take. 'What on earth's happened to your face, Chloe? It looks awfully sore. Come here and let me have a look.'

I went over to her side of the table and sat down. I could tell by her expression that things hadn't got any better on the raw cheek front. Hard to decide at that point what to be most miserable about.

'I had a close encounter with the pavement running for the bus,' I said. 'Do I really look like a freak show?'

'I'll get some cream, love,' said Mum, starting to get up. 'You'll be all right, it's not so deep. Just very sore. You poor lass.'

'Don't get up, Mum. We can do that later,' I said. 'Just tell me what's going on.'

'Well. You're not to worry,' said Mum (ha). 'But I found a lump on my breast, and they've been doing some tests. They took a bit out of the lump and had a look and they, well, they didn't think it looked very good.' Mum paused. She suddenly got up and went over to the sink.

With her back to me she stood looking out of the window and went on, 'And today they said they're going to have to remove it altogether, and then they're going to have to give me some treatments. Chemotherapy, they think, and maybe radiotherapy.'

She turned round and came and sat down at the table again. She looked at me with what I think was meant to be a reassuring smile. 'So I might be a bit substandard for a while, love. After the op and then maybe for six months or so. But they say they think they've caught it quite early. They say I should be OK in the end.'

She took my hand and gave it a squeeze. Her hands felt warm and familiar, and for a second I felt safe.

Then it all started to sink in. So much stuff went through my head.

So it *was* Capital Letters Serious, I thought, looking

hard at the pattern on the kitchen table. And that's why she always seemed so tired lately. That's why she's been so pale and sleepy. But have they got it right, have they really caught it early? How do they *know*? And does it mean Mum's going to go bald, and be sick all the time? Why her, why someone who doesn't do anything wrong? And how long will it go on for? And will she have to stop work, and does that mean we won't have any money? And, oh, how are we going to manage if she's not the strong one holding us together? And above all, WILL SHE BE ALL RIGHT?

'OK,' I said, even though it wasn't OK at all. 'When do they want you to have the operation?'

'They said as soon as possible, probably next week,' said Mum, looking a bit relieved. Perhaps she was glad that it was out in the open. 'I'll be in hospital for a week or so, and then they'll start the treatment a week or so after that. I think we might have to ask Gran to come and look after us all, love.'

At this, Ghastly Ralph, who'd been staring morosely at his teacup, looked up and gave a groan.

'Ralph thinks he can manage, but I'd feel a lot better if you had Gran to look after us all. She can come down and stay here when I'm out of hospital. I'm going to be a bit poorly until the treatment starts.'

'And you're going to be a lot more poorly after the treatment starts,' said Ralph, looking even more morose. I wasn't sure how helpful that comment was. Maybe it was just Ralph's way of sympathising.

Or maybe he was dreading the arrival of Gran.

Gran. She of the bouffant hair, the Crimplene trouser suit, the lace-up shoes, the walking stick with rubber on the end... Gran. The one whose scorn for The Younger Generation knew no bounds, the one whose dislike of anything electronic extended even to Mum's elderly mobile phone, and the one who knew for an absolute certain fact that This Country is Going to the Dogs.

She was Mum's mother, so there must be some great genetic good in her to have produced Mum. But sometimes it was really hard to believe that they were of the same stock.

It was no wonder that Ralph was looking so extra morose. Apart from their deep-rooted dislike of all things Left Wing, he and she had very little – or, more accurately, nothing – in common.

I wasn't at all sure what it was going to be like with Gran in the house; I hadn't seen that much of her, what with her living somewhere very dark and a long way away. (The dark is all I can remember about going to see Gran. Sitting in the back of the car for a million hours, arriving in the dark in the evening, and then going back in the dark in the morning because it was such a long journey. It's possible that the part of the country she lived in was nice, but since we never set foot outside the door of her tiny bungalow when we were there, we wouldn't know.)

'Chloe?' Mum was looking at me with the worried expression back on her face. 'I'm sure it's all going to be all right, love. And I know you'll be my brave girl and help us get through this.'

I felt the edges of my mouth start to tremble, and there was a definite stinging in my eyes. But of course, being brave, I didn't cry. I could save that for later.

'I'm going to tell Steve about it all this evening. It's so lucky he's coming home on Sunday,' Mum went on. 'Now. Let's get some of that cream and see if we can't make your cheek a bit less sore.'

Later that evening, lying on the bed with my cheek smarting from Mum's magic cream, with the door banged shut and the duvet over me, I let myself have a good cry.

Quietly, of course. With my face in the pillow.

I woke up early the next morning, and for one and a half seconds felt bright-eyed and full of beans. Then I remembered. Mum. And instantly had a sick feeling in the pit of my stomach.

If there was anything like a silver lining to this terrible cloud, it was that the misery of my disillusion with Mark had plummeted down the scale of things to be sad about. Perhaps there is only so much capacity for sadness in the human make-up, and now Mum was taking up most of mine.

For now, Mum was getting us all ready for work as if life were as usual. She even managed to find some of her old-fashioned foundation to put on my offending cheek. It didn't make me look any less bumpy, but it made my face look a little less startlingly scarlet.

We set off for the bus stop in plenty of time to catch the bus that hadn't wanted to be caught the day before, and arrived *chez* Helmet-Hair all too soon.

I was immediately set to work sweeping up non-existent hair, and washing clean hairbrushes. I tried not to notice Mum ask HH for a private word. And then I tried not to keep looking at the back office after they'd both gone in there and shut the door.

After an age they came out and I saw that Helmet-Hair had an expression of such concern on her face that I had a feeling I might have to hate her a little less.

The rest of the day passed relatively harmoniously, although I was as knackered as ever by the end of it. I don't think I'll ever get used to being a bit player in the drama of hairdressing life.

As we were getting ready to go, Mrs Cadwallaby took me aside.

'Chloe,' she said, 'It's been quite helpful to have you around. If you'd like to come back again, then we'd be happy to have you at Happy Hairliners.' She stood back to see the effect her words had on me. Clearly she thought she was conferring great favour on me by saying nice things. 'But until then, I hope things go well for your mother. I'm sure you'll look after her properly and we'll see her back here soon.'

'Look after her properly.' Huh. How else would I look after her? And just when I was starting to hate Helmet-Hair a little bit less.

Mum and I managed to get a seat on the bus that evening, even though the rush hour was at its worst, and doing its worst.

We didn't say very much; we just looked out of the window, watching the world go by very slowly.

I was stopping off on the way to go and see Sally. We had decided that between us we could surely find something in Liv's bathroom cupboard to practise hiding our various deformities. Bad enough going back to school without some super-smooth summer tan, but going back in various shades of bright red and yellow didn't bear thinking about.

What with one slow bus and another, I was late by the time I rang Sally's piercing front door bell.

'You're late,' she said when she opened the door. And then after a brief pause, 'Also, your face is looking *very* weird.'

I do sometimes wonder how Sally made it to the status of my BFF. I'm sure when I last checked, best friends were supposed to support each other, look out for each other. Not tell them off and pour industrial quantities of salt into their various wounds.

'And there speaks the girl with the *totally* normal complexion, the one where the yellow and grey bits hardly clash *at all* with the red bits,' I said.

Well. She asked for it.

'That's mean!' said Sally. 'You're supposed to be my friend!'

'I am,' I said. 'Course I am. Come on, let's go and

check out Liv's products.' Life, I decided, was too short to explain the complexities of the concept of friendship to Sally. Anyway, we had work to do.

Liv was in the kitchen, and called out to us as we were going past. 'Chloe! How *are* you? No ill effects after eating that Brie, I hope?'

I wondered if Mr Pinot Grigio had scrambled her memory. Perhaps she thought that it was me who'd eaten a whole plate of cheese. This was the sort of awkward social encounter they don't teach you about at school. Dealing with grown-up alcohol memory lapses: to mention them or not mention them?

'I mean Albert, of course,' Liv went on. 'I know it wasn't you who ate all that cheese!' And she gave a rather nervous laugh. Probably one of relief that she'd remembered what had happened after all.

'He's fine, thank you, Liv,' I said. 'I'm very sorry about the Brie though.'

'We're off upstairs, Mum,' said Sally, thankfully breaking up the Awkward Social Encounter.

We settled down in the bathroom. Every available surface, and some that weren't available, was covered in bottles and potions and tins and tubes. Plus there were two big cupboards with three or four shelves in each to go through. We would be some time.

'So have you found out what that phone call to your mum was about?' I asked Sally as I started to inspect some tubes with promising-looking words written on them like 'conceal' and 'complete'.

'No. She won't say. She just says it's nothing for me to worry about. But I'm sure it's something to do with Dad. Honestly. Parents shouldn't be complicated, they should just look after you, shouldn't they? Isn't that what they're for?' said Sally, sticking her finger in a tub of exfoliating body lotion.

'Guess so,' I said, feeling sick again. 'They're not supposed to be ill and go to hospital and have operations anyway.' I sat down on the edge of the bath and looked up at Sally.

For a moment Sally looked completely confused. Then it seemed to dawn on her that this was serious. 'Oh no,' she said. 'It's not your mum, is it? What's wrong?'

'Hospital. Next week. Operation for breast cancer. And then treatment and all the trimmings. They say they've caught it early. But they never know for sure, do they? Anyway. It's all horrible. And Gran's coming to stay.' I found using very few words was the best way of conveying this sort of grim information.

'Oh your poor mum,' said Sally looking as if she

were going to cry. 'And poor Chloe. How awful.' And she came and sat next to me on the bath and gave me a sideways and uncomfortable but very heartfelt hug.

We stayed like that for a while. It was nice being comforted.

'We can help, can't we?' said Sally eventually. 'I mean, we can take you out and cheer you up and things. And then when your mum's out of hospital we can come round and cook things for you.'

I didn't know whether to laugh or cry at the thought of Sally trying to cook something in our kitchen under the eagle eye of Gran. But she meant well. Plus it was good to know that she understood what friends were for after all.

I decided we should focus on our work. I told Sally to find at least three things that she thought would disguise her grey and yellow face (which was starting to look a lot better than it had done, but still needed considerable camouflage) and I'd find three things that would make me look less bumpy and scarlet, and then we'd compare notes.

Twenty minutes, and several mistakes later, we were both able to look ourselves in the mirror and think we looked quite presentable. Putting my chosen potions in my bag (Sally said Liv wouldn't notice, and anyway even if she did it was the least she could do for me) we went downstairs.

All was strangely silent. Perhaps Liv had sedated Harris and Jock and then sedated herself. But it meant we could have some comforting ice cream in peace before I set off for home.

Even though we lived a bus ride apart we agreed to go to school together in the morning. When it's the first day of term, and you're sad, and heavily made-up, there was safety in numbers.

Education, Education, Education

So far so good, I thought. Sally and I had had a nice time on the bus telling each other that our faces looked fine. Plus the sun was shining, we weren't late, and there was no sign of QBM and her cohorts standing in their usual place at the gates to the school. (On most days you could be pretty sure of having to walk the walk of humiliation, as she pointed out your peculiarities loudly to the world in general and her cohorts in particular.)

'Perhaps she's moved and gone to another school,' said Sally, the eternal optimist. 'Or perhaps she's been asked not to come back because everyone thinks she's such a cow. Or perhaps she's had a terrible accident and has had to have her legs cut off.' Her voice trailed away. We both knew that somehow or other Queen Beeyatch Maggie wasn't going to leave our lives that easily.

We headed towards our new classroom, wondering who our form teacher for the new year was going to be. So long as it wasn't hideous Miss Grunbar (Maths), ultra boring Mrs Slopeth (Biology), or ultra bored Miss Daniels (History), we might be all right.

Amy and Gemma were both already in the room. Amy was showing something to Gemma on her phone and I could tell that Gemma was only pretending to look interested. And not actually succeeding.

She looked up with relief when we arrived. 'There you are,' she said. 'And well done. You two look almost normal.'

With friends like that…

'I was just showing Gem some pics of me and Charlie running up a mountain,' said Amy. 'Look. Doesn't it look beautiful?'

I just thought it looked ridiculously steep. I mean running is bad enough, but why would anyone want to do it *uphill*?

'Chloe's got some bad news,' said Sally abruptly, not even going through the motions of admiring the mountain. 'Her mum's got cancer. So we're going to have to be very kind and nice to her.'

Amy and Gemma looked horrified. Amy's face seemed to crumple and she came up to me and gave me a long slow hug. Gemma looked as if maybe she'd give me a hug, only someone had got there first and so what can you do?

At that moment I could sense that everyone suddenly seemed to be standing to attention. I looked round.

It was Mrs Slopeth (boring, Biology) and behind her a rather short youngish man busily adjusting his tie. He was wearing thick-looking spectacles and was blinking far more than a normal person should. I reckoned he was very, very nervous. I also reckoned he had good reason to be, because just behind him was one helluva Queen Beeyatch.

Maggie had come into the room just behind the two of them, and what they couldn't see but we all could was that she was busily adjusting her virtual tie and blinking hard. It was a horrible imitation, mostly because it was so accurate. Already I felt sorry for Mr Tie Man.

'Girls,' said Mrs Slopeth in her most bossy, stand-no-nonsense tone. 'This is Mr Carson. He is your new form master and he is also going to be teaching Religious Studies. I'm sure you will show him the courtesy that can be expected from all the girls at

Queen Mary's.' And with that she turned on her heel and left the poor man blinking, and alone.

'Sir, sir,' said QBM as soon as Mrs S had gone. 'Are you related to the O'Genics in Ireland? I'm sure they had a son called Carson. Or, hang on, maybe he was the one who died of cancer, what with being Carson O'Genic and all. What do you think sir?'

There was a roar of sycophantic laughter. I'm sure half the class didn't know that 'carcinogenic' meant cancerous. Perhaps I wouldn't have done not so long ago... But as cruel bits of psychobullying go it wasn't completely unclever. Which was what made the Queen Beeyatch so very good at her job.

'Hello,' Mr Carson said, trying to pretend nothing had happened. 'I'm looking forward to getting to know you all.' Oh dear, oh dear, he had a slightly plummy accent. 'I will take the register now; please make yourself known to me when I call your name.'

Hideous. He'd laid himself wide open to all sorts of Beeyatchery. Starting with everyone answering to someone else's name.

It was going to be a difficult year for Mr Carson.

Our first piece of teaching for the new term was scheduled to be a French class with Madame de Bellaire (whose real name, we had recently discovered, was Doris Bracegirdle. I kid you not). Madame de B was rather vague about everything – up to and including discipline and grammar, but especially concerning what time lessons were meant to start. So the four of us reckoned we had plenty of time and went the long way round through the schoolyard at the back, spinning out the moments until we had to go back into Education.

'Your poor mum. And poor, poor Chloe,' Amy said as we went out of the fire exit at the back of the hall. 'As if you weren't sad enough already what with Mark being so…well…what with Mark.'

'How's your mum being about it, Chloe?' said Gemma. Her own mother had abandoned her for another woman (no, really) eight years ago, and she was only recently reunited with her. We'd had a few quite deep talks about how important mothers are, and I knew she really felt for me underneath the cool.

'I think she'd known something was wrong for some time,' I said. 'And she's sort of relieved that they're now doing something about it. But she's worried about us. And I'm sure she's frightened too. We all are.'

'And then there's her ghastly stepfather, and

she's got her gran coming to stay too,' said Sally, not terribly helpfully.

'It's OK,' I said quickly, not wanting to talk about Ralph and Gran. 'We'll manage. Main thing is Mum.'

Despite the deliberate dawdling, we were still first into the classroom, so our reward was to be able to bag the back seats. All the better to write notes to each other.

Madame de B seemed as reluctant as we were to get back into the swing of lessons. Dressed in a tight blue jersey dress, she came bustling in, perm and everything else bouncing away, and immediately turned on the A-V system.

We were going to hear people talking in French about various forms of transport, she said. She obviously thought it was a lot easier to have us listen to a pre-recorded voice grumbling about not getting a seat on the Metro, than teach us about the pluperfect of 'aller'.

Especially since I think her knowledge of the pluperfect was almost as hazy as ours.

I'd just started to drift off into speculation as to whether or not there was a Mr Bracegirdle, and whether he liked his wife's perm and if so why, and if not doesn't he really owe it to her to tell her how peculiar it made her look...when the words 'school', 'trip' and 'Paris' penetrated my consciousness.

'...for those of you taking French, and for those of you who will be doing Art. It will mean an early start, but I think we can be sure that you will get a Lot Out of It.' Getting a Lot Out of It was a bit of a mantra with Madame de B. And mostly she applied it to how we'd feel when we'd learnt some more French vocab, but on this occasion I thought she might have a point.

'Miss.' It was QBM, also sitting at the back. She was calling Madame de B 'miss' because Madame de B told us – often and emphatically – that her name was 'Madame'. 'Miss, did you know there's a famous museum in Paris full of English things? Can we go and see it? It's called the Bracegirdle Museum.'

Everyone tittered and sniggered as they always seemed to feel they have to when the QB's up to her tricks.

Madame de B went bright red, and turning her back on us started to fiddle with the A-V system. 'There will be further details sent to you and your parents,' she said without turning round, 'that's all for today, you may go.'

As we headed off to our next lessons in the science labs I reckoned one thing was clear: the summer holidays had done nothing to make the Queen Beeyatch any less of a Beeyatch. Until someone came along and sent her to another school and/or cut off her legs we'd have to watch our backs very carefully indeed.

But the good news was that a school trip to France might just take our minds off everything. Plus surely Boy Watching, French-style (*Garçon Regarder?*), was bound to teach us a whole load of new tricks.

For most of the rest of the morning I was reminded of why the term 'back to school' fills most people with gloom. Chemistry seemed more pointless than ever, Physics more incomprehensible – and the thought of an afternoon filled with things like Religious Studies was almost enough to make me pine for the joys of washing clean hairbrushes. Almost.

But at least there was a small window of normality in the middle called lunch. When you could talk to your friends about really important things like what you'd done on your last holidays, what you were going to do on your next holidays, the weekend, and Boys.

The four of us stood in the queue for lunch just behind some of the least nasty cohorts of QBM. I was vaguely speculating as to whether to have the salad and baked potato or the stew (by far the most interesting decision of the day) when I started listening to what they were saying.

'...my sister knows her and says Georgie's coming here. That's what I heard anyway,' said one.

'But wasn't she going to go to St Thomas's?' her friend said.

'Dunno. Maybe they want her to go to an ordinary girls' school if she's going to be a TV star and all that,' said the first one. Then they started talking about stew versus baked potatoes. Which suddenly seemed to me to be the most least important thing in the world.

'Georgie' must be Mark's sister. He'd said that she was going to go to St Thomas's as a rare girl in the sixth. Plus their mother was in TV so it made sense she might be in a TV show. I'd only met Georgie once, and she seemed so nice. But then her brother had seemed so nice too...

And now I was going to be at school with her. There was a time when that would have been lovely news, for I had been convinced that just like Lizzy Bennet and Mr Darcy's sister, Georgiana, we would end up close friends. But now it just seemed like one more unattainable thing to be sad about.

'I've got the perfect excuse to get me out of netball ALL TERM!' said Sally, putting a huge chunk of butter on her baked potato and reminding me that I already had close friends.

But I very much took the view that getting out of netball was NOT sporting, in any sense. If one of us had to suffer netball, then we should all have to suffer netball.

'Why? How? You can't just get out of a whole term. You'd have to be really ill or break something,' I said.

'I'm going to get a bunion,' said Sally. 'Mum's got a bunion and she's had to stop going running. The doctor says she can't do any sport for weeks and weeks.'

'I think you'll find that bunions aren't infectious,' said Gemma, putting a little bit of salad on her plate, just like a supermodel. 'Plus they happen to middle-aged people, not people in Year Ten,' she went on, taking four large pieces of bread and hiding them in her sleeves for later. So not really a supermodel.

'Oh,' said Sally. She looked...I think the word is crestfallen.

'But you can't not want to play netball!' said Amy. 'It's such good fun, and anyway, I thought you played brilliantly in that match last year.' There. That's what separates Amy from the rest of us. Incredible niceness

116

and an inexplicable enthusiasm for running about.

But before anyone ran anywhere we had this thing called Religious Studies to go to.

I find Religious Studies can go either way. Either you get given endless unmemorable facts about World Religions, or everyone gets to sound off about what they think about God and Death and other Things With Capital Letters.

Except this time there was the horrible curiosity factor of how on earth blinking Mr Carson would cope.

We went into the classroom and sat down. I could see QBM was obviously gagging to get started on a spot of psychobullying. Then in came Mr Carson and it was immediately clear that he, too, was going to rely heavily on A-V.

'Religion,' he began in his semi-plummy voice almost before we had sat down, 'or the lack of it, frequently determines our attitudes to death and suffering. And to evil.' He glanced at QBM as he spoke. 'So I want us to listen to a few people talk about how suffering has affected them, and affected their beliefs.'

Before anyone could interrupt he quickly flicked a switch and the screen was filled with a young man talking about his brain tumours. And then someone talking about their daughter dying. And then someone talking about their mother dying. Swiftly followed by someone who'd been tortured and someone who had cancer.

They were either bitter or stoic, unbelieving or religious. None of these things were really very surprising, but they were certainly depressing.

Eventually there was a pause in the transmission. Mr Carson stood up again, blinking more than ever. 'So the question I want you to think about is: does suffering serve a purpose?'

Everybody had something to say about that, and everybody started to shout so loudly that we almost didn't hear the bell.

As we left the room I thought about what a waste of time school can be. I'd just been taught two things, and I already knew them both. The first was that horrible things happen to people, and some of them can bear it and some of them can't. And the second was that whoever had encouraged Mr C to go into teaching had a rather sick sense of humour.

That End of the Week Thing

Of all the days of the week, I usually find that the Friday is one of the best. It's often an easy day at school (Art, English, that sort of thing), there's a sense of oh-well-it-can-wait-till-Monday amongst the grown-ups (I find this to be true whatever the 'it' is), and of course it's only a day away from the good thing that is the weekend. And the anticipation of the good thing is often as nice as the thing itself.

But this particular Friday wasn't quite so nice or good, even though the sun was shining bright and cheerfully through the curtains. As I lay in bed, thinking about getting up, my list of things to worry about over the weekend seemed to get longer and longer. Especially about Saturday night.

What on earth was going to happen at the Shedz gig – will he be there? What will he say? What will I say? What shall I wear? What will happen about Rob, who still hadn't made a proper arrangement to meet up with Sally? What about Jack? And Jezza?

'Come on, love, up you get. It's getting late,' said Mum from outside my door.

How she knew I was still in bed, I don't know.

When I got to the school gates, I realised I'd forgotten to worry about one other thing. The QB. She was standing in the middle of her usual cohorts, saying something I couldn't hear but which they were all, of course, laughing at.

As I got nearer, they seemed to move together in a group and started to surround me. Like cows in a field. Certainly cows, anyway.

'Here she is,' the QB said. 'Come on, everyone, let's check her out. Let's have a good look at the girl who thinks she's Mark Anderson's girlfriend. Let's see what she thinks she's got that we haven't? Is it the mud-coloured hair? Or the deformed right cheek? Or maybe it's the suede wedges with dog poo on them? You've got to laugh. Haven't you, everyone?' And she looked around at them and sure enough they all started laughing.

They were so up close and in my face I could have slapped them. How I longed to slap them. The thought of slapping them – the surprised look on their sucky-uppy faces, false laughter dying away – somehow kept me going. Surely it would soon be time for the QB to move on to making someone else's life a misery? But anyway, it wasn't like she could give me a brain tumour or secondary cancer. Being psychobullied by Psycho Maggie wouldn't actually kill me.

Maybe Mr C's lessons in Suffering and Evil were putting things in perspective after all.

I went as quickly as I could without it seeming as if I was running away, up the steps and towards the Sally meeting-place. She was there, fiddling with her phone as usual. Normally this annoys me very much indeed – Sally is always, *always* fiddling with her phone, even when she should be looking at me while I'm talking to her – but on this occasion I thought she looked very sweet and very reassuring.

Amy came up at that moment, too. Just the sight of her made me feel better. I decided they didn't need to know what had just happened.

'Hey,' Sally looked up from her phone, smiling a big triumphant kind of smile, 'guess what? I've finally had a text from Rob. He says we must all meet up in the park before the gig. They're going to play football and we must come and watch. How great is that?'

Only quite great, I reckoned. After all, football is football, even if it's being played by the boys in our lives who we all love, or would like to love. But it would be interesting to practise Watching Boys in a sporting environment anyway.

'I knew he was going to ask me out,' Sally went on, 'I just *knew* it.'

Which was odd because I was sure I remembered Sally telling me how she knew, just *knew* that she'd never hear from him again.

'That's brilliant, Sal,' said Amy with one of her nice smiles that reminded me how much more properly good she is than me.

I wondered if there'd be time to go shopping first – I'd decided that what with the bright sunshine and the important need to look cool I needed a new pair of sunglasses. The only ones I had were completely squashed after an unfortunate encounter with Ghastly Ralph's bottom. I'd been very angry with him at the time, but perhaps I shouldn't have left them down the back of the sofa.

I was thinking important thoughts like whether or not charity shops sell designer sunglasses, and if so how much they might cost, and whether I should go for large or small frames, when we arrived at our English

Lit class. It was time to discuss Wilfred Owen's poetry and the death and despair of thousands of young men on the battlefields of the First World War.

I hoped it didn't show that deep down I was having shallow thoughts.

We were taught English Lit by Mr Fanshawe who, rather unusually and slightly revoltingly, seemed to have a perpetual cold. It was often quite disconcerting to be having a lesson on *Bride and Bread Yudish* or *Of Bice and Ben*. But he was actually quite good at pointing things out in books that I'd never have noticed myself. Which I guess is quite a good skill to have if you're an English teacher.

I could immediately see that today was an extra-specially bad cold day for Mr F. His eyes were puffy little slits, his nose was a pale purple colour with a blob of red at the end, and there was a generally damp look to his whole face.

Despite the smart jacket with the red handkerchief in the top pocket, and the rather fetchingly tight trousers, the overall effect wasn't great. In fact, the more I looked at him the more I felt the urge to grab the handkerchief out of his pocket and give his face a good wipe.

Bunged-up or not, Mr F was in full flow: '...and of

course many people think that Wilfred Owen's poem "Strange Meeting" is in blank verse,' he was saying. That'd be me, I thought. 'But actually he uses a form of slant-rhyme that emphasises the feeling of sadness, and makes you feel uneasy long after you've finished reading it.'

Out of the corner of my eye I saw Gemma looking utterly puzzled and disbelieving. And I must admit that even as a future prize-winning writer I sometimes find English Literature a bit bewildering.

Later, much later, there was only Art standing in between us and freedom for the weekend.

There was a rumour that our Art teacher, Mr Pampledousse, who was Greek and even hairier that Mr Underwood, had been on holiday to Newfoundland. Because that's where a History teacher called Mr Horriday was recovering from a nervous breakdown brought on – everyone agreed but didn't dare say – by an epic episode of psychobullying by QBM. (Like I said, very good at her job.)

I'm pretty sure the rumour was started by Gemma, who is convinced that the two of them are an item, and that Mr Pimplemouse (which of course is what we call him) was pining away ever since Mr Horriday suddenly disappeared.

'I know I'm right,' said Gemma as we headed off to the studio. 'Bet you anything. Ask him.'

'We can't just ask him. How embarrassing would that be?' said Sally, squawking a little bit.

'OK then. Leave it to me,' said Gemma, now looking much more interested in her education than she had done for years.

We all sat down at desks around the studio and seconds later Mr Pampledousse came through the door.

He certainly looked a bit better. Perhaps he even had an outdoor Canadian glow to him (we'd googled Newfoundland – nothing but seals, moose, and a distant view of the Canadian coast. Definitely a spot to get away from it all if you're having a bit of a breakdown).

'Hello, everyone,' he said in his thick Greek accent. No sign of any Canadian twang there.

'Today we will do animal,' he went on. 'You have clay. You have magazine here for inspiration. And you will do motion. Your animals must be move.' So no Canadian mastery of the English language either.

Fortunately we were used to being instructed in the

original Greek. And knew that what we were meant to do was find a picture in the magazines lying on our desks of an animal in motion, and try to recreate it out of the lumps of clay in front of us. A tall order. Especially if you had never done anything like that before and had absolutely no idea where to start.

Perhaps this was inspirational teaching, or maybe it was just easier for someone with only a hazy grasp of English to encourage a bit of experimentation.

'I rather think,' Gemma's voice rang out from the corner of the room, 'that I would like to make a seal. Can you help me, sir? Have you ever seen a seal? Or maybe I would like to make a moose. What do you think, sir, have you seen one of those?'

'Yes, you are in lucky,' said Mr Pampledousse. 'Here I have.' And he pulled his phone out of his pocket, fiddled about with it and then, with a satisfied, 'ah', showed it to Gemma.

'That's great, sir,' said Gemma. Anyone who didn't know her might almost think she was trying not to laugh. 'Really great. He's a fine figure of a moose, isn't he? Did you get close to him?' And she gave a small snort, which you could easily mistake for a stifled giggle.

'I think that enough,' Mr Pampledousse seemed to

realise that he'd been in some way set up and put his phone away. 'You can do cat. Here.' And he pointed to a picture of a small tabby cat in the nearest magazine.

As we got on with the business of ruining a great deal of perfectly good clay, I reckoned we might just have learned the most interesting thing we were likely to learn all week. Plus, I hoped that somewhere out in the Canadian ocean, Mr Horriday was having a nice holiday.

Before I knew it, it was Saturday and time to decide what to wear to watch a game of football that I didn't want to watch, and see a boy who I didn't want to see.

It was a difficult brief, but in the end I went for a total denim look topped off with Mum's sunglasses. As Mum's sunglasses weren't exactly the designer knock-off I'd had in mind, I decided to plant them artfully on my head so that they kept back some of my hair but not all of it. A last check of me in the mirror and I reckoned the overall effect was pretty good.

Must remember to tell Sally, I thought, how I'd managed to do all this without the advice of a twenty-three-year-old on a YouTube video.

I headed downstairs, slightly dreading the whole day, but determined not to show it. I would walk to the park, where I was going to meet the others under a particular tree (Sally's idea. She was quite sure we'd know which tree she meant when we got there. I wasn't so sure; parks tended to have quite a lot of trees in them as a general rule, and a lot of them looked rather the same), and we would have a picnic there while we assessed the boys as they got ready to play football.

Boy Watching was hungry work, so I was going to get a bumper extra super big bag of crisps and other salty snacks that you're not supposed to have too much of.

So far so good. All plans in place, I thought, as I opened the front door. But then, dilemma! It was a brilliantly sunny day. Dazzlingly brilliant. A day where you really, really needed sunglasses.

I disentangled the artful creation and brought the shades down to fulfil their original purpose. How annoying was that?

As I got nearer the park, I could tell that the tree identification plan was exactly as bad as I'd thought. Every tree I looked at looked like the one Sally had described. If it wasn't for the fact that I could see Amy in the distance, I would probably still be walking round the park looking at trees even as I write.

'Hiya!' Amy was waving and shouting. She was in the middle of a group of people I didn't recognise, but I could see Sally and Charlie standing behind her. 'We're over here.' Brilliant, I thought, Amy's caught the Bennet habit of pointing out the obvious.

I set off for the tree they were under (which didn't look like Sally's tree at all) getting rather hot by this stage and wishing I'd bought some of those fizzy drinks you're not supposed to have too much of.

'Hi, Chloe,' said Charlie, who was looking exceptionally good in his football kit. (Football does have something to be said for it, after all.) 'You look a bit hot. Have a drink to cool you down.' And he handed me a can of forbidden fizziness.

'Fantastic, thank you,' I said. So handsome, and so thoughtful. What a lucky girl Amy is. Is what I didn't say, because that would have embarrassed all of us.

'Isn't he clever to think of bringing cold drinks?' said Amy, looking at him a bit goofily. 'And doesn't he look handsome in those shorts?' OK, so Amy could do all that embarrassing stuff for herself.

'Hey, tosser, over here!' Charlie was facing the other way, and looking at someone behind me. I was just thinking how amazing it is that boys always seem to greet each other with great insults and perhaps there's some lesson we can learn from this in our Boy Watching records when I turned round and saw who it was.

It was him. He was with Rob and two other boys I didn't know. They were all kitted out in the full football gear. If I hadn't suddenly felt incredibly nervous and faint and surprised and horrified all in one go, I might have found time to think how unbelievably handsome he looked. He was wearing a red and white striped T-shirt and black shorts, and had a perfect tan and the same floppy hair. Taller than the others, and handsomer by far, he was smiling with such a confident, relaxed, warm, easy, friendly smile.

'Tosser yourself!' he called out back to Charlie.

And then he saw me. For a moment I thought he looked all happy and pleased to see me, and for a moment I felt all happy and pleased too. I'd been longing to see him again for so long, and there he was. Looking perfect and lovely and just exactly as wonderful as I remembered.

But then his face changed, he looked away and his smile faded. He seemed to slow down, and he let the others get to our group first. I moved slightly to one side. Perhaps he'd come over and talk to me first; perhaps he was going to say something that would make it all all right. And if he did, then I didn't want anyone to hear us.

But he went straight up to the others, slapped Charlie on the back, gave Amy a quick hug and started talking to one of the boys I didn't know.

Thank goodness for Mum's sunglasses, I thought.

No one was looking my way, so I quietly set off in the direction of some more trees. Once they started playing football, I'd go back and watch, but right now I just couldn't pretend to be all jolly and normal.

I thought the bandstand looked like a good place to go. It was full of people in uniform, with their brass instruments glinting in the sunshine. They all looked rather old, but very happy and smiley. I expect they loved their work.

I walked towards the bandstand to get a closer look.

Maybe I should learn a musical instrument, I thought, as they got out their music and started arranging it in a rather sweetly self-important way. Properly learn it, not like my ten chords on the keyboard. The trumpet, perhaps. Then I could play in a brass band, or maybe with an orchestra. I'd be the only prize-winning writer who also had an international record deal.

As I was mentally designing the poster for my concert at the Albert Hall, the band...struck up, I think is the expression. The tune was enormously merry, with lots of oom-pahs and banging on the drums. Everyone standing around was laughing and clapping.

I felt depressed all over again, and turned round to go and find somewhere quieter. They still hadn't started playing football, so it wasn't safe to go back.

I wandered over to a group of trees where there didn't seem to be anyone about, looking down at the ground so that I didn't have to look about me at all the people having such a good time.

'Chloe,' said a voice just behind me. 'Chloe, wait a minute.' It was him.

I stopped and waited for him to catch up, looking at the ground, fixating on a clump of grass. 'Chloe,' he said again, now much nearer. 'What's going on? I've been trying to call you. Did you get my letter? What's happened? What's the matter?'

I looked up at him. Thanking goodness for the sunglasses yet again.

'Nothing's the matter,' I said, because that sort of untruth is one that always seems to come easily at moments like this. 'Nothing's happened. I think I've just got things wrong, that's all. I feel a fool, if you must know. And I don't want to talk about it. Not now. Not ever.'

For a moment his nearness had almost made me lose my nerve. Almost made me forget for a second that he wasn't the boy I'd fallen for. But he couldn't ever undo the hurt, and I'd just have to get over it. Starting now.

I set off back up the hill and towards the quiet woods that I'd spotted earlier, and didn't look back. I wasn't playing games. I didn't want to be followed, I just wanted to stop it all and try to move on.

The jolly oom-pahs of the band followed me up the hill. But Mark Anderson didn't. Perhaps deep down he was relieved that we could put an end to something that had never really started, and now wouldn't go anywhere.

Later, much later, I could hear shouts and yells at the bottom of the hill where they were playing. Even at this distance, I could hear the 'Pillocks' and 'Wazzocks' and 'Tossers' and 'Dingbats'. Clearly they were all having a splendid time. There must be a formula for the proportion of insult given to fun had – it looked like there was a lot of both going on at the bottom of the hill.

As I got nearer Sally caught sight of me. She was in the middle of a big group of girls and a lot of picnic mess. A part of me found time to worry that we were going to have to clear it all up some time and did we have enough plastic bags. And then another part of me told me to shut up, as there were more important things to worry about than litter control right now.

'Hey, Chloe,' she called out, tottering slightly on some quite high and probably – given that we were in a park situation – ill-advised heels. 'Come over here. You've just missed the last sausage roll.' She sounded vaguely triumphant, as if she'd personally managed to ensure that they'd run out before I arrived.

I tried not to be too irritated. Besides, it wasn't as if I wanted anything to eat. Probably wouldn't want anything to eat ever again, what with having had all my illusions shattered and all my hope of happiness gone for ever.

Amy headed my way. 'Don't you think they look fabulous, Chloe? Shall we have a new section in the Boy Watching charts for sport? We could have points for Handsomeness in Shorts, and for Playing Nicely.'

'Yes,' said Sally, filming them all as they shouted and ran about and sometimes connected with the ball, 'and I think Rob wins – look at him, doesn't he look great?'

Actually Rob didn't look great. His football kit made him look rather stocky and short, plus he had that grin on his face that he seemed to have whenever he was running which made him look like a slightly out-of-condition serial killer.

Mark, on the other hand, looked sensational. He seemed to be faster than everyone else, and yet didn't seem to collide with people all the time like the others did.

I turned away from this particularly painful bit of Boy Watching. And found myself looking into the eyes of a girl with a long dark ponytail, designer sunglasses casually on the top of her head, and an oversize yellow T-shirt. Georgie. Sister of the more famous Mark.

'Hello there,' she said smiling at me. 'Chloe, isn't it? We met at the bowling alley. You're at Queen Mary's, aren't you?'

I was just about able to smile and nod like a normal person.

'I've just started there. Year Eleven. Very strict and old-fashioned, isn't it? I think my parents have made me go there as a punishment for wanting to be an actor.'

'How exciting.' Sally had put down her phone and was gazing fascinatedly at Georgie. I was glad someone else could do the talking as I couldn't seem to get a word out. 'Are you in anything? Do you know any famous people? What's it like being an actor?'

'Well, yes, no and I don't really know yet,' said Georgie, smiling at Sally in a really nice Georgiana Darcy kind of way. 'I'm in this pilot for a comedy show. I'm the daughter who goes off the rails. Think that's why I've ended up at Queen Mary's. Mum wants me firmly on the rails in real life.'

'I met your mum,' I found myself saying. 'I was working at the hairdresser's she goes to. I thought she was great.'

'She *is* great,' said Georgie. She started to say something else but at that moment we were interrupted by a loud, 'Hey, Georgie.'

Three of the boys were waving at her. The game had finished and there was a lot of general yelling from the football area. They were all high-fiving each other as they headed our way.

Perhaps it was just as well that my conversation with Georgie was interrupted. She probably still thought

I was a friend of Mark's, and I couldn't bear the thought of having to explain that I wasn't any more.

Meanwhile, the sweaty sportsmen were now amongst us, treading all the rubbish into the grass and spitting just like they do on television. Every other word was post-watershed bleepable. It must be something to do with the testosterone released by football, I decided, that shows The Boy at his least attractive.

'Don't they all look fantastic?' said Sally, gazing particularly intently at Rob.

'I think I prefer them fresh out of the sea.' It was Gemma, suddenly in our midst. She had Jack 'Surfer Boy' Harrington with her, and she smiled flirtatiously at him as she spoke. I wondered why she was coming on so strong, and then I saw Jezza in a group just behind her. He had noticed Jack, and the flirting, I could tell, even though he was pretending not to look.

I had to hand it to my friend: she was good at this.

Jezza went towards the football players and separated out the ones who were going to go and perform with the band. Jezza himself didn't do football. Perhaps because he already had a perfectly natural sheen of sweat without troubling himself with any form of sport.

They headed off towards the Student Union where

137

the concert was going to be. The Union was a scary place. I guess when we're a bit older it will be a perfect place to do Boy Watching, but for now the students seemed more like men than boys – out of our league anyway.

'Come on, Chloe,' said Gemma from behind me. 'Let's go and watch some boys. Your favourite kind of thing, isn't it? After First World War poetry of course.' And she smiled at Jack in an eye-rolly way that managed to be quite irritating, but didn't actually make me hate her.

(Note to self: after we've published our copyright-protected, scientifically-proven Boy Watching charts – *The Complete Guide to the Habits and Behaviour of the Boy of the Species* – we might help the very boys we watch by giving them some Girl Watching advice. I shall save the chapter about Gemma until the very end. Because I think you'd have to have a pretty good understanding of Girls in general to have a hope of understanding Gemma in particular and the effect she has on people.)

'If we get there early we've got some hope of being in the front,' said the one from the last chapter. And she linked one arm in mine and the other in Jack's.

As we walked off across the park towards the Union

I told myself firmly that I mustn't turn round to see if anyone was watching us go.

I didn't turn round. Perhaps I was on the road to curing myself of my hopeless passion. Perhaps one day I'll look back on all this and laugh.

Perhaps.

Camouflage...

We were just arriving at the Union when Jack turned to me: 'Cool shades. They look good on you.' Beautiful surfer Jack must have been listening in charm school. Plus who knew Mum's shades would score me a compliment? 'Do you really like poetry? I remember you were reading *To Kill a Mockingbird* that time on the train to Cornwall.' Yup. Definitely listening.

I was just about to get started on one of my favourite topics – the genius of Harper Lee – when we were almost run over by a million enormous boys.

This is only a slight exaggeration. Half of them were in sports gear, huge and covered in mud, and the other half were just huge.

'Rugby,' said Jack. 'Half of them have just been playing and are going to watch the World Cup match later, and the other half are just going to watch the

World Cup. Reckon you have to be huge to watch rugby as well as play it.'

At that moment a particularly enormous and quite muddy rugby player, approximately seven times my size, cannoned into me. I didn't go flying because he instantly grabbed hold of me for what was really rather a nice moment.

'Hey there,' he said in a lilty voice – Welsh, I thought – 'nearly knocked you out, very sorry.' And he let go of me just a fraction later than he need have done.

He had bright blue eyes and a head like a lump of rock, all craggy. It had a bandage tied round it to protect what looked like giant ears. He looked down at me from his great height and grinned. 'No harm done?' he said.

I felt a bit dazzled and winded. Also a bit overpowered by the strong whiff of manly sportiness. I'd never been so up close to so much boy. 'No, not really,' I said. 'I'm fine, thank you.'

There we go again. Sounding like a middle-aged person at a tea party. One day, I thought, I'll get the hang of the instant sexy repartee. I hoped I'd do that before I started being middle-aged and going to tea parties for real.

As Mr Sweaty Giant headed off with his mates,

I decided we needed to have a rugby section in our Boy Watching researches. Perhaps we should have a group outing to a match, to make informed comparisons between Rugby Boys and Football Boys. I got quite excited thinking about all this. 'A dedicated researcher never rests' should be our motto, I thought, or maybe 'the quest for truth is never-ending'. Or even 'all this takes my mind off the pain'.

We fought our way through the crowds to the front of the hall – via someone offering me a voucher for an all-you-could-eat burger joint (no, thanks), someone else who wanted me to have a free tattoo (probably not, thanks) and someone else who wanted me to have free membership of the Punk Pirates Society (definitely not, thanks).

Once we were in the front, things started to hot up. Literally as well as metaphorically – the whiff of sportiness was all around me. Probably even coming from me, if I had to be honest.

At last Jezza and the Shedz guys came onstage. I realised that Gemma had cunningly put Jack in between her and me. So Jezza, looking at us from the stage, couldn't really see which one of us Jack was with. Jezza was a cool dude and deserved none of my sympathy, but he sure was being kept on his toes.

For now, though, he was doing what he does best. Strutting and singing and caressing the mike in the way that only Jezzas can do.

I always hated to admit it when I saw Shedz play, but they were good. And I could tell that the audience were loving it.

From the front we had a good view of them all, even of Rob the backstage drummer. I looked all over, but I couldn't see where Sally was in all the noise and crowd. I hoped she had a good view and could see her beloved as well as I could. (He had the same rictus-grin/serial-killer expression on his face as he drummed that he had when he played football, but now it was more like the expression of a serial killer preoccupied with trying to keep time.)

By then Shedz had done their last number, and it was nearly time to meet up with The Dad Who for our lift home.

I headed out of the hall after Gemma and Jack into the crowds of people leaving. I hadn't seen Sally at all since we'd left the park and was starting to feel a bit anxious when I felt a sharp tug on my carefully carelessly arranged hair.

'Hey, Chloe,' said my BFF. 'How great was that? Wasn't Rob brilliant? Did you see him in that last bit?'

'Yup, I saw him in all the bits, and he was just as great as he usually is,' I said a bit gracelessly, because she had disappeared, plus – and I do know this is beneath me – she hadn't saved me a sausage roll.

'I was with Georgie,' Sally said. 'Didn't you see us? We had a great chat. But, Chloe, you might be cross.' Sally looked at me a bit sideways, as if calculating the danger.

'What do you mean, cross?' I said crossly. 'Anyway, we should head over to the car park and find Amy and her dad.'

'It's just,' said Sally. And then she stopped.

'It's just what?' I said, getting a bit irritated with her, and the two girls in front of me who were taking so many selfies and pictures of each other that they'd come to a full stop and were blocking the way out.

Just amazing how some people seem to think real life and real people don't matter in the slightest compared to taking the ten thousandth selfie.

'What?' I said again, as Sally still seemed to have dried up.

'Well,' she said slowly as we were pushed by the crowd against the two girls still taking selfies. 'I was talking to Georgie. And she was telling me about all her TV and acting and stuff. And then we

144

got to talking about football.'

Ouch. Someone had trodden on my toe. Now I was really cross. Sally's tale had better be good.

'And I was talking about how some people didn't like football. In fact, YOU didn't like football.'

'Okaaaay,' I said, thinking that there was nothing too terrible here. What's with Sally's nervousness? Most people know I don't like football.

'And she said...' said Sally. 'And she said, "Yes, I know. It's a shame, because Mark loves it. And it was one of the things he thought would be difficult." And I said—'

'Yes?' I said, now beginning to get the picture and starting to feel furious and sick at the same time.

'Well, I said, "I think it's already difficult, because Chloe saw him going to a football match when he said he was still away."' Sally had stopped at this point and was looking fixedly at the floor.

'And what did she say?' I said very icily indeed. I couldn't believe that Sally was palling up to someone she didn't know and telling her all my secrets. The whole *point* was that he had lied and cheated and I didn't *want* him to know I knew and for him then to tell me more lies. What was the *point* of that?

'And she said, "Oh, I seeeeee," like that. Like she

145

suddenly understood something. And then she said, "Look, best not tell Chloe we've talked about this," and then someone came up and started talking to her and we all got split up and then the concert started and that was that. But I've told you now, haven't I, even though she told me not to, because it's you that's my friend not her.' Sally was now looking anxiously at me.

At that point there was a big push from the crowd behind us and we were both sent flying into the people in front of us who were sent flying into the people in front of them. At least that's stopped people taking selfies, I thought, as my nose was squashed into an evil-smelling anorak.

By the time we escaped from the crowd and were heading towards the car park the inner me had calmed down a bit. I was still very cross with Sally, but at least she'd told me about it.

It was all too much to think about at that moment, so I focused on finding The Dad Who in all the crowds. I walked fast and determinedly towards the car park.

'Chloe,' Sally was pattering along behind me, I knew her heels had been a mistake, 'you're not cross, are you? Chloe?'

Finally I spotted The Dad Who. 'Quite cross,' I said to Sally as we went towards The Dad Who and his ancient people carrier. 'But right now I think I just want to get home.'

And suddenly that was very true. It had been a traumatic and noisy day, I'd been full of angst but very little food, and suddenly home and bed seemed incredibly appealing.

The flat was dark when The Dad Who dropped me back, so I let myself in carefully and quietly, grateful that I wouldn't have to talk to anyone. I'd had enough human interaction for one day.

I'd reckoned without Mum being Mum, of course. She'd waited up for me, which I suppose is part of a mother's job description.

She came quietly out of her bedroom, dressed in an astonishingly unflattering nightie that looked like an electric blue tent that had been left out in the rain. 'There you are, love,' (bless her and her line that keeps on giving). 'I hoped you wouldn't be too late. We've got Steve and his friend coming first thing, so you'd better get straight to bed; it'll be a long day.'

Something else to look forward to, I thought as I cleaned my teeth: my oiksome brother and a nameless army friend filling up the house and generally interfering with my Sunday.

I looked in the mirror and saw that my right eyebrow was still somehow bigger than my left, that my scraped cheek looked as scraped as ever, and that something suspiciously like a spot was starting to appear on my nose. Also, my hair was looking all bedraggled even though I'd only washed it that morning, and I looked bright white and exhausted.

Fantastico, I thought. Obviously the stress and trauma of my life is making me lose my looks. Just my luck if Steve's friend turns out to be some unbelievably gorgeous, well-read and brilliant hunk who plays rugby and makes me laugh with his outrageously cunning wit. He'll take one look at me and my spots and scars and greasy hair, head straight back to barracks or whatever they're called, and tell all his unbelievably charming army friends that Steve's sister is even uglier than Steve.

All this was churning and churning around in my head, together with the memory of my non-conversation with Mark, the news of Georgie now knowing all about his betrayal, and, always, the worry of Mum and her operation. It felt like I lay awake all night, but I suppose I must have gone to sleep at some point because I had a dream that I was trying to play the trumpet in a blue tent where Mum was lying on an operating table surrounded by rugby players. Just as Georgie came in, dressed as a nurse and carrying a tray of sausage rolls, Mark and Steve and Mr Carson in army camouflage uniform arrived and started to throw footballs at the sausage rolls.

I think it was the noise of the footballs that woke me up. Because they turned into the sound of doors banging and voices. Mostly male voices.

It was only seven in the morning. Way too early for anything to happen, especially on a Sunday. But clearly the army chucked them out early on their days off.

I wondered if I could make it to the bathroom without being seen. I could feel the spot had come along a treat during the night and would require massive concealing. Plus I had to have another go at washing my hair, which I could feel looked horrible. Just my luck if the door handle chooses this moment to come off in my hand, I thought, as I started to gently ease it down and towards me.

As I pulled very smoothly and firmly I could feel the door start to come. Hurrah. And then with a loud creak it sprang open, the handle came off, and I found myself face to face with a strange young man in just the sort of camouflage army uniform I'd just been dreaming of.

'Hello,' he said, looking almost as dazed as I felt. 'I'm Ethan. You must be Chloe.' He was tall, a bit taller than Steve, and older. With sort-of blond hair and stubble. He certainly didn't look very hunky and six-packed, in fact he looked rather skinny and borderline anaemic. More likely to play rounders than rugby. And of course it was too early to judge, but he didn't look like he read EM Forster or the war poets either. All this I computed in a nanosecond, but decided that on balance he looked quite nice. Better than Steve's BMF Kevin-the-clone anyway.

'Yes,' I said, 'nice to meet you. I'm just going to the bathroom.' Marvellous. Still doing perfect middle-aged tea party conversation, but now also adding unnecessary and embarrassing information.

'Oh,' said Ethan, because after all what else could he say? 'Right.' Again, what else was there to say?

I put the door handle down on the floor and walked towards the bathroom, which happily was free, and shut the door behind me.

Looking at myself in the mirror I could see that I had been right about one thing: my spot had sure come along a treat during the night.

A few moments later, there was a bang on the door.

'Chloe.' It was the ghastly one. 'How much longer are you going to be? You've been in there for hours. There are other people in this family, you know.'

Which was rich coming from Ghastly Ralph, the most selfish slob in the known universe. There wasn't, though, any point in arguing the toss, so I finished my concealing work as best I could and opened the door.

'About time,' said my revolting stepfather. 'Go and help your mother get breakfast.' I could see Ethan in the background looking a bit bemused.

I went into my room and put on my purple jersey (I *think* it was purple in a good way), brushed my soaking wet hair (it was going to be another hopelessly lank day, I could tell) and pulled on the furry boots that may or may not look cool.

With my self-confidence bouncing around the low to lowest mark, I went into the kitchen. Ethan was standing by the cooker looking like on balance he'd rather be running up a hill with a fifty-pound pack on his back. Mum was frying an egg, and Steve was sitting at the table fiddling with his phone.

He looked up when I came in and said, 'Hi, Chlow,' and went back to fiddling with his phone.

See how hard it is to love a brother like this? On the one hand he calls me 'Chlow' which he knows I hate.

And on the other he barely looks at me because his eyes are pretty much glued to his phone. Which he also knows I hate.

Steve was wearing the same camouflage as Ethan was. I had to admit that he did actually look a little less oiky and oily in a uniform. Something about those light brown suedey-looking boots and the brand-new material and belt made him look altogether cleaner and stronger.

But he still had loads of spots. Even more than me. And he was STILL LOOKING AT HIS PHONE. If Ethan hadn't been there I'd have let rip.

As it was: 'Hi, Steve, nice to see you too, how have you been, hope you've been having a good time, we've only got one day together, and we should make the most of it, shouldn't we, especially with Mum being ill,' I said all in one go with my best sarcastic voice on.

'Oh,' said Steve properly looking up. 'Yeah. Right. Mum, I'll lay the table, yes?'

I reckoned this was as near to a victory over my poxy older brother as I was going to get.

I noticed Ethan looking at me and smiling a bit nervously. Perhaps he'd report back to barracks that not only was Steve's sister incredibly ugly, what with the spots and the greasy hair, but she was also a right little bossy-boots.

'That would be nice, love,' said Mum to Steve, who was actually heading towards the drawer where the cutlery was kept. (Who knew he knew? Amazing.) 'But you mustn't worry about me. I can still look after you and cook you all breakfast, you know.'

'What can I do to help, Mrs Bennet?' said Ethan, who I could now tell had a bit of a lilty accent. But not lilty like the rugby hunk's lilty more...Irish, that's what it was!

'You're Irish!' I interrupted suddenly and brightly. Goodness, my conversational skills were on fire.

'Yes, that's right,' Ethan turned to me, still looking a bit bemused but with his polite face on. 'I'm from County Mayo.'

'And no salad dressing jokes, please, Chloe,' came Steve's voice from behind me, as he made loud clattering noises, obviously trying to identify the various bits of cutlery one from another.

If Irish Ethan hadn't been there, I would so have clouted my horrible brother. On what level could he possibly think I could be so gauche as to make a joke about mayonnaise? On what level could he imagine that I wasn't perfectly capable of making incredibly amusing conversation without making some stupid pun?

'Where's County Mayo?' I said.

There. What did I say about incredibly amusing conversation?

'It's on the left. Sort of opposite Dublin. We live on the coast. It's lovely but it's sometimes a bit wild and windy,' said Ethan in his nice accent.

I started to think this was all shaping up quite well. Perhaps Ethan would get to know and love me and Sally and Gemma and Amy and he'd ask the four of us out to County Mayo, where we could check out another sort of Foreign Boy (Ireland was definitely foreign, what with it being a separate island) and have a whole new chapter in our Boy Watching records.

Ghastly Ralph came into the kitchen just as the smells of frying reached their peak. 'Ah,' he said rubbing his hands and smiling in the way that only the greedy can when they smell food. 'You're in luck, Ethan, Gill cooks a mean breakfast,' he said eyeing up the large pile of bacon, which looked anything but mean.

If you're the ghastly one this was probably the best compliment you could possibly pay your wife in Ralph World. And I guess that after years and years of practice with butter, eggs and processed meat, Mum was indeed a pretty good fryer.

But since there was nothing really to say to this we all sat down in silence – there was always something rather silencing about the presence of a Ralph anyway.

Mum brought over a huge plate of bacon and sausages and everyone rearranged their cutlery so they could get stuck in. (You really would think that a sixteen-year-old boy, all ready to join the army, would have noticed how people generally laid knives and forks. The one being on the right and the other on the left. Not so Captain Mini-Brain across the table from me.)

'What would you boys like to do with your day off?' said Mum to the poxy older brother and his Irish friend. 'It's a sunny day so we could go for a walk in the park, and then perhaps have lunch at the pub, and then they might have a good movie on at that new cinema.'

Good old Mum, I thought. What a proper old-fashioned Sunday. It just needed tea with the vicar and we could be in a TV series c. 1978.

'No, you're all right, Mum,' said Steve. (Why do people say that? And anyway, the last thing Mum actually was was 'all right'.) 'We've got some unfinished business with an Xbox. Ethan and I are neck and neck so we'll just get stuck in when we're done here.'

'You'll come with us to the pub, young man,' said

155

Ghastly Ralph. 'Your mother hasn't seen you for weeks, and you won't be spending the day in your bedroom playing some game.'

Ethan still had his polite face on, but now it was starting to look apologetic and a little bit alarmed as well.

'I expect the boys need to let off a bit of steam,' said Mum – seeming to confuse her oikish son with a small boy wanting to play in the garden. 'But let's all go together for lunch at the Hand and Arm later. That would be nice.'

Those of us familiar with the Hand and Arm couldn't agree less. It was a horrible place full of horrible music and horrible smells and the most hideous orange carpet in the history of carpets. I'd rather hoped it had fallen out of favour after Ralph had had a fearsome row with the landlord over the size of his pints.

I sighed. 'I might go and see if I can take Albert for a walk,' I said. 'Then I've got to read *A Room with a View* so I think I'll just stay here afterwards.'

'And you, missy,' said Ralph, getting up from the table in what he clearly felt was a rather commanding way, and letting loose a small burp as he did so, 'will be a part of this family and come with us too. Dunno who you think you are with all that reading. I suppose you think it makes you cleverer than everyone else.'

There was no safe way to respond to that, so I thought it best I didn't try. Happily lilty-Irish Ethan came to the rescue. 'I really like *Room with a View*,' he said surprisingly. 'I did it for my exams. I thought it was great.'

I looked at him in a whole new light. I was right about the six-pack, but wrong about EM Forster. Perhaps underneath the stubble and the camouflage uniform there beat the heart of a poet. Perhaps he'd be a war poet, and be famous.

'I'm off to set up the game,' said Steve, who of course didn't have anything to contribute to a debate about EM Forster. 'Come on, Ethe.'

I could see I wasn't going to be able to discuss *A Room with a View* with 'Ethe', so I gave him my best attractive and intelligent smile as he got up to follow Steve. I began to hope that he might think that ugly and bossy I may be, but perhaps I had an interesting and educated mind.

Although maybe that wouldn't be much of a selling-point back at the barracks.

The Hand and Arm(s)

There had been no sign of Mr Underwood or Albert, so I decided to forget exercise and fresh air for the morning.

On the whole, I was glad to have a day without going to the park. The park was fraught with danger these days, what with football, and girl gangs, and things to tread in by mistake. Also, I remembered that we never did clear up the picnic, so I'd probably be arrested for littering too.

But I didn't see why I should be the only one to suffer lunch at the Hand and Arm, so I sent a firm message to Sally to say she had to get Liv to take her there too. Plus we still didn't know what her mysterious phone call had been all about. Maybe if Liv was all mellowed up by the best fine wine the Hand and Arm could provide we could find out what was going on.

With the ghastly one watching TV, and the 'boys' letting off electronic steam, I took my book into the kitchen to keep Mum company.

I was soon in the land of EM Forster and in the middle of Florence, willing Lucy and George to get together and live happily ever, and constantly amazed at how little freedom even quite grown-up girls had in those days.

'Chloe, love, give me a hand with the dishwasher.' Mum's voice jolted me out of Edwardian Italy. Freedom and dishwasher-emptying versus repression and idle holidays in Florence. As I took the still-hot mugs out of the top layer of the dishwasher, I thought how nothing is ever perfect.

'How you feeling, Mum?' I said, rather dreading an honest answer.

'Not too bad, love,' she said. 'Be glad when it's over, though. At least I won't have to worry about looking after you all once Gran's here.'

I'd forgotten about that. Or at least I hadn't allowed myself to think about it. Crimplene-clad Gran and her wooden walking stick. A grim thought indeed.

After we'd finished all the clearing up, and as if by magic and knowing it was safe to do so, the menfolk *chez* Bennet came into the kitchen.

'Best get going,' said the ghastly one, starting to do the hand-rubbing-together thing that seemed to go with his realising there was room inside for some more food.

We set off to the Hand and Arm, me trying hard to be at the back so I could talk to Ethan about *A Room with a View*.

'So do you still get to read and things now you're training for the army?' I asked Ethan, as I got myself next to him, making sure that I was on the right-hand side so he couldn't see the full glory of the spot and the scraped cheek.

'Not much, no,' he said in his lilty voice. 'I miss it a bit, but it's full on in the army all the time, and if you're reading anything it's regulations and stuff you have to learn.'

'I guess you'd get teased anyway, reading EM Forster,' I said. 'You've got to be all tough and rufty-tufty if you're a soldier, haven't you? I mean, not that reading is girlie, but you don't want to show off being in touch with your feminine side and all that, do you?'

I was looking ahead at Mum as she leaned rather heavily on Ralph and I didn't notice that Ethan had gone silent. Then I saw out of the corner of my eye that he'd also gone a bit red.

Perhaps he was one of those boys who didn't like anyone to think he had a feminine side, I thought.

And then I went all silent myself, remembering a certain boy who I'd once seen deeply engrossed in *The Diary of Anne Frank.*

I couldn't ever imagine myself liking, *really* liking, a boy who didn't read. It had been one of the categorisations that I'd wanted in our Boy Watching studies: the ability to read proper books (with pleasure and without use of forefinger to follow the words) and discuss them interestingly. But I think I was the only one who thought that important. We had points for Looking Good in Jeans instead.

Since Ethan still seemed a bit silent, I tried again. 'So are you all really fit? Do you have to do all that scrambling over walls stuff, with a backpack, carrying jerrycans, and wading through mud up to your knees?'

In an idle moment, when I was meant to be doing French homework, I'd looked up Army Training: A Day in the Life and there seemed to be an awful lot of physical endurance tests. Ethan seemed to be on the spindly side for all that activity.

'Yes,' he said, 'there's quite a lot of that.' He paused and looked a bit thoughtful. 'And I'm not very good at it. It was Dad's idea this army thing anyway. I wanted to be an actor.'

Before I could pursue this interesting line of investigation – Tough Dad Wants Spindly Son to Follow in Tough Footsteps, Not Be Poncy Actor, sort of thing – we arrived at the Hand and Arm.

We were there so early that it was eerily empty. Which meant you had plenty of opportunity to admire the dirt on the orange carpet, and listen to what a pub sounded like before they turned the music on. Neither of these things made me any keener on the whole experience.

I followed Mum and Steve and Ethan into what they cheerily called 'the family room'. Which was another way of saying the place where you put all the tiresome underage people while the grown-ups got up close and personal with the likes of Mr Pinot Grigio.

I watched Ghastly Ralph roll towards the bar, and hoped that Sally and her mum wouldn't be long.

About an hour, and two and a half Ralph pints later, we were sitting quite silently (the music now being on and very loud) at the table when in came Sally and Liv. Close behind them were the terrible twins, Harris and Jock, and Patrick the gardener.

Sally headed over to our table.

'You won't believe it,' she shouted into my right ear (close to the spot and the deformed cheek). 'But Mum says Patrick's coming to live with us. Apparently, he's going to look after the garden and the twins permanently. Plus he's going to be Mum's personal trainer.'

This was quite a lot of information to compute, and not what I'd expected at all. Having built up quite a detailed picture of Sally's dad-the-spy coming home covered in glory and/or terrible wounds from having been blown up a couple of times, it was a bit odd to hear that the future lay with Patrick-the-gardener.

I decided that the mysterious phone call to Liv was dad-the-spy telling Liv that all was over between them because he'd been nursed back to life by some glamorous foreign girl in some glamorous foreign country and he was never coming home. All of which was a bit tough on Sally and Harris and Jock, but perhaps as they'd never really known their father, they didn't know what they were missing.

Then I thought of my own – real – father, who I could just about remember even though I was only three when he died. I could remember his presence, and his soft voice, and the fact that everything felt safe when he was there.

As I watched the ghastly substitute, Ralph, as he

rolled back from the bar with another pint, I started to feel really quite sorry for myself and my fatherless friend down the other end of the table.

I looked at Patrick as he sat down and started to show the twins how to do whatever it was they were trying to do on their phones. He was very handsome, and obviously very fit, which I guess is what you'd expect, what with the personal training and the gardening.

Liv sat down next to him, clutching a large glass of something light yellow in colour, the sort of light yellow that we'd come to associate with Pinot Grigio. And Liv.

Whether it was because of the glass, or Patrick-the-gardener, she looked much happier than she had done on the day of Albert and the Disappearing Plate of Cheese. And judging by the acute angle of her right shoulder, I'd say she probably had her hand on Patrick's knee.

Sally came and sat next to me at just about the point when the music got less loud. Which meant that everyone could hear her when she said, 'Hey, Chloe, don't you just love Patrick's muscly arms?'

I blushed, because I had been thinking something pretty much along those lines, and Sally blushed because everyone had heard, and out of the corner of my eye I saw that Ethan blushed. But even as he blushed he still carried on looking at Patrick.

Thankfully – and I can't believe I mean this – at that moment something really horrible from the 1980s piped up on the music system. It had a very loud beat, incomprehensible lyrics, but was beautifully welcome for its drowning out all possibility of conversation or thought.

There was a bustle of getting up and getting Cokes and burgers and lots of salty things on the forbidden list, and the moment of Patrick and the loveliness of his arms had passed.

The rest of lunch passed without incident or accident, although I noticed that Ethan was even more silent than before. But then it was hard to be anything else in all the noise.

Eventually, Sunday lunch came to its natural end. Ralph heaved himself up from the table, taking some of the evidence with him (five empty pint glasses), and he was followed by Mum (one empty tomato juice glass) and Liv (six empty wine beakers) as they went to pay the bill.

Sally grabbed my arm as we headed towards the door. 'So what's with Ethan, Chloe? Has he got any Boy Watching points? Will you be seeing him again?' she said.

'He seems nice,' I said. 'And he can read.' Sally looked a bit confused at this. 'I mean books. Proper books. Like EM Forster. I think it was actually nice of Steve to invite him to ours, because he's miles from his family – he's Irish, they live in Ireland – County Mayo,' I said, realising, too late, what was going to happen.

'What did the mayonnaise say when someone opened the fridge door? Close the door, I'm dressing!' said Sally before bursting into peals of laughter.

Yup, I was right.

'Do you think Ethan knows that one?' said Sally. 'Shall I go and tell it to him?'

'No,' I said, watching Ethan leaning politely down towards Mum, offering his arm for support. 'I think he'd rather get back to Xbox or whatever on his precious day off than listen to daft jokes.'

Sally looked a bit downcast at this, but really, I was only saving her from herself.

For the rest of the afternoon everyone behaved rather satisfyingly according to type. Ralph fell asleep – loudly and uglily – in front of the TV, the 'boys' carried on with their electronic games, Mum sat in the kitchen with her Sudoku and I went back to Edwardian Italy.

When the time came for Steve and Ethan to pack up their kits and head for the bus and the barracks, everyone was distinctly quiet. Ralph because he was probably still half asleep and woozy from all the pints, and Ethan because he internalised everything. (I had come to this conclusion about Ethan. Perhaps it was on account of being a frustrated actor, or something.) And Steve because even he felt that he couldn't just grunt goodbye this time, yet saying things was even more difficult if you never had any practice.

'OK, Mum,' he said, obviously making a big effort. 'You'll be all right, won't you?' Which wasn't so good. He was just seeking reassurance, which didn't really help. 'I mean, they know what they're doing and stuff.' Ditto.

'Yes, love,' said Mum, 'it'll be fine. You mustn't worry.'

The relief on Steve's face was clearly visible. Licence not to worry. What could be better?

Spindly Ethan made an effort too. 'I do hope it all goes well, Mrs Bennet; thank you for having me.' They must bring them up properly in County Mayo, I thought.

As they stood around the front door, Steve seemed to be trying to make a decision. After a moment he suddenly turned to me and said, 'Gemma all right, is she? Still got lots of boyfriends?'

Oh dear. Still carrying a candle, or a torch, or whatever it was. Perhaps hope would always spring eternal in the Steve breast.

'Yes, she's fine,' I said. 'Brilliant in fact, and yes, more boyfriends than ever.'

You can only do what you can do.

As I watched the two of them head downstairs, I started to have a few thoughts about unrequited love. Something about how unfair it was that we could be wired to really, really like someone who was really, really never going to return the favour.

It was but a short step from this to thinking about a football-loving boy who'd recently returned – early – from America.

I went to my room in another slough of despond.

Lessons to Learn

The slough of despond lasted all through Monday and Tuesday. It even lasted through History, and Eng Lit (two of my favourites), and was particularly bad in Chemistry (ugh) and Maths (double ugh).

So by the time we got to Wednesday, Hospital Day, I was properly dismal.

Mum, on the other hand, was incredibly cheerful. We sat around at breakfast not eating very much, and Mum nothing at all – nil-by-mouth, I think it's called – waiting for the minicab to take her to the hospital.

'...a whole week of being waited on hand and foot,' Mum was saying. 'And they say that the drugs and things they give you to knock you out make you feel nice and woozy.'

I had to hand it to Mum: she could give master classes in looking on the bright side of life.

As she and Ralph set off in the taxi, I headed for the bus to Queen Mary's. I'd rather hoped that I might get a compassionate day off, but apparently you've got to be the one having the operation for that to happen.

Amy had convened a meeting at her house for the evening as it was generally deemed I'd need cheering up. So that at least was something to look forward to, I thought as I sat in the back of the Maths class (incredible how often Maths is on the timetable). The loathsome Miss Grunbar, thin dark hair shaking with anticipated irritation, was in full flow, explaining the theory of the quadratic equation.

She had a rasping voice and a constantly sarcastic tone, as if she expected that anything we said would certainly be wrong and probably be stupid. There was something of a self-fulfilling prophecy in all this, because she seemed to scare us into being dumb.

Sally and I had managed to sit together at the back. Generally they tried to separate us, but new term, new rules. Sally had suggested that we should take our minds off the pain of Maths by making a Boy Watching subsection and make 'Snog/Marry/Avoid' lists of boys in St Thomas's Year Twelve (excluding Mark and Rob, the two who really mattered, naturally).

I thought this was rather a childish idea, but – just

to keep Sally happy of course – agreed. Soon I was utterly caught up in whether I would rather snog or marry a boy called Dave who always won the 200 metres race at Sports Day when a raspy voice penetrated my consciousness.

'...perhaps Chloe can tell us the answer as she's obviously been very busy working it out.' I looked up to see Miss Grunbar's beady eye was focused on me with an expression of half hatred, half glee. 'Let us have a look at your workings, Chloe,' she said as she advanced towards me.

Too late for Sally or anyone to pass me something mathematical-looking, too late for me to scrunch into oblivion the results of my 'workings' – basically a list of all the Year Twelves I knew because I hadn't wanted to forget anyone. Too late...

Miss Grunbar took the offending piece of paper from my desk and looked at it with an expression of scorn and then one of triumph. Somehow I found time to wonder why she should be so pleased that someone in her class was so totally not listening to her teach.

'New year, new rules, Chloe,' said Miss Grunbar, uncannily echoing my earlier thoughts, but not in a good way. 'From now on anyone caught *deliberately*' – she gave the word a huge long-drawn-out emphasis

– 'not concentrating will be sent out of class and reported to the headmistress. No ifs. No buts.'

Great. Not just to be sent out, but to be put on Mrs Munroe's, the headmistress's, black list. Mrs Munroe was so humungously scary, that the idea of being in her black books was a major disincentive to bad behaviour even among the most badly behaved.

I must have looked as dazed as I felt. 'Get up then, Chloe. No excuses; it means you. Go out into the corridor.' And she walked to the door, opened it and made ushering motions to me.

I was still a bit dazed when the door shut behind me and I found myself standing in a silent corridor. How quiet everything is, I thought, when you are in disgrace and everyone else is busily learning away behind all those closed doors. Somehow the silence and the row of doors made me feel extra alone and extra punished.

Outside one of the Year Eleven classrooms, there was just one rickety chair to sit on. I had no phone, no book, no one to talk to, but perhaps if I sat down I'd look less conspicuous if anyone – God forbid Mrs M – should walk past.

Seven minutes crawled by. Maybe I'd be allowed back in after fifteen, I thought. Then I heard some footsteps – running fast – coming towards the corridor.

Running of course being strictly not allowed, I already liked whoever it was who was running that fast.

Then round the corner came Georgie, pink in the face, ponytail flying from side to side. Focused on the door to my left she only noticed me at the last minute.

'Chloe!' She skidded (literally, kind of sliding and leaving a mark) to a halt. 'What are you doing – have you been bad?' She smiled in a sympathetic and also mischievous way.

I felt my scarred right cheek go flaming red underneath the layers of Liv concealer. 'A bit, I suppose,' I said, with the blush now coming on a treat. 'Made the mistake of not listening in Maths.' The exact reason for my expulsion now seemed beyond childish and I was determined not to tell Georgie.

'Bad luck to get caught then,' said Georgie. 'Actually I am now so, SO late for English that it's probably best I don't go in at all. Wanted to talk to you anyway.' She looked a bit more serious now.

For some reason – or for lots of reasons – I started to feel a bit nervous.

'We had a great time in America,' she suddenly said. 'Went to New York, North Carolina, Los Angeles, all over. Brilliant holiday. Did you hear about it?'

'No, I – I mean I didn't, that is…' Difficult to say what

173

I meant, when I didn't even know what I meant. All I could remember was that Georgie knew that I'd seen Mark at the football ground, and knew that we hadn't been in touch.

'We had to come back a bit early, though, because Dad's got some big case on. It's a big fraud case, and he's prosecuting.' Even in the midst of my confusion I was pleased that Mark's father was a barrister. I'd always found barristers with their wigs and big brains rather fascinating. 'But he wasn't too upset because it meant he could go to the league semi-final.'

Georgie paused, looking at me rather carefully.

'That's league semi-final as in football,' she went on. 'We do know that you and football don't exactly get on. But honestly, it's not all evil, and neither are the people who watch it.' She was now frowning, as if willing me to understand what she was saying.

I so liked Georgie, and wanted her to like me, just like I wanted her mother to like me, but mostly like I wanted her brother to like me.

Unless I was being very stupid (and though that was always a possibility I didn't think I was), Georgie was telling me I needed to get over myself and my hatred of football and understand this was a family outing and not necessarily blame Mark. Although she didn't know about the QBM element, did she?

I looked back at her earnest expression. 'I know. Maybe I feel a bit – well…' I tried hard to find the words to say that perhaps I wasn't completely right and Mark completely wrong, and maybe I shouldn't have damned him utterly and totally, when a door along the corridor opened.

'You may return, Chloe,' said Miss Grunbar as she held the door open, revealing a vision of Maths Hell behind her.

I turned to Georgie. 'Thanks…' I said quickly, feeling that was the only thing I could say, slightly illogical though it was, and I went towards the entrance to the classroom, brain even more whirring and confused by my recent conversation than it would have been carrying on with quadratic equations.

I went into English and Drama at exactly the time that Mum was scheduled to go into the operating theatre. Theatre/theatre, I couldn't stop myself thinking as we waited for Miss Brewer to come to the class. Odd to have the same word for high entertainment and for the messy business of mending people.

Miss Brewer was uncharacteristically late, which of course meant that, unsupervised, everyone was getting noisier and noisier. This was probably partly because this term everyone was very excited about English and Drama...for the simple reason that the end-of-term play was a scene from *A Midsummer Night's Dream*, and half the cast and crew would come from St Thomas's School for Boys.

Amazing how everyone's interest in theatre and drama had got so intense recently. Even those who didn't have a part were showing a sudden interest in a career in stage management.

To my delight I had, at the end of last term, been cast in the play – I was to be the Wall as played by Snout in the play within a play. Mark, of course, was to be Theseus, the Duke of Athens – 'of course', because he was by far and away the most handsome and dukely boy in the whole of St Thomas's. At first I'd wanted to be his queen, but he'd assured me that I was better off making people laugh. I *think* he'd meant it kindly...

Finally Miss Brewer appeared. She looks quite a lot like Edna Mode in the film *The Incredibles*. And if that doesn't conjure up a picture of someone small and powerful with huge glasses, a deep voice and a way with putdowns then you've obviously never met either Edna or Miss Brewer.

She (Miss Brewer, that is) is a fierce but inspirational Drama teacher. She also commands respect from even the most talentless and vicious of pupils (QBM, you know who you are); Miss Brewer has an air of great authority about her – despite being even shorter than the most talentless and vicious of pupils...

'Welcome back to a new term and a lot of hard work,' said Miss Brewer with a fleeting and not very convincing smile. 'Today we're going to run through some key scenes in *Midsummer Night's* so that you all have more of an understanding of the play as a whole.'

This was altogether disappointing, and much too much like real work.

'The course of true love never did run smooth,' said Miss Brewer. Too right, I thought, not very originally. 'When Lysander says this, do we think that he and Shakespeare are mocking the progress of love, or love itself?'

Jeez, I thought. And looking around me at the expressions of total puzzlement, it seemed that everyone else thought that too.

As sometimes happens when you're at school, I was going to have to concentrate.

And it was good to have to concentrate, I decided, because it exercises the brain and takes your mind off things.

By the time I came out of English and Drama, it was nearly time to go home and Mum would have had her operation.

Sally came with me as I went to our book bags to get my phone. I had arranged to ring the Ralph to find out the news.

'I hope she's all right,' Sally said.

She meant well, but sometimes her statements of the obvious surpass even mine and Mum's.

'So do I,' I said in a voice that might have sounded a bit sarcastic.

'Chloe.' Ghastly Ralph picked up on the first ring. 'So it's you.' (And no, I wasn't going to rise to that, not at moments like these.)

As nothing more seemed to be forthcoming, I said rather impatiently, 'So what's going on, is Mum all right?'

'Yes,' he said, 'they say it went OK and they'll know more soon. She's sleeping now. I'll go and see her later. You can come with me tomorrow.'

I was relieved enough not to resent that 'you're first after me' thing he had going.

After I'd disconnected, I realised that Amy and Gemma were lurking with Sally in the corner of the hall; they were all trying to look as if they weren't really waiting for me to get off the phone.

'It's OK,' I said as I walked towards them. 'The operation went all right, and that's all they can say for now.' Everyone looked properly relieved, which was nice to see.

'If we were blokes,' said Gemma, who, with her gorgeous hair, rich make-up and tight top, was definitely the Girl Least Likely to Be a Bloke, 'I think we'd probably all go to the pub and get drunk at this point.'

'But we're not,' said Sally – always the least hypothetical of all of us – 'so let's just go to Amy's and hang out.'

I'd never been a great believer in the activity they call 'hanging out', but on this occasion it seemed like the absolutely perfect and best thing to do.

Sometime later we were in Amy's bedroom deep in the

middle of a particularly strenuous game of 'Would You Rather…?'

Having vetoed 'Snog/Marry/Avoid' because of its painful memories, we'd started looking at our Boy Watching charts to see what we'd learnt recently that added to the huge sum of wisdom we'd gained since we started.

But we got distracted from the serious matter in hand by discussing Rob and asking Sally questions like 'Would you rather he had a hand the size of a roast chicken or a head the size of a pumpkin?' or 'Would you rather kiss Mrs Munroe and no one would know, or not kiss her and have everyone think you had?' And from there it was but a short step for us all to try to decide whether we would rather share a toothbrush with Miss Grunbar or kiss Mr Pampledousse on the mouth.

At this stage, there was, I must admit, a lot of giggling. Which was probably what made The Dad Who call upstairs and tell us to 'pipe down'.

I reckoned this was the equivalent of the pub landlord telling us we were too drunk and needed to go home. But giggling, I decided, was just as therapeutic.

And besides, we'd feel much better in the morning.

While it's true that none of us had thumping hangovers the following morning I, at least, felt a bit gloomy.

Ralph had come back from the hospital the previous night, just as The Dad Who dropped me off home. Mum, apparently, was very woozy (so she was right about that bit, anyway) and had only really started to come to when the ghastly one had to leave.

And since the doctors hadn't yet examined the tumour thing we didn't yet know how much treatment she was going to have to have.

So the day went by in a bit of a whirr, what with thinking about Mum and Mark and Georgie and football and, very occasionally, wondering whether I would rather have a third arm or a second mouth.

I came to, though, when we found ourselves back in Madame de B's boudoir, or Year Ten French class as it's more commonly known. Doris Bracegirdle (as she isn't more commonly known) seemed to have recovered her poise after QBM's bout of psychobullying, and started proceedings by – rather radically – teaching us something about French verb tenses, in this case, the future conditional: 'You would finish what we would eat', that sort of thing.

Or 'You would watch what I would hate', as I mentally translated it.

Which brought me back to brooding about Mark, of course. We'd have to meet soon at the first play rehearsals. Should I contact him before then? I wondered. I didn't want to have some serious conversation with him in front of everyone. Maybe I should send him a message, maybe—

'And what about you, Chloe?' Incredible how my thoughts were so often interrupted by teachers asking intrusive questions. I gazed rather dozily at Madame de B, unable to pretend I had a clue what she was talking about.

'The trip to Paris, Chloe. Will you be going? It's in two weeks' time, so everyone who wants to go needs to get their *patins* on.'

Note to French teachers: introducing French words in English sentences in this way might seem like a good idea. But it really only works if you actually explain that *patins* meant skates.

Also it only really works if you have the undivided attention of your class. And on this occasion we were much too preoccupied with working out who we needed to get to sign which form for the Paris trip. Because there was a rumour that some boys from St

Thomas's were going to go to Paris too.

Garçon Regarder AND Boy Watching. What could possibly be more educational?

Get Well Soon

Charlie lived near Mum's hospital, and as he and Amy were going off on a run together later that evening (of course! – the fun never stops for them) they were going to come with me and Ghastly Ralph to the hospital. And where we went, Sally would of course come too. ('I'm coming if they're coming,' she'd said. Which I *think* was just supportive and not at all competitive.)

As we got on the bus, Ralph headed towards the front and a place where he could fill two seats with one bottom. Sitting behind him, I felt really glad to have my BFF and my sweet-natured, curly-haired friend and her kind and bouncy boyfriend with me. I'd never been to a hospital before, and although hospitals are *good* things (I kept telling myself) and all about *mending* people, I was dreading going inside one.

So it was great to listen to Charlie's chatter – he

was a very good chatterer – and not have to say anything much.

'So there are these trips to Paris some people are going on,' Charlie was saying. 'Have you heard about it? The guys are all going for the rugby, but the girls are all going for the culture. Says it all, really, doesn't it? Apparently the boy/girl ratio is brilliant. Who knows who I might meet?' And he winked at me over Amy's head.

'I'm not going, and you're not going because we're both going to my training!' said Amy. 'And I saw you wink at Chloe. Stop winding me up, you pig!' All this was said v. lovingly. In fact borderline yuck.

Partly to interrupt this sickly love-fest, and partly because it was a genuine worry, I asked Charlie what he meant. 'When you say brilliant boy/girl ratio, Charlie,' I said, 'I take it you don't mean there'll be loads of boys and only a few of us?'

'Yup,' he said, 'That's right. One boy to three girls, apparently. You girls might have to find some local talent. But not you, Chloe, eh? You wouldn't trade in my mate Mark for some passing French hunk, would you?'

So maybe Charlie still didn't know that it was all over between us. This was a great tribute to Amy's discretion, and also to Mark's. Plus it must mean that no one thought that Mark and the QB were an item. What a lot to think about...

I must have looked as surprised as I felt, because Charlie said, 'Yup, I have heard a bit about it and I do know you two aren't exactly going out, Chloe, but I just think one of you's got to get off their high horse. Eh? Well, that's what I think anyway.'

'Charlie, stop it; leave Chloe alone. Remember the old expression about your business and minding it?' said Amy.

Bless her. But it was the second time in two days that I felt I was being a bit told off. I decided to think about it later.

For now, I had enough to worry about as we approached the huge reception area of the hospital. Everywhere you looked there were brisk-looking nurses and ill-looking people. Some of them were standing outside in the chill afternoon air, attached to a drip like the ones you see on television, and smoking a cigarette. They looked so desperate it was enough to put you off the whole idea of smoking.

We followed Ralph up the escalator to Ward F where Mum had been moved to that morning.

'Left at the top of the escalator, and then second on

the right and it's at the end,' a nice nurse had told us.

The wards seemed to go on for ages, but we found F relatively easily, helped by it being in between Wards E and G.

I could immediately see that Mum was at the end by the window. She was asleep, and even at a distance I could tell she looked very peaceful.

Bit too peaceful, I thought, as we got nearer. Then someone dropped a cup from their bedside table, and she woke with a start. It was good to see her come alive, and then even better to see her smile when she saw me. It was what I thought of as her particular Chloe-smile when I'd done something good and she was happy with me.

I smiled back, and tried not to show how shocked I was by how frail and tired she looked. Perhaps it's just the anaesthetic, still wearing off, I thought.

'Hello, love,' said Mum. 'Sorry, I didn't mean to be asleep when you came. I've been looking forward to seeing you all day.'

Which of course made me want to cry. As if she couldn't be asleep if she wanted to be.

'Hi, Mum. You're looking much better than I'd thought you'd be,' I lied. 'Sally and Amy and Charlie wanted to come and see you too. Hope you don't mind.'

'If you're a bit tired, Mrs Bennet,' said Charlie with his best kind crinkly smile, 'we'll just say hello and goodbye and leave you to talk to Chloe.'

And after a few moments, and ever so tactfully, my friends slid away with a 'see you outside later'.

Ralph had sat down on the only available chair and was thoughtfully eyeing up the untouched tea and biscuits on Mum's tray. I sat down tentatively on the very edge of her bed.

'I didn't bring you anything, Mum,' I said. I realised to my horror that everyone else had cards and things on their bedside tables, and Mum didn't have anything. What an idiot I was. 'But I'll bring you lots of stuff tomorrow.'

'Don't worry about things like that, love. It's just you I wanted you to bring,' said Mum, smiling her Chloe-smile and making me want to cry all over again.

'What happens next? When do they let you out?' I said, wanting to get back to practical things that would stop me crying.

'Five days or so, they say. I'm all hooked up to things until then,' said Mum, showing me some wires and pipes coming out of her arms. I tried not to look away, but couldn't help it. After all, it wouldn't make either of us feel any better if I took one look at her and fainted, would it?

At bit later, and after Ralph had eaten Mum's biscuits, a nurse came up to us and said it was time to check Mum's drain. This was absolutely all I needed. I really, really didn't want to know what sort of a drain, how you checked it, where it was and what it was doing.

'OK, Mum, I'd best leave you to it,' I said, getting up quickly. 'I'll see you tomorrow and at the weekend. And I'll bring stuff – you must think if there's anything you want.'

'It's all right, love,' said Mum, smiling at my haste. I guess she didn't get to be my mum without knowing exactly how squeamish I was. 'Just come when you can. It'll be lovely to see you.'

Later, outside and with the others, I told them how ashamed I was of being horrified by my own mother.

'Don't be silly,' said Amy. 'She just wants to see you. She doesn't expect you to nurse her and do stuff for her.'

She's a wise bird, is Amy.

Friday brought with it two new distractions. The first

was the challenge of getting the paperwork together for the Paris trip, and getting Mum to sign it. It was going to feel soooo selfish to swan into the hospital with a form for Mum to sign for me to have a holiday – I mean an educative trip that I would 'Get a Lot Out of' – when she was all bandaged up and attached to her drain.

So I decided to create something wonderful for her in Art so the selfishness wouldn't show so much. I hoped Mr Pampledousse would let us play with clay again, and I could make something sweet that would fit on a bedside table.

The second was the Mystery of the Disappearing Gemma.

Gemma has a lot of previous when it comes to disappearing. Often she would just turn up to school very late – and only sometimes with a doctor's note – and sometimes she would just disappear for a whole day, or even two. Somehow there was always a reason, or a piece of paper, to satisfy 'the authorities'. After all, she had Merv under her thumb or tied round her little finger or whatever the expression is, so a parental note was easier to come by if you're Gemma.

And we all reckoned she got away with it partly because she was the Girl with the Runaway Mother.

Gemma's mother, Marianne, had left the revolting Merv over eight years ago and had run off with her school friend Juliet. This was already extremely exotic, but when we discovered that Juliet was a millionaire West Indian artist with a big house in Cornwall overlooking the sea, well, it was all just beyond exotic. (Also, very good for winding up Ghastly Ralph – just telling him how rich my friend's wonderful gay West Indian artist stepmother was, was guaranteed to turn him purple.)

When Sally and I had been down to Cornwall we'd seen all the exoticism for ourselves. It was such a beautiful part of the world, full of beautiful surfer boys (like Jack Harrington) to watch, and Marianne and Juliet were so cool it almost seems impertinent to say so. (I like 'impertinent', it's my new favourite word.)

But none of this explained Gemma's latest disappearance. There'd been no sign of her in Madame de B's boudoir or at the end of school. (I'd tried not to be hurt that she hadn't come with me to the hospital, but I hadn't been surprised. Somehow Gemma and hospitals didn't seem to go together.)

And now there was still no sign of her in our last lesson of the day, Art.

'I've just sent Gemma another text, and not a word,'

said Sally as we headed towards the Art room. 'So RUDE,' she added.

'It might be rude if it weren't so worrying,' I said. 'I've sent her loads too. So it's not just you...'

'What do you mean it's "not just me"?' Sally started to say indignantly, when all of a sudden my phone pinged.

Thats enuff msges. Am OK. Cum & c me 2moro eve. G x

Well, that was a relief. So much so, in fact, that I was hardly irritated at all by the deliberate misspellings and lack of apostrophe.

Also it would be nice to have some gold-plated pizza after Saturday's visit to the hospital. I could leave the ghastly one home alone with the remote and the match, and generally let him stew in his own Stupid Juice.

We settled into our places around the studio and waited for Mr Pampledousse to grace us with his presence. I was still hoping that Mr P's plan for our lesson would be more clay, more animals – and less teaching.

Mr Pampledousse came in ten minutes late. 'Bet he's just got off the phone from Newfoundland – he's so in lurve,' whispered Amy to me. She seemed to have embraced the whole idea of the Mr Horriday/Mr Pampledousse love affair with incredible enthusiasm. I think she just thought they both looked so sad, and in her nice way of wanting everyone to be happy, had decided that Lurve was the answer.

Also, like most people happily In Lurve, she wanted everyone else to be too. I've noticed that a lot with people like her. And find it quite irritating.

'We are back doing the clay,' announced Mr P, to everyone's obvious satisfaction. 'Today I am hoping one of you will be good enough to be fired.'

I'd decided not to have anything to do with 'firing', it would all take too long. My plan was to smuggle out a small creature who could just dry out happily in Ward F.

I had my eye on the very creature: a meerkat peered out from one of the pages of Mr P's magazines. He was clearly the one on watch, looking out for his meerkat chums. He looked utterly charming.

Twenty minutes later and I was beginning to have a new admiration for people who could look at something and then draw or make a something that looked like the original something. At this rate my meerkat was going to be a sort of abstract expressionist meerkat, with unequal paws and a head half the size of his tail.

But I had a deadline, and it focused my mind and my fingers quite amazingly. At 3.29 on the dot I had something in front of me that you could almost mistake for a meerkat on watch. Amy had quietly found a small box hiding behind the sink, and just as the bell rang we popped Maximilian (the smaller the creature, the more the syllables he should have in his name, I'd decided) into it for his onward journey to the hospital.

But as I was leaving school, I had a message from the hospital that Mum wasn't able to have visitors as she was having a small 'procedure' that afternoon. I didn't know what sort of procedure a 'procedure' was; apparently it could be something really quite small or something really quite big.

I tried very hard not to think about it, and went home, clutching Maximilian's box closely to my chest like some sort of good-luck talisman.

When I got home I went straight to my room and managed to spend the whole evening pretending that I had the house to myself and my ghastly stepfather wasn't in the living room watching football.

Knowing how the whole hospital thing worked made

my second visit a bit less gruelling, and I followed Ralph through the wizened people and their drips and their cigarette ends without either staring or feeling a bit sick.

Mum was awake and looking a bit more like Mum; plus she didn't seem to have so many wires and pipes coming out of her. Presumably, whatever the procedure had been, it had proceeded properly.

She gave me a very good Chloe-smile when she saw Maximilian – he'd come with his own greetings card, which I'd found in the hospital shop – and now Mum's bedside table was looking much better.

As Ralph settled himself down into the chair and started reading the sports pages of the newspaper he'd brought for Mum, I got out the forms for the Paris trip and passed them to Mum, trying to make as little of it as possible. But because she was very good at being a mother, she knew which way was up straight away.

'You mustn't let me being here get in the way of your having a nice time, you know,' she said, 'you've got to get on with things and not think too much about me.'

See what I mean? SUCH a good mother.

'They think I'm going to be here till Wednesday now,' went on Mum. 'Gran's going to get to us on

Monday to be ready. I'm afraid I'm not going to be much use for a while.'

'You don't have to be useful, Mum,' I said, 'we can do everything, you've just got to get better.' I put my best bright smile on, although inwardly my heart was sinking at the thought of she of the crimplene trouser suit and the stick with the rubber on the end. 'Monday' was really, really soon.

I walked out of Ward F waving goodbye to them, still with my best bright smile on. Although I suppose I did have something to smile about: Maximilian was looking very proud of his new position guarding the bedside table, Mum was looking a little bit better, and I had my Paris trip papers safely signed and in my bag.

Chinese Whispers

When I got to Gemma's house, there seemed to be something weird going on. The electric gates were open, and on the drive I could see two enormous truck-like cars with darkened windows. Perhaps I'd seen too many of Steve's favourite films, but I felt that any second now the doors would open and out would pour lots of huge bearded men in camouflage uniforms waving pump-action shotguns.

Maybe they'd be hitmen paid by Russian oligarchs to target Merv because he owed them thousands of pounds. Or, looking on the positive but less exciting side, perhaps this was the entourage of a major Hollywood producer who wanted to invest in Merv's dodgy TV format. Either way, it was kind of fascinating.

Just at that moment two more cars drew up.

The first was missing a bumper, made a noise like

an ancient motorbike in the wrong gear, and had Jezza at the wheel. He had shades on even though it was early evening and cloudy, and he was obviously in the middle of a huge argument with his passenger, Gemma. The car stopped and neither of them got out, they just carried on shouting at each other. More kind of fascinating.

But also very annoying not to be able to hear what they were saying.

The other car was shiny, silver, and almost completely silent. It slid to a halt and I could see that the driver was Patrick. He was looking as handsome as ever – I could even make out the muscles on his famous and much-admired arms – and was wearing the sort of designer tracksuit that only people who are professionally fit would wear.

He was smiling nicely at *his* passenger, Sally. She appeared to be in full flow, in the way that she sometimes has when she feels that if a thing's worth saying once it's worth saying six times. Patrick's smile, I could now see, was rather pasted on.

I couldn't help thinking that he must be really keen on Liv to take on her whole family – Sally, lovely though she is, and Harris and Jock, not to mention Mr Pinot Grigio.

The Jezza car then suddenly gave a roar, as if Jezza had put his foot on the accelerator in a fit of fury. Which he probably had, judging by the way Gemma flounced out of the car and slammed the door. At the same time, Sally's flow seemed to have dried up and she got out of the shiny silver car. Patrick immediately slid silently off, presumably to a quiet night with his beloved and her menfolk.

'Hi, guys,' said Gemma, as if nothing much had just happened. 'Come on in. Merv's got some Chinese friends for tea, but they needn't bother us.'

Goodness, our friend supplied all the best drama, I thought. I immediately decided that *obviously* the Chinese friends were opium dealers, and they were calling in a bad debt.

'Gosh,' said Sally from behind me. 'Look at those big cars, don't they look scaaaaaary?'

'The bigger the car, the bigger the cretin,' said Gemma, rather boldly I thought, because the cars did indeed look scary. 'Come on, follow me.'

We edged round the cars (definitely scary) and aimed for the side door to the kitchen. I had a vague vision of finding a lot of bearded Chinese in camouflage suits sitting around drinking Earl Grey and eating buttered scones. But happily the kitchen was empty and there was no sign of Merv or the Chinese, cretinous or otherwise.

'How's handsome Patrick settling in?' said Gemma to Sally. 'Seems Liv's got him well trained if he's driving you about? Or maybe he just wants to get out of a house filled with Harris and Jock?'

'He's all right, I think,' said Sally. 'He's out running a lot, which annoys Mum, because she can't go too. What with the bunion and things.'

Gemma was getting stuff out of the giant shiny fridge. As much pizza and pasta to supply a small Italian restaurant, and enough fizzy drinks for us and several Chinese armies.

'So what's going on, Gem?' I said, because the bunion discussion was all very well, but Gemma had a whole day and a half's disappearance to explain. Also I needed the script of what was going on in the car with Jezza.

'Well, you won't be surprised to hear that it's all about Jezza,' said Gemma. 'He told me on Thursday afternoon that his family are going back to Scotland. Suddenly. They're not telling him why, but anyway he's got to go too. He's not happy about this, so being a very grown-up caring sort of person, he's taking it all out on everybody else. Like me.'

'But it's hardly your fault,' I said. 'And anyway, isn't it quite a good thing to have a rest from Jezza?' I had always felt that Jezza wanted his own way too much – as in all the time. I know you're not supposed to diss your friends' boyfriends, but in all our Boy Watching activities no one ever came close to Jezza for selfish and thoughtless behaviour. Even Gemma had to agree that he deserved all his minus points.

'So what were you doing yesterday?' said Sally. 'Why weren't you answering our texts?' Clearly this was what really rankled with Sally. Not worrying about Gemma's mysterious disappearance.

'Nothing much, but Merv wasn't around – and Jezza wanted me to go round to his. He's got this new car. Well, when I say NEW – you saw it. Knackered thing, but he wanted to take me for coffee in it, some place near the racecourse,' said Gemma.

'Godssake, Gemma,' I said. Because I know I've got this reputation for being po-faced, but really how RIDICULOUS to risk getting into so much trouble just for coffee in some dive near the racecourse. Is what I thought, but didn't say.

'You're crazy,' I said. 'Just crazy. What on earth's the point of risking getting into serious trouble just to have coffee with Jezza in some dive near the racecourse.'

So, I was wrong about that. I didn't just think it.

'It seemed like a good idea at the time,' said Gemma a bit sheepishly. 'School's so boring at the moment. Or most of the time really. And he'd actually said he was going to take me somewhere exciting. How was I to know it was just, as you put it, Chloe, some dive near the racecourse?'

'So why haven't you been expelled, or suspended, or whatever?' said Sally, with the air of someone who rather likes a bit of bad news. I don't think she DOES like bad news. I mean, I'm not saying she would be one of those women knitting by the guillotine as the revolutionaries cut people's heads off and threw them into baskets, but there's a sort of eager anticipation going on there that sometimes worries me.

'Maybe I have,' said Gemma. 'Won't know till Monday, but I reckon I can get Merv to do the decent thing and come up with the right paperwork.'

Incredible.

Except the mention of paperwork did remind me of Paris.

'Did we know, people, that there's a bit of a ratio issue with the Paris trip?' I said. 'According to Charlie it's a hot ticket at St Thomas's because there are going to be three girls to one boy. Which, given that Amy's not going, means that mathematically speaking, there is one boy out there for us three to share. And I don't know about you, Sally, but I don't fancy my chances against our friend here.'

'I thought you were only going for the Art and the Architecture and the Culture, Chloe,' said Gemma, a bit unnecessarily, in my view.

'And the science!' Sally piped up. 'After all, we all know that Boy Watching is not just a hobby it's a science!'

Quite. There are times when I remember why my BFF is my BFF.

'Exactly,' I said. 'I think we could learn a lot from observing the English boy abroad, and the French boy in his native habitat. So of course we need as many specimens as possible to make it all properly scientific.'

'Well, we're going, and there's not much we can do about persuading a whole load of new specimens to come too. So let's not think about it for now, and get stuck into this pizza,' said Gemma, extracting huge wheels of pizza from the oven.

Moments later we were halfway through our weekly allowance of sugar, salt and fat. (We knew about this sort of thing because Sally had an app for measuring the ingredients of everything – except she never used it on pizzas. Possibly because she liked pizzas too much to want to know what was in them.) And we were just getting on to the ice cream course when the door opened and in came the dreaded Merv.

His denim was blue this time, but its seams were still straining against the strain of containing Merv. And somebody should tell him that thin, greasy shoulder-length grey hair, and grey stubble, doesn't make you look like a movie mogul.

'Hello, hello, girls,' he said rubbing his hands in that borderline sinister way that he has.

'We all having a nice time? Got everything you need, have you?' he went on, for all the world like a normal, likeable father.

He gave us a wide smile, which had the unfortunate effect of showing us quite how many teeth he was missing. (You'd think someone with state-of-the-art electric gates could afford to go to the dentist.)

'We're fine, Merv,' said Gemma in that contemptuous tone of hers that she seemed to reserve for her father. 'Hadn't you better get back to your Chinese friends?'

'They're not the Chinese ones,' said Merv, now

a bit subdued. 'They're from Hong Kong, but they're Korean. Unfortunately.'

There was a silence. None of us really had anything to contribute to a debate about the possible nationalities of Merv's business associates.

'Why "unfortunately"?' said Gemma.

'Because they've taken over the business of my Chinese friends, and we're not getting on so well.' He paused. 'Not really so well at all.'

'Then you'd better not leave them alone,' said Gemma coldly. 'Let us know when they're gone and it's safe to go in the living room and watch TV.'

Merv didn't say anything. He just looked at his daughter, then at the floor, and then turned and walked slowly out of the kitchen.

'Oh my gosh!' said Sally, when he'd gone. 'Do you think he's caught in the middle of some gang warfare? Do you think they're going to kidnap him and hold him to ransom?' She sounded rather excited. I tried not to be reminded of the knitting and the heads rolling into the baskets.

'I don't think we want anyone we know to be stuck in the middle of gang warfare, do we?' I said a little bit coldly, and then went on: 'Plus I wouldn't want you in my gang, if you think that you should kidnap the person you want to get a ransom from.'

'Exactly,' said Gemma. 'It'd be me they'd need to kidnap. And for all sorts of reasons I hope they don't. Not least because I wouldn't bet on Merv stumping up.'

Not long after that we heard sounds of voices, and then of heavy expensive car doors shutting, the growl of big engines starting up, and then the sound of big engines fading into the distance.

Moments later we could hear Merv head out to the garage and start up his own big engine. As he growled off into the distance, to go wherever Mervs go when they've had a Korean scare, we knew it was safe to go into the living room, turn on the enormous screen and sink thankfully into the world of Saturday night reality TV shows.

I spent a lot of Sunday re-bonding with the one reliable male in my life.

I hadn't seen Albert much since his adventure with Liv's plate of cheese. In fact I'd been rather worried that he'd been a bit silent every time I'd been past his door. But I needn't have worried. By the time I'd walked him twice round the park, we were both very tired and very bonded.

It had been a good way of spending a Sunday – leaving the ghastly one behind, being in the fresh air, quality time with Albert, that sort of thing. Plus it gave me time to do a bit of thinking.

By the time I got back, and had handed Albert back to Mr U, I had made a number of momentous decisions.

First that I would absolutely make a point of being super nice to Gran and even to Ghastly Ralph when Mum came home. Whatever it took not to worry her. And I would make Steve come back for another visit soon to cheer her up. These were all good decisions, for which I deserved many brownie points.

And second I would write to Mark: a proper email or maybe even something on actual paper with an actual pen, and ask to see him before rehearsals started. This was quite a selfish decision, for which I deserved no Brownie points. But everyone – Mum, Georgie, Charlie especially – had said I shouldn't cut myself off.

Besides, I wasn't sure how much longer I could go without seeing him. One way or the other.

Grandmother's Footsteps

Monday morning had an odd feel about it right from the off.

This was partly because the ghastly one had taken the day off to prepare for the arrival of Gran. So he was slobbing around at the breakfast table in his tartan dressing gown (unnervingly like the one Mr Underwood downstairs had. In fact, if I allowed myself to think about it, the two of them were unnervingly alike in more ways than one).

Secondly, the hall was full of Steve's stuff from his bedroom, which was having to be emptied to make way for Gran and hers. It was oddly disconcerting to have to walk around skateboards, piles of jeans and boxes of old DVDs. And to wade through duvets and posters covered in the shields of whichever football team Steve supported (see how hard I try not to know about this stuff?). It was almost like my brother was being thrown away.

'You'll be back in good time today, won't you?' the ghastly one said, as he reached across me for the marmalade.

'Yes, of course,' I said more abruptly than I'd meant to according to my new resolution. But the whiff of Ralph that came my way after he reached over the table would be enough to make anyone tetchy.

'Because your gran hasn't seen you for over a year, and she'll want to spend a bit of time with you before your mother gets back from hospital,' said Ralph.

'Yes, of course,' I said again.

'Also, I'll be out,' continued Ralph. 'Gotta see some mates about a job.'

So he was lining me up to keep Gran happy while he went down to the pub. Great.

I got up, got my school bag, negotiated a pile of discarded boy socks and football boots and went downstairs. I didn't trust myself to say anything – it would be a pity to break my resolution so soon.

It was pouring with rain when I left, and pouring with

rain as I came back. The walk from the bus stop is quite a long one, so I was nice and damp by the time I got to our front door.

Albert must have recognised my squelchy step, because he barked vigorously as I put my key in the door. I felt bad not knocking on his door to say hello or take him for a wet Monday walk, but I had visions of Gran, sitting in solitary state at the kitchen table getting crosser and crosser as it got later and later and her granddaughter still hadn't appeared.

Nervously I walked up the stairs to our flat. All was very quiet: no sound of cases being unpacked, no sign of unfamiliar bags in the hall. The only strikingly different thing was a very, very strong smell of peppermint.

They say that there's nothing like a smell to trigger a memory. As I started to feel like I was being strangled by a giant Polo mint, I understood what they meant. It was the essential Smell of Gran, and it took me right back to her dark bungalow a million miles from here. Sitting on the scratchy sofa in front of Gran's ancient TV which was turned up so loud you couldn't think, with a plastic plate of tinned spaghetti loops on my lap. Glad of the darkness, because it meant I couldn't see the greenish colour of the food, the clumps of hair on the carpet, or her bizarre and terrifying collection of china dolls that sat on the shelf above the TV.

As I got nearer the kitchen, the smell got stronger and I heard a snorting noise. I looked round the door and there was Gran, standing at the cupboard over the cooker, leaning on her stick with one hand and rummaging around in the jams and marmalade with the other.

She had on exactly the kind of crimplene trouser suit that I remembered so clearly. A sort of pale brown colour, it was baggy in all the wrong places and the trousers were so short you could see her elasticated socks.

As she turned around, I quickly looked away in case she caught me staring. She was wearing a large pair of blue spectacles that Dame Edna Everage would have been proud of, and which perfectly matched the blue tinge of her bouffant hair. She was looking at me with an expression of disapproval.

'Hello, Gran,' I said.

'There you are, Chloe,' she said. Clearly, stating the obvious must be firmly in the genes. 'You are very wet,' she added with a frown which made me feel that somehow it was my fault it was raining.

'Yes, it's raining quite hard outside,' I said. I wondered if we could actually maintain an entire conversation like this – making statements of blinding obviousness without actually exchanging any real information.

'Well, it's nice to see you, dear, wet or not,' said Gran, and she gave one of those smiles that disappears almost before you've noticed it. She had an accent a bit like Mr Carson's – sort of not-quite-convincing plummy. 'It's very hard on your mother, this cancer business, and on you too. I expect you're glad I've come to look after you, aren't you, dear?'

'Yes, Gran,' I said, because that was the only safe answer. 'Are you all right in Steve's room?' I asked, wanting to move it all on a bit.

'It's a bit smelly in there, dear,' said Gran, wrinkling her nose in a way that made her look like a pug. 'But I've brought my air freshener, so I expect we'll be all right.'

The peppermint air freshener. Never without it. That's Gran, for you. But if she filled the bathroom with Eau-de-Polo-Mint, that had to be better than Eau-de-Methane.

I smiled my best granddaughterly smile. 'Were you looking for anything particular in the cupboard, Gran?'

'Yes, dear,' said Gran. 'I was looking for something for our tea. I'm sure your mother must have some tinned spaghetti loops somewhere, mustn't she? They were always such a favourite of hers, I'd expect her to have a cupboard full.'

Mum hated tinned spaghetti loops almost as much as I did. But I suppose since nobody had ever had the heart to tell Gran that, it was our own fault that we were now doomed to eat tinned spaghetti more or less on a...loop.

'Let's just have cheese on toast today, Gran. Going to have a shower, back in a mo.' I suddenly felt the urge to warm up and wash away the smell of peppermint.

Later, sitting over the remains of baked beans, bacon and sausages – I guess there never really was any escaping processed meat in our house – Gran put down her teacup with what sounded like a decisive clatter.

'And so, Chloe. What about boyfriends?' She looked at me over the top of her monstrous glasses. 'You're much too young, of course, but these days it seems that Anything Goes. And children your age seem to think they should have a boyfriend.'

Ah. Anything Goes. The other sign of This Country Going to the Dogs.

Of course I hated being called a child. And even

more I hated being grilled about boys.

'There isn't anyone in particular, Gran,' I lied. 'Some people have boyfriends, but not everyone. And some people make them up, and some people pretend they don't care, but mostly we don't talk about it much. Too much work to do.'

I reckoned God would probably forgive me for the little untruths in that statement.

'That's good, Chloe,' said Gran. 'Time enough for all that sort of thing when you're older. The main thing is to pass your exams. You're going to pass your exams, aren't you? You're a clever girl, so they shouldn't be too much trouble.'

'Thanks, Gran. But I'm not that clever. In fact... I think I'd better go and do some homework now, if you don't mind. Shall I help you wash up?'

There. What a perfect little granddaughter I was.

I fled to my room in relief that the inquisition was over. It was a bit true that I had work to do. But the only work I actually wanted to do was write my English essay for the Queen Mary Creative Writing Prize.

For a future prize-winning author, it seemed to me that I'd better start practising winning prizes. And the Queen Mary prize was the only one for creative writing, so of course I needed to win it.

The trouble was that every time I sat down to write, something happened to my brain, and I found myself fiddling around on the internet when I should have been honing my adjectives and plotting my plot. It had got so bad that I was beginning to wonder if the internet wasn't actually Evil. How could it be that checking out my star sign (Sagittarius – optimistic, adventurous, large-hearted and tactless according to my latest find), the St Thomas's website (of course), the houses of the rich and famous, even the *weather forecast* had more appeal than settling down to the work that I loved.

It was a worry.

But right now, Gran didn't have to know that I had a butterfly brain and probably wouldn't write a word that evening. Or at least not a word except several texts to Sally to see if she was looking at the same websites, or to Amy to see if Charlie was going to go to Paris, or to Gemma to see if Merv's Korean friends had come back.

I heard revolting Ralph get home when I was in the middle of testing Albert's IQ. (Turns out, according to this website, that Albert was an especially bright dog.) I could hear some stumbling up the stairs, and then some banging about in the kitchen, then Steve/Gran's door opening and then some footsteps going into the kitchen.

Kind of intrigued to see how the Gran/Ralph dynamic was going to play out, I eased open my door, hoping the handle wouldn't fly off and give me away.

I could hear low voices. First Gran's rather, terse I think is the word, voice and then some monosyllables from Ralph. Then more terse, and then one more monosyllable and the kitchen door flew open and I could see Ralph roll into the sitting room. He shut the door and then all went quiet again.

It seemed to me like the first blood had gone to Gran.

As I started a Google Fight between Jane Austen and Zac Efron (Zac by quite a whisker) I felt a lot more warmly towards my crotchety crimplened grandmother.

Unbelievably, I did actually manage to write seventy-eight words of my creative writing essay that night. I had set the scene of an old man going through his dead wife's things, and finding a mysterious letter. I thought this was brilliant, and a cunning way of setting up unanswered questions and mysteries about who she'd been before she met him. I hadn't quite got to the stage of deciding what the mysteries actually were, so I had to go back to checking the characteristics of people born under the Aries sign (Mark's birthday was in April). Most websites seemed to agree that Aries and Sagittarius are very compatible signs.

But then, as we all know, astrology is nonsense. Isn't it?

Breakfast the following day was an odd affair. I could tell that Ralph's policy was going to be one of saying very little if anything at all, and it was a policy that seemed to suit Gran very well. I managed to insert the odd harmless comment into the psychotic silence, but was then mightily relieved to head off to school.

Somehow school had started to seem rather safe and reliable – nobody there was having an operation, or an affair with my worst enemy, or was telling me I was too young to think about boys. Plus I could be with my friends most of the time, which was – most of the time – good.

The three of them were already in our usual spot by the gates when I arrived. As I got nearer I realised they were staring in fascination at Sally's phone. I was, of course, very used to seeing Sally hypnotised by her phone, but for it to have that power over all three of them meant there was something super good on it.

There was something super good on it.

'Hi, Chloe,' said Sally cheerfully. 'Guess what! We're Boy Watching!' And then she looked back at her phone and gave a guilty start.

'What's the matter?' I asked, because she'd started to blush.

Apparently someone had uploaded videos of the St Thomas's auditions for the play. And as luck would have it, ha, they had just got to the part where Mark was auditioning for the part of Theseus.

'Let's have a look,' I said grabbing the phone before anyone could stop me. 'I mean, it's not as if I can't bear to look at him or anything.' And there he was, in shirtsleeves, tie askew, running his hands through his luscious floppy hair.

'The lunatic, the lover and the poet, are of imagination all compact,' he was saying. How true, how true.

I looked closer at the gestures, his elegant hands seeming to illustrate what he was saying, and the pauses for emphasis where he gazed into the camera:

'And as imagination bodies forth
The forms of things unknown, the poet's pen

Turns them to shapes and gives to airy nothing
A local habitation and a name.'

How beautiful was that? And I expect it would be even more beautiful if you knew what it meant. I pressed Pause, so I could admire the expression and the gaze to camera.

Goodness, he was handsome. When they say your heart skips a beat, they're not kidding. I felt a bit faint what with the thumping heart and the forgetting to breathe. I'd forgotten what it was like to see him properly, living and breathing and talking. Declaiming even.

I realised I was wrong. It *was* sort of unbearable to look at him.

'Isn't he brilliant?' said Sally. 'You've got to get back with him. Then we can go on a double date, because guess what? Rob's said, "How about meeting up for coffee on our way home today." Isn't that great? I mean that's a date, really, isn't it?'

'Or he might be going to break it to you gently that he's leaving the country or got another girlfriend or both,' said Gemma, rather acidly. The good news had been that she had indeed (just) got away with bunking off school, but the bad news was that it seemed like her row with Jezza had really got to her.

'That's good about Rob,' I said, trying hard not to think about what I'd just been looking at. 'Where are you going? Can we all come too? We could watch from a distance, and if he tells you he's leaving the country we can come and pick up the pieces. But if he gets down on one knee and offers you a ring, well, then we'll leave you to it.'

'Don't be silly, Chloe,' said Sally, 'he's not going to ask me to marry him.' See what I mean about literal?

'I didn't mean he'd *literally* get on one knee and *literally* ask you to marry him, dingbat,' I said. 'But why don't you get him to take you to the Sunny Beach Café? Then you can go to the bottom floor and we can be on the top floor and look down on you. Sort of guardian angels.'

I thought this was an excellent idea. And as the Sunny Beach Café (which justified its name by having a picture of a beach in the sunshine behind the bar, but was otherwise dark and wooden and exactly like any other café) was a favourite haunt for all sorts of boys – from St Thomas's to the art school – we could catch up on our Boy Watching skills as well as look after Sally. Everyone would be, as they say, a winner.

'OK, I'll text him,' said Sally. I do like it when she

does what I tell her to do. (I guess I like it when anyone does what I tell them to do.)

'Come on,' said Gemma. 'We've got a whole day of school to get through first. Give Sally her phone back, and let's get into class. It's English, your favourite, Chloe. Don't want to be late.' For a second I was gobsmacked at Gemma's sudden enthusiasm for lessons, but then I remembered that she was within half a hair's breadth of suspension, and she needed to Be Good. That should be worth watching in itself.

As we set off for Mr Fanshawe's class, I hoped it wouldn't be too difficult a lesson. That we wouldn't have to concentrate like crazy as we did when we were reading Wilfred Owen. I wanted to be left alone with my thoughts for the day. If I could find a safe place at the back of the class, perhaps I'd even start to write my letter to Mark.

As it turned out there wasn't a moment to think about him. Mr Fanshawe, still clearly good at his job, wasn't going to let us daydream and/or write important letters.

Instead he introduced us to the world of *The Lord of the Flies*.

I already had a hazy notion of what happened in *The Lord of the Flies*, and knew that we were in for another bumpy ride. As if, I thought, it wasn't difficult and tragic enough to be a teenager in This Day and Age, without being asked to read about such terrible traumas.

After all, I'd only just about recovered from the sadness of the death of Boxer in *Animal Farm* when we were plunged into the bloody horrors of the First World War. And now we were going to be terrified by being trapped on an island with a lot of increasingly psychotic boys, gradually intent on murdering each other. Probably the grimmest piece of Boy Watching you could have dreamt of.

But at least these things had the advantage of interrupting my Mum Worries. She was on track to come home on Wednesday, so only one more day until I had to be extra nice to everyone at home.

Sun and Sea

We arrived at the café ten minutes before Rob was due to be there, so we lurked outside with Sally. If you are going to be stood up then the last thing you want is to be on your own. (Although, as we know, Sally is never alone, what with having her phone surgically attached to her.)

Then in the distance we saw Rob. He was with six or seven other boys, some of whom we didn't know, one of whom looked vaguely familiar, and two of whom looked very familiar indeed.

Vaguely familiar, I worked out, was the hunky rugby player with the lilty accent who'd knocked me down and picked me up. Very familiar were Charlie and him.

I gasped. How could I not? After thinking about Mark so much, it knocked me for six to see him in real life. The usual blush was starting to work its way up to my face, and I moved quickly behind the others so he wouldn't see me.

He was walking with Charlie and smiling. And then when Rob said something to the lilty hunk I could see him burst into laughter. I felt angry with him for being so carefree, and then I just felt overwhelmed by how wonderful he looked, how he walked – quickly and confidently – and how relaxed he seemed as he talked to the others.

'Hey, Chloe,' said Sally. 'Look who Rob's got with him! It's Mark! Isn't that amazing!'

'Yes, it's relatively amazing,' I said as I edged further towards the wall and behind the three of them. 'So amazing, in fact, that I'm going to go inside and hide in the Ladies. You'll be fine now Rob's here, so just text me when it's safe to see you two upstairs,' I said to Amy and Gemma.

And with that I rushed as quickly as I could without actually running into the café and out to the Ladies at the back.

I breathed a sigh of relief as the door shut behind me. The joy of the Ladies toilets: completely safe, the only place where you simply couldn't ever be caught unawares by A Boy.

I looked around and saw that there was an old lady

and a short girl looking at themselves in the mirror.

Both of them in their different ways were completely absorbed in what they saw – the old lady brushing her hair lightly and carefully, the girl putting on an extra thick layer of eyeliner with intense concentration.

So I had a moment's grace before QBM looked in my direction and recognised me.

So much for the safety of the Ladies. It was only full of my greatest enemy. Maybe she's here because she's got a date with Mark, I suddenly thought. A sense of hopelessness and wretchedness washed over me. I darted quickly into one of the toilets, pretty sure that she hadn't seen me.

I waited till all was silent outside before coming out again. I texted Amy and Gemma. Still in toilets, QBM here. Is she w Mark?

I looked at myself in the mirror while I waited for the answer. Eyebrows not too bad today, hair quite bouncy, cheek scar almost invisible under Liv's concealer, new jeans looking tight in a good way and blue jersey quite pleasing. And then I thought, what's the point of being 'in good looks', as Jane Austen would say, if the person you wanted to look at you didn't want to look at you.

The sound of frogs croaking made me jump. How could there be frogs in a Ladies toilet, I thought, before

I remembered that Sally had changed the alert on my phone. Shes w her gang. M's with us. Cum on out! read the message from Amy.

OK, I thought. This is it. With Amy and Charlie there it couldn't be that awkward, could it?

I breathed in and out very slowly three times. I'd read somewhere that that's what you should do to calm nerves. It made me feel a bit better, but I could still hear the blood pumping and thumping in my head.

The café was packed as I emerged. I could make out the QBM in a distant corner surrounded by her cohorts. She was saying something and making big gestures as she did so. All the girls sitting on the bench with her looked as if they were trying to outdo each other in listening intently and laughing at her jokes. If they could only see themselves, I thought. Sooooo sycophantic, so mindless, so frightened.

Not that I wasn't frightened myself, I reminded myself as I ducked down and headed in the opposite direction in the hope she wouldn't notice me.

I spotted Amy and Charlie and him by the window. The three of them were sitting together; there was no sign of Rob and Sally or Gemma, and the lilty hunk and the unfamiliar boys seemed to be talking amongst themselves.

They all looked up as I approached.

'Hey, Chloe,' said Charlie, loudly and cheerfully. He got up and gave me a hug. It was a nice hug, and smelt of warm wool. I emerged from it feeling definitely stronger.

I looked down at Mark. He was looking up at me with a thoughtful expression on his face.

'Hello, Chloe,' he said. He looked rather serious when he said it, and didn't go on to say anything else.

'How's your mum doing?' said Charlie, now looking rather serious himself. 'She recovered from the anaesthetic, I hope?'

'She seems a bit better now, I think,' I said. 'I made her a meerkat.' I couldn't imagine why I said that, but I suddenly had such a strong image in my mind's eye of Mum in bed with her bedside table and my clay model.

'He's called Maximillian,' said Amy helpfully. 'And he's very handsome, isn't he, Chloe?'

'Actually, he's rather out of proportion and his tail could fall off at any minute, but I suppose it's the thought that counts.' I couldn't *believe* we were having this conversation.

I sat down next to Amy.

'I'm sorry about your mum, Chloe,' Mark said, leaning forward and looking me in the eye. 'It's very tough. But they're so good at treating cancer these days, and she's in a good hospital.'

'Thank you,' I said, blushing and looking down at the floor. Lots of bits of fluff on it, I noticed.

'Rob and Sally and Gemma have gone outside,' said Amy after a pause and it had become apparent that I was incapable of saying anything more. 'I think his mates are having a cigarette. All those rugby guys seem to smoke.'

I remembered the desperate people on drips outside the hospital, dragging with all their might on the last bits of roll-up. 'I think visiting Mum in hospital has finally cured me of wanting to do that,' I said, realising that I actually meant it.

'Good girl,' said Charlie with a smile. 'You are wise beyond your years. Unlike me, I'm afraid. Just going to join them for a little bit. Come on, Ames.'

'Charlie, you are so BAD,' said Amy, getting up to follow him outside. 'I'm coming, but only so's to make sure you only have one.'

They headed off outside. Anyone would have thought that it was all a set-up job, especially because I was ninety per cent sure that Charlie didn't smoke.

'And then there were two,' said Mark, with a wry smile. 'So come on now, Chloe, tell me what's going on. I'd been looking forward to seeing you, but you seem to have cut me off completely.' He looked into my eyes as he spoke. 'Please tell me this isn't about football.'

His deep brown eyes seemed to bore into me, as I tried to think of the words to say what I wanted to say, even though I scarcely knew what that was. I didn't know how to explain that I just wanted him to be the boy I loved, and not the boy who walked into a secret football match with a loving arm round my worst enemy.

'Oh my GOD,' a voice suddenly screeched from behind me. 'You're HERE. That's amaaazing because Jimmy's here and he's dying to see you. Come on over, the gang's all here.'

The Queen of Beeyatches herself.

She moved in front of me, completely and totally ignoring me, leant down to Mark and reached for his hand.

'He's not going to be here much longer, let's go!' And she started to pull Mark up from his seat.

'Chloe, I'm sorry,' he looked down at me, 'but I've been trying to get together with Jimmy for ages. He's in charge of the photography exhibition at the art college, and he's been looking at my submissions.

We'll catch up later, won't we?' And he looked hard and seriously at me for a moment.

Then he turned round and followed the evil one to the back of the café. He hadn't let her carry on holding his hand. But apart from that there was absolutely nothing to be happy about.

For a moment I sat there, horribly alone in the middle of a banquette meant for two. Of course no one was actually looking at me, staring at the loser, taking photos and posting them on Instagram. No one was actually laughing at my total inability to say anything more than five or six words throughout the whole encounter, or at how I'd blushed and stared at the fluff on the floor.

But it sure felt like it.

Mark had by now completely disappeared into the back of the café and was swallowed up by crowds of people.

I got up briskly, as if that's what I'd meant to do all along, and headed off towards the door.

Outside, the sun was shining brightly. All we needed was a beach and we could almost be in the picture behind the bar.

Among the crowds of people outside, half of them talking, half of them looking at their phones, I could make out Rob and Sally. I headed over towards them to see how they were getting on. Plus I desperately needed to think of something other than what had just happened.

At first sight the signs didn't look great. It looked a bit like Rob, surrounded by his smoky rugby friends, wasn't taking any notice of my BFF, who was standing slightly to one side half looking at her phone.

Then all of a sudden Rob turned away from his mates and put his arm round Sally briefly and said something which made her smile. He then turned back to his huge friends and carried on laughing and talking with them.

As I got nearer, I thought how this behaviour pattern seemed to bear out some of our Boy Watching reports. The Boy gets points for asking the Girl out. Boy gets caught up in Boy Gang. Girl has to take back seat as Boy becomes more intent on showing off to Fellow Boys than impressing Girl. Boy gets minus points.

Whereas the other way round the Girl in her Girl Gang, will abandon Gang at first sign of Boy, and do everything to try to impress and please The Boy.

This is all a bit of a generalisation, of course, but then most science is like that when you only have a finite number of specimens to observe. Boy Watching is a slightly inexact science because of that, which is why you have to do so much of it.

Sally was back to looking at her phone as I got nearer, so she didn't notice me coming. Lilty hunky rugby player did, though.

'Hey there,' he said, separating himself from the others and standing in front of me.

I looked up at him – there was quite a lot of 'up' as he seemed to be well over six foot four. He smelt a lot nicer than he had last time we'd met, and he looked a lot less muddy. Also his head looked less like a lump of rock when it didn't have a bandage tied all round it to protect his ears. Although I could now see that his ears probably needed a lot of protecting as they were borderline huge. Plus they looked all the bigger coming out of his buzz-cut head. (The buzz cut is not a good look, I don't think. It makes a boy's head look bigger and him therefore thicker. But perhaps if you're a lilty rugby hunk you can't afford to have luscious locks which might be pulled off in the heat of the scrum.)

'I'm glad I didn't squash you the other day. You wouldn't look nearly so pretty if you were squashed,' he said in his Welsh lilt.

'Hi,' I said. 'I'm glad you didn't squash me too. Thank you.' There I go again. What am I thanking him for? Not squashing me? Saying I was pretty? But you don't actually *thank* boys for saying that, do you? For a moment I wondered what Gemma would do. Something cool, no doubt.

But I couldn't imagine what that might be.

'Rob says you and Sally are going on this Paris trip in a couple of weeks' time. Don't tell me you're there for the rugby!' said lilty hunky rugby player. 'I'm Owen by the way,' he added, almost as if he could see inside my head and thought 'lilty hunky rugby player' wasn't a real name.

'And I'm Chloe,' I said. 'But no, I didn't know there was rugby on in Paris. They only tell us about the museums and galleries.'

'Well there is,' said Owen. 'It's a big one. World Cup. Paris will be full of men and boys talking about rucks and scrums and conversions.'

'Don't women follow rugby too?' I said, instantly kicking myself for sounding like some sort of Eighties feminist.

'Sure do,' said Owen. 'I'd ask you along, but the tickets are like gold. And anyway, you probably *would* get squashed before you even got to the stadium.'

What a great distraction from the miseries of moments ago. Who knew I'd practically be asked out on a date in *Paris*? Only he wasn't really asking, and it wasn't really a date. And I knew I was still miserable deep down.

I felt a tug on my blue jersey. The BFF.

'Chloe,' said Sally, looking up at Owen as she spoke in rather wide-eyed astonishment. I guess he was quite an imposing sight. 'Rob's got to go, and the others have disappeared, so let's get the bus now, shall we?'

I needed to hear what had been going on in the life of Sally, so I turned to Owen the Welsh Giant to say goodbye.

'See you then, Chloe.' Owen got there first. 'See you in Paris!'

'Bye,' I said, with my usual *savoir faire.*

I turned away and followed Sally to the bus stop. So many boys, so many questions. So few answers.

'No ring then?' I said to Sally as we made our way to the back of the bus.

'No, silly, of course not,' said Sally. 'But he said there's going to be a joint band playing the night of the school play. And he says I can play drums in the last set. That's good, isn't it?' She looked a little nervous as she said it.

I was pretty sure that this might have had something to do with the fact that it had been so long since we'd practised in our band together. OTTO (Overgrown Throttle and the Tempted Obscurity – to give it its full name) consisted of me on keyboards and vocals, Amy and Gemma on guitars, and Sally on the drums. We'd got used to rehearsing in Merv's garage, on kit which we managed to squeeze in between the Jeeps and motorbikes and unused exercise machines. We weren't at all terrible, but somehow or other we'd got out of the way of playing. I wasn't even at all sure that I could remember my ten chords, and I thought there was a very good chance that Sally's drumming skills might have gone the same way.

'We'd better have an OTTO session soon, so you can have a bit of practice. But it is good, yes, because you get to spend time with Rob at rehearsals. Was he nice to you? Was he paying you enough attention?' I felt we had to get this stuff out into the open.

'Yes, he was,' said Sally. 'He calls me Dork, but in a nice way.'

OK. I couldn't help feeling that 'Dork' wasn't exactly 'Darling', but still, if it made Sally happy.

'What about you, though?' Sally asked. 'Last I saw, they were leaving you alone with Mark.' Ah. So it *was* a set-up. 'Have you kissed and made up, Chloe? I do hope you have.'

'No, Sally.' I sighed. 'I couldn't think straight. And before I had a chance to try to say anything sensible who should come up and take him away but the class cow herself.'

'Noooooo!' said Sally, eyes wide in horror. 'So how? What? Did he go off with her?'

'Sort of, because she said she had some guy called Jimmy with her, who he wanted to talk to. Dunno what that's about, but she got him to follow her.'

I looked out of the window at an old man and woman shuffling along the pavement, arm in arm. They looked totally old, and totally content. I guessed they had each other and nothing else mattered.

This time my sigh was longer and sadder.

Between Rocks and Hard Places

It was now over a week since Mum had come home. She still looked very pale, and she moved rather slowly. But she seemed very peaceful and glad to be back in her house. She was even glad to eat the spaghetti loops, and listen to the silences that seemed to reign between Gran and Ralph.

I did a great deal of tea-making, and had adopted a policy of simply going to my room if I thought I was going to get cross and say something that I or anyone else might regret.

Since this was a policy that ended up with my having quite a lot of quality time in my room, it meant that my Creative Writing essay was coming on a treat (well over a hundred words), and so were my notes for our Boy Watching file – the results of so much observation and thought would make a good book, I reckoned… And I was hardly distracted at all by trying to find the perfect mate for Albert on FindYourDogaPerfectMate.com, or researching the best ways to stop yourself blushing, or trying to learn the rules of rugby.

Only another week and we'd be off to Paris. I was getting quite excited in between the worries and miseries of the rest of my life. I hadn't heard anything from him, and had managed to avoid her – the QB – for the whole week. There were so many times when I wanted to swallow my pride and ring him or text him, but always I held off at the last minute. The first rehearsals with St Thomas's were happening after Paris, so that would be a test of whether he seeks me out, I thought.

Meanwhile, on this particular Saturday, we had a Mission. The object was to get Sally's drumming skills up to speed so that Rob's 'Dork' didn't disgrace him at the end of term. We'd settled on spending the whole morning in Merv's garage and then rewarding ourselves with a little light shopping in the mall.

I sometimes have an uneasy relationship with shopping – if you haven't got enough money to actually *buy* anything, there's a limit to how much fun you can have walking around shops – but on this occasion

I had an Endgame: my quest for the perfect pair of black boots.

After a lot of online research, I was pretty sure I'd found The Ones. They were expensive, so I had to come face to face with them in real life before I could know we were right for each other. As the boot shop was next to the ice cream shop, just across from the coffee shop where we did some of our most productive Boy Watching, that was pretty much the afternoon sorted.

I had just got off the bus and was heading down the road towards the familiar electric gates, when I heard a loud honking behind me. Usually on these occasions the honker is a middle-aged bloke driving a white van, and often the honkee is someone older and more glamorous than me, so I did what I normally do and kept calm and carried on walking.

But then the honking got hysterical, and as there was no one else around I realised I must be the honkee.

I turned round. Jezza.

He was in his beaten-up car, on his own and looking very stubbly. He wound the window down as he drew up alongside me.

'Hey, Chloe,' he said. 'Look, don't tell anyone I'm here, but I need to see Gemma.'

'Okaaaay,' I said, thinking how pale and sweaty he looked and how incredible it was that everyone seemed to find him irresistible. Also how rude he was. 'But if you don't want anyone to know you're here how are you going to see Gemma? I mean, if she's going to see you she's going to know you're here.'

'Quite the little pedant, aren't you, Chloe?' said Jezza. Like I say, rude. But also surprising – who'd have thought he'd heard of the word 'pedant'? Then he must have remembered he wanted a favour because he said, 'OK, sorry. But can you ask Gem to ring? She's not answering her phone, and I've got to go back tonight.'

Without thinking, I said, 'We're going to the mall this afternoon. Shopping in all the usual places. She'll be there with us.' Too late I wondered why she wasn't answering her phone to him, probably precisely because she didn't want to see him. Lord.

'OK, fine,' said Jezza. 'See you then.' And he stepped on the accelerator, made the engine roar, and sped off.

Leaving me with a slightly sick feeling at the thought of telling Gemma what I'd done. Also at the thought of seeing Jezza again.

The electric gates drew back to reveal an empty

drive. Good. At least the Korean mafia weren't in residence. I went into the side door and made my way to the garage where I could already hear sounds of music. Or at least someone was playing the drums and someone else was tuning a guitar.

When I went in everyone was already there. Gemma had her guitar artfully draped over her shoulder but was looking intently at her phone. Ouch.

She looked up. 'Hi, Chloe,' she said. 'Amazing how bad news travels fast. Apparently Jezza's going shopping this afternoon. Thanks for that.'

'Sorry, Gem,' I said, because I really was. 'I didn't think – it just came out.'

'Well, we can always not go,' said Gemma. 'It's just that I've had it with the guy. And anyway, he's supposed to be in Scotland, what's he doing here?'

'He's pining away for love of you,' piped up Sally from behind the drum kit. 'He's probably driven all the way from Scotland, through the night, 'cos he can't live without you.'

'More likely he wants a favour,' said Gemma. 'Anyway. Let's get on, shall we? Sally needs all the practice she can get.'

We spent the next hour making a great deal of noise, not all of it in tune or in time, but some of

241

it didn't sound bad at all.

Which was why we were puzzled when someone started banging loudly on the garage door.

'Gemma,' shouted Merv. 'Can you come out, please? Now, if you don't mind.'

We looked at each other in amazement. Merv being so assertive with his cool daughter wasn't the Merv we knew. Curiosity must have got the better of Gemma because instead of shouting back at him she went to the garage door and switched on the motor to open it.

As the huge door rose slowly and noisily up, we could see the legs of Merv – in his peculiar pointy brown shoes and tight denim jeans – and the feet of someone else. Someone wearing elegant high-heeled black shoes, and floaty silk black trousers.

As the door got higher and higher, I recognised the tall, elegant figure as Marianne. Gemma's mother, Merv's ex, partner of Juliet. She looked stunning in her black trouser suit, her thick blonde hair waving gently in the breeze. Her expression, though, was one of extreme displeasure.

But then, as she saw Gemma, her whole bearing changed, she seemed to soften in front of our very eyes, and she smiled a small but warm smile.

'Mum!' said Gemma, for once unable to be cool.

She rushed towards her mother, where she was hugged long and deep. For a moment they looked like a rather beautiful grown-up Madonna and child.

'Darling,' said Marianne. She stood back and looked properly at her daughter. 'It's lovely to see you,' she said and then she looked at us. 'And Chloe, Sally. And you must be Amy.' Amy had missed out on our Cornish holiday, so she was the only one of us who hadn't met Marianne and Juliet.

Then Marianne turned to her ex-husband, her expression resuming its air of great displeasure. 'I'm here because your father and I need to sort out a few financial matters,' she said, looking coldly at Merv. 'Things have got a little out of hand, haven't they, Mervyn?' If looks could have shrivelled, then Merv would have been a little pile of shrivel on the drive.

'We're going to go inside now, and see if we can make some progress,' she went on. 'And then I have to go to a meeting. They're making a TV documentary on Juliet, and I'm staying with the producer here. But I'll see you tomorrow, Gemma. I'll come and pick you up about ten. OK?'

'That'd be great, Mum,' said Gemma, smiling in a rather nicely unguarded way.

'All right then, darling. I'll let you get back to your

music,' Marianne said, smiling back. And she walked back into the house, the little pile of shrivel nervously following in her footsteps.

Gemma switched the motor back on and the door started its slow descent. Once it had safely landed, everything felt terribly silent. What an encounter. Clearly the formidable Marianne was going to have Merv on toast and eat him for breakfast or whatever the expression is.

'Gosh, your mum's amazing,' said Amy. 'But I'm glad I'm not Merv.'

'Everyone should be glad they're not Merv,' said Gemma. 'But you're right, Mum is rather amazing.'

'Do you think Merv's gone bankrupt and is going to have to go to jail?' said Sally ever so slightly gleefully. That vision of knitting needles, guillotines and baskets just won't go away...

'God knows,' said Gemma. 'But it may be that he'd prefer that to being in the hands of his Korean friends. Couldn't happen to a nicer man, anyway.'

We'd decided our concentration was shot to pieces, what with one drama and another, so we packed up all the music kit and got ready to go Boy Watching in a retail environment. Or shopping as some people call it.

Much later we were sitting in the outside bit of the ice cream shop, full of ice cream and watching the comings and goings at the coffee shop. It had been a successful afternoon. I had decided that the black boots were The Ones, and asked that they be put aside for me for a few days, by which time I hoped to have negotiated a loan from the ghastly one or Mum. It would mean spending virtually the whole of Christmas washing clean hairbrushes and sweeping up imaginary hair, but I reckoned it was worth it.

'Great boots, those, Chloe,' said Gemma, which made me feel even better about my new love – Gemma had firm and reliable views on what was 'great' and what wasn't. 'And I expect you'll get loads of pleasure out of that T-shirt, Sally.'

Sally had bought a T-shirt featuring a ginger-haired cartoon girl above the words 'I Woke Up Like This' written in ginger writing on a green background. The girl bore more than a passing resemblance to Sally. You had to admire Sally's fearlessness; she was a great one for supporting the ginger cause.

'I think that's meant to be rude,' said Sally a bit poutily. 'Just 'cos you're cross about Jezza, you don't have to take it out on us.'

'I'm not, dingbat, it's a good look on you,' said Gemma more kindly. 'Green and ginger, magic combo,' she added, less kindly.

Amy, meanwhile, was due to meet Charlie in the coffee shop at any moment, so she was looking at the shop with that faraway look in her eyes that always meant she was thinking about him.

'Hey,' she suddenly said. 'Isn't that Madame de B and Pimplemouse over there?' So it wasn't the faraway look of love, it was the keen eye of the scandal spotter.

And indeed, slightly to one side was a small table with our hairy Greek Art master on one side, and our be-permed French teacher on the other. Mr P was talking very intensely and leaning towards Madame de B as he spoke. Even from where I was I could see that Mr Pampledousse was in such full flow that spittle was flying everywhere. Every now and then Madame de B would use her napkin to discreetly wipe herself down.

'Well, they're not having an affair,' said Gemma firmly. 'Pimplemouse would never be unfaithful to Mr Horriday over there in the land of seals and mooses. He's probably just telling her how he's planning to run away to Newfoundland.'

'Or he's plotting a coop,' said Sally. 'You know, like

246

in the French Revolution. They're going to overthrow Mrs Munroe and put themselves in charge.'

'It's pronounced coo,' I said, because I knew Sally would want to get it right. 'And I can't believe anyone would dare to challenge Mrs Munroe. Least of all Doris and Pimplemouse.'

We were so busy looking at this unlikely couple and speculating ever more wildly that we didn't notice Charlie approach from one direction and Jezza from another.

'Hi, Ames,' said Charlie as he got nearer. 'Hi, everyone. Finished your girlie shopping?' He gave his nice crinkly smile as he said this, which definitely took the edge off what he'd just said. I'll give him 'girlie', I thought.

Happily for Charlie, our attention was distracted by Jezza arriving at our table moments later. He looked, if possible, even whiter and more damply shiny than usual. His stubble looked even stubblier in the bright lights of the mall, and his hair had an oiliness to it which I thought looked half scientifically fascinating, half revolting.

But clearly Jezza wouldn't have been interested in my theories about grease and hair; he didn't have eyes for me or anyone except Gemma.

'So where were you last night, Gemma?' he said, looking at her angrily. 'I waited like an hour, and you never showed. What's *with* you?'

'Nothing's *with* me,' said Gemma coldly. 'It was never a date. I never said I'd go to the gig, you just assumed I would. Anyway, you had plenty of other dates there to choose from. Half of Queen Mary's, from what I hear.'

'Look, we need to talk,' said Jezza. 'Come on. Come for a walk with me. I've got to go in an hour, then you won't see me again.'

'OK, Jezza,' said Gemma, in a rather world-weary way. 'We'll go outside for ten minutes, but I can't stay longer than that.' She got up and followed him as he marched off down the mall. A little later, he stopped and waited for her. I could see him try to put his arm round her, but she shrugged him off.

If he was hoping for some sort of romantic reconciliation before he set off back to deepest Scotland, well, good luck with that, I thought.

'Respect,' Charlie said, as he looked at the two receding figures. 'If there's anyone who can cut Jezza down to size, that's got to be Gemma.' He looked at Amy. 'She's something else, your friend, isn't she?'

'She sure is, but she's not available – and neither

are you!' Amy now had her goofy telling-off voice on. I could tell that any minute now there was going to be a lot of teasing and flirting and hugging...and generally it was time to leave them to it.

'Time to go, Sally,' I said. 'Our work here is done, and I've gotta get back to Mum.'

We gathered our stuff together and set off. There were several dramas left unresolved, but it was nearly kick-off time for 'the big match' and Mum would need rescuing.

Gardening for Dogs

On the whole, the Bennet family had risen to the challenge of being nice to each other for Mum's sake fairly well. Ghastly Ralph had been quite low key – hours spent in front of the football on TV and Stupid Juice consumption had gone down, and he'd even been known to load the dishwasher once or twice.

Gran seemed to be making an effort too. Once or twice I could see that some of Ralph's outbursts had been too much even for her. She had a way of saying 'I think you'll find...' before telling everyone what to think. But even she seemed to have found that there was no telling Ralph. The ghastly one knew everything there was to know, was always right, and don't you forget it.

Mum seemed to be making the most of being made a fuss of (well, fuss Bennet-style) and got up even later than I did at weekends.

Soon she'd be having her treatment, as she called it. Odd how 'treatment' and 'therapy' sounded like something soothing and expensive that you might have in a spa. But I knew there was nothing soothing about chemotherapy – although it probably scored quite highly on the expensive front.

In all my online researches, I'd resisted the temptation to look up the details of what Mum was in for. Whenever I found the mouse hovering over 'what to expect from chemotherapy', I made sure the mouse found its way to fabulous black boots, indelible eyeliner or the World's Best April Fools' jokes.

That Sunday was the last before the Paris trip the following weekend, and the last before the chemo started, so I was going to spend the day with Mum being sunny and lovely – making cups of tea for her, emptying the dishwasher, and generally entertaining her with my coruscating conversation. ('Coruscating' is a new favourite. Brilliant, sparkling, shining – like most Sagittarians.)

But first I had a date with the most-reliable-male-in-my-life.

Albert hadn't had as much of my attention lately as he deserved. I felt sure he was pining. So I was looking forward to collecting him at eleven o'clock, on the dot, as the hairy Mr U had specified.

I was in the kitchen with Gran and Mum. I'd emptied the dishwasher, taken the next batch of bacon out of the deep freeze and found Mum's special Sudoku pencil for her. I reckoned I was on track to being allowed out, but I had reckoned without Gran – who I suddenly realised had her special 'And Another Thing' face on.

'And another thing,' she said, looking at me as she settled down into the chair opposite Mum. 'I think it's a bit selfish to spend all this time with your friends, shopping and the like, when your mother's so poorly. And not only that, but you seem to expect her to pay for these – what was it? – black boots, when you know money's short. Hm? What do you say to that young lady?'

'Oh, it's all right, Gran,' said Mum. In the middle of my irritation, I found time to think it must be odd to call your mother Gran, and I wondered if I'd call Mum Gran when I have children. If I have children, that is. If I ever get married. 'Chloe needs to get out and see her friends. She mustn't stay indoors with us old things all day.'

I could see that Gran was taking exception to being

called an 'old thing', but the debate was put on hold by a loud banging on our front door.

Mr Underwood. Clearly impatient to get Albert off his hands so he could go off and do whatever Mr Underwoods like to do on a Sunday.

'Sorry,' I said as I opened the door, as it's always safest to be in the wrong so far as Mr U is concerned.

'Here he is and here's his lead and don't bring him back before two,' said Mr U with all his usual dazzling charm. And he handed the lead to me and shooed Albert inside and up our stairs.

'Thanks,' I said to Mr U's back. There was no time to say more because there were the sounds of what can only be described as a commotion upstairs.

'Get this wretched creature out of here,' I could hear Gran shouting. As I reached the kitchen I saw Mum hanging on to Albert's collar for dear life as he barked and growled and yapped at Gran, who was waving the rubber tip of her stick at him.

'I'm sure he likes you, really,' I said loudly and untruthfully over Albert's barking. 'Perhaps best not to wave your stick at him.' I clipped the lead to his collar and pulled him towards the door.

'Fleas,' said Gran firmly. 'I'm quite sure the wretched creature is riddled with them. Riddled. You should wash your hands, dear, after touching him,' she said to Mum.

Presumably after a week in hospital Mum's resistance was low – in every sense – and she got up to do as she was told. By this point Albert had quietened down and was sitting at my feet looking up at me with an expression of such sweet innocence it would melt the hardest heart.

'Wretched creature,' said Gran again, her hardest heart clearly showing no signs of melting. 'You'd better take him away. He obviously can't be trusted.'

Not wanting to discuss the wretched creature, or my selfishness, or the price of black boots, I backed out of the kitchen, pulling Albert with me. 'Bye then,' I said to Mum, as I didn't really want to look at the other 'old thing'. 'See you a bit later.'

I'd decided to take Albert for lunch at Sally's. After all, what else are best friends for if not to offer shelter to you and a furry friend when you've been exiled from your own home.

But as I marched down the street, Albert pulling happily on his lead as he inspected revolting thing after revolting thing, I had a message from Gemma. Cum 4 lunch w me and Mum. Pik u both up from Sally's. Gx

How lovely, I thought. It was an especially nice

254

message to receive when you've been exiled, AND Gemma must be feeling extra well-disposed towards me because she actually put an apostrophe in the right place.

Liv opened the door almost as soon as I'd rung the bell. 'Oh,' she said, looking rather surprised and not very pleased. 'It's you.' I tried not to be hurt by this not very welcoming welcome. And then thought perhaps it was Albert she wasn't very pleased to see.

'Yes, I'm afraid so,' I said, and then felt cross with myself for apologising for being me. 'Sally and I are going to be picked up in a moment to go out. Can I come in?'

Liv looked at me, and suddenly seemed to remember how this sort of doorstep social interaction should go: 'Yes, of course, Chloe. Nice to see you. Sally's upstairs practising.'

Puzzled by the 'practising' but relieved by the politeness I started to lead Albert upstairs. In the distance I could hear quite a lot of banging and Sally's voice shouting, 'One and a two and a, a right and a left, left and right and a one and – oh damn.'

As I opened the door to her bedroom, I could see the cause of the problem. Her open laptop was showing a video of some drums and a guy doing something complicated on them quite quickly with his sticks. Sally was gazing intently at him as she held two drumsticks in the air ready to join in.

It didn't look like it was going well.

'Come on,' I said, trying to stop Albert jumping up at the sticks. (Obviously sticks in Albert World only had one purpose – and he couldn't understand why Sally wasn't throwing them a great distance for him to retrieve.) 'We're being picked up any minute. You can do this later.'

Sally looked more than usually flustered. I thought perhaps it was the unexpectedly close contact with Albert, or the frustration of not being able to count like the guy in the video, but apparently life's never that simple *chez* Liv.

'I think Patrick's gone,' she said without any of the customary hellos. 'Mum had another mysterious phone call yesterday evening, and then I could hear her rowing with Patrick, and we haven't seen him since.'

Curiouser and curiouser. So maybe it *was* Sally's dad on the phone and Patrick realised he couldn't compete with a handsome spy and the father of Liv's children. Or something. I had to stop my speculations because the noise of frogs croaking (my phone) and the Tardis (Sally's) flashed up a message. Outside, we were both told. Sometimes you had to admire Gemma's economy of language.

The three of us headed out of the front door, Sally still looking confused (and for once I could sympathise), Albert bouncing up and down with his usual loveable zest for life, and me trying to stop Albert bouncing into the middle of the road.

In front of the gate was a large 4x4 car, rather battered and covered with mud. I remembered it from going to Cornwall at half term in the summer. It made me want to go back to Marianne and Juliet's beautiful house by the sea...

The window was wound down on the driver's side and Marianne was looking at us with the kind of smile that made her look a lot less scary.

'Hello, you two,' she said. 'Who's that you've got with you?'

'It's Albert,' I said. 'Most of the time he's quite well behaved. But he'd probably better go in the back just in case this isn't "most of the time".'

We put Albert in the back beside a lot of rugs, wellington boots and picture frames. He immediately curled up beside the muddiest pair of boots, gave them a quick sniff and then shut his eyes and started to give a good impression of a well-behaved dog.

As we got into the back seats, Gemma turned round and said to us, 'We're having lunch where Mum's been staying. It's a house in Pickwick Grove.'

The name sounded familiar, and not just because it had a cosy Dickensian ring to it.

And then I realised that Pickwick Grove was the road round the back of the town hall, full of old-fashioned houses. Where Mark lived.

And then it all fell into place. The TV producer for Juliet's documentary was Patricia Anderson. Dear lord, we were going to have lunch at Mark's house.

Would he be there? Would Patricia? She knew who I was, but did she know there was a – sort of – connection with her son? And all those puppies? Would Albert get into a fight and eat one of them? Mark would see me even more tongue-tied than I was the last time I'd seen him. What with being in awe of Marianne, *and* his mother. And him. How I wished I'd washed my hair, worn my new black top, had some proper shoes with heels on…could think of something to say.

'Chloe?' Gemma was saying. 'What's the matter?'

I gazed back at her; it took me a moment to realise that my mouth was still half-open, frozen in shock.

'It's Mark's house,' was all I could get out.

'Gosh,' said Sally cheerfully. 'That's great. So you

get to meet Mark's mother again, Chloe. You really liked her, didn't you? And maybe Mark will be there. Wouldn't that be fantastic, Chloe?'

There are times when the phrase 'could cheerfully strangle' doesn't even come close.

'Oh, have you met Patricia then, Chloe?' said Marianne, fortunately focused on driving round a tricky roundabout, so she couldn't see my expression of utter goofiness. Or, at least, I don't think she could.

'Er, yes,' I said. 'I sometimes work at the salon where she has her hair done. I thought she was awesome – in the true sense of the word, not in the sense it's used now.' There I go again. Somehow I *have* to make some point about language and how people don't use it properly. I *have* to be a pedant, just like Jezza said, even when I'm trying to impress and be normal.

'I agree, Chloe,' said Marianne. 'I agree she's very impressive, and I agree that "awesome" has sadly lost its real meaning.'

I wondered if Marianne knew that from that moment on she had a most devoted fan in her back seat.

'Here we are,' she said, perhaps not entirely unaware of the trauma going on behind her. 'Let's get Albert back on his lead, just in case the puppies are loose.'

The house was old, with bare brick and lots of ivy growing up it. It looked quite dilapidated, but in a nice way. We all got out of the car, and followed Marianne to the front porch, which you could see was full of just the same sort of rugs and boots as Marianne's car. The house had an air of lived-in comfortableness, and looked particularly welcoming in the bright September sunshine.

Happily, Albert seemed like he was about to make a lot of Albert noise, so I could hide my tenseness and embarrassment by trying to make him be quiet and good.

Patricia came to the door. 'Hello, everyone, come in, come in. I've just put the puppies in the back room so we'll be able to have lunch in peace.'

Which was the moment Albert chose to bark his little head off.

I bent down to look him in the eye and tell him to shush, feeling myself getting redder and redder. I could see that Patricia Anderson was looking rather taken aback at her noisy and unexpected guest. I suppose if you've carefully and thoughtfully shut your own noisy dogs up, you don't really expect people to bring their own noisy dog.

'I'm very sorry,' I said to her over the barking.

'I'll put him in the car. I think he might be happier in there anyway.'

'No, don't worry. Little chap can't have Sunday lunch on his own. Take him round the side of the house to the garden. Just shut the gate behind you and he can't get out.' And she turned to follow everyone else as they went inside.

I led Albert round the side of the house, holding firmly onto his lead.

'You are a very bad and noisy dog, Albert,' I said to him as I opened the gate. 'I can't take you anywhere, can I? You'll never be asked again if you make such a racket. Now, if I take your lead off you must promise to be good. OK? No barking, and definitely no eating puppies.'

I was so busy giving him a good talking-to – eyeball to eyeball – that at first I didn't notice someone standing right by me.

I unclipped Albert's lead, watched him shoot off into a hedge, stood up and came face to face with Mark. He was wearing jeans and a thin white T-shirt, and his hair was still wet from a shower. It made him look even more exceptionally handsome.

I suddenly felt so happy to see him, so overwhelmed by his being just centimetres away – I could have reached out and touched his hand, and in fact, only a superhuman effort of will stopped me doing so – that I just looked at him. Even more completely tongue-tied than I thought I'd be.

He looked searchingly at me, and seemed to be about to say something serious.

That was the moment Albert chose to hurtle out of the hedge and race towards a table by the back door that was laid up with sandwiches and drinks, ready for a garden lunch.

We both saw him at the same moment and raced towards him. Mark got there first, and fell on Albert with a dramatic rugby tackle just as Albert was about to pull the tablecloth off the table.

'Hah!' he cried, as he lay on the grass, cradling Albert like he was a particularly precious rugby ball. 'Gotcha, you naughty dog. And you ARE a naughty dog, aren't you? You were all set to make a mess, weren't you, Albert? You were going to eat half our lunch and spread the other half all over the garden, weren't you? BAD dog,' he said, looking Albert in the eye with a smile.

For a moment I thought how lovely Mark looked lying on the grass cuddling Albert, and how his smile emphasised the dimple in his left cheek. I smiled down at him, but he was busy making a fuss of Albert and I couldn't catch his eye.

'Who is this BAD dog then?' It was Georgie, coming out of the back door with a tray of fruit and cheese. 'Oh hi, Chloe,' she said, turning to me and watching me disentangle Albert and his lead from her brother. 'Haven't seen you in the corridors of shame lately. Does that mean you've been being good?'

'I think so. Or not found out, or something,' I said as Patricia and Marianne came out of the back door and looked over at me and smiled.

I started to feel unexpectedly overwhelmed by the whole occasion. Here were most of the people I most admired, plus him, all in one garden. I felt like everyone was looking at me, and sizing me up. Of course they weren't. Of course not everything's about you (I said to myself), but then you are you, and you are the centre of your own universe (I also said to myself). And I so wanted to present myself in a good light, I felt tense with nerves.

Then I saw Sally step out of the back door carrying a plate of biscuits. She adjusted her sunglasses, missed her footing, tripped on a paving stone and dropped the plate of biscuits. In the 'never minds' and 'so sorrys' and 'don't worrys' that followed I had a moment to catch my breath.

By the time we were all sitting down, and even though I'd actually ended up sitting next to Mark, I felt a bit calmer, thanks to my clumsy friend. Still absolutely and utterly unable to eat anything, drink anything or say anything, but a bit calmer.

I had various bits of food on my plate, which I moved around in a nervous and unhungry manner. (That would be the ultimate diet book, I thought. You'd just need a Falling-In-Love potion, and bingo, *Thin Thighs in Thirty Days*.)

None of this seemed to be affecting Mark in the slightest – of course, why would it? I watched him calmly help himself to a couple of sandwiches, and calmly eat them as he calmly talked to Marianne about art and Cornwall and Juliet's documentary.

He was saying things about artists at the Tate St Ives, and sculptors, and photography that I had no idea he knew. But then I didn't really know what he knew, I suppose, because I didn't really know him.

This made me think about a whole new section for the Boy Watching files. The business of finding out things about The Boy, and what you have in common, and does it matter if you have different interests. Which of course brought me round to thinking about football...

I decided it was definitely better, for every possible reason, not to think about football.

I tuned back into his conversation. He and Marianne were now talking about artists, and painting vs photography. They were using the kinds of words that some of the people at Juliet's exhibition in Cornwall had used – 'abstract' and 'meaning' and 'flowing' and 'naturalistic'.

Then I remembered why he'd gone off with the QB that time in the café. Something about his photography submission for the art college.

Football and art in one person. Who knew?

'...maybe combine it with photojournalism, spend time in Africa, something like that,' Mark was saying, his elegant left hand lying on the table only centimetres away from my right hand. I gazed transfixed as he reached out for the jug of water. 'Want some, Chloe?' he said.

I could only nod, and stare at my glass as he carefully filled it up. I took a breath to say 'thank you' but he had already turned back to Marianne. I wondered if he knew the effect he was having on me by being so distant, and rather thought that he did.

It seemed like only a moment later that Gemma at the other end of the table announced that we needed to go because Marianne had to start the long drive back to Cornwall, and Sally and I needed delivering home.

Everyone got up and there was a swirl of 'goodbyes', 'thank yous' and 'come agains'. I don't *think* I disgraced myself in all of this, but I was so focused on Mark's every move and trying not to let it show, that I have no idea if I succeeded in appearing normal or not.

Eventually I was bending down releasing Albert's lead from the table leg, which happened to be just next to Mark.

'Bye, Chloe,' he said casually. 'Keep an eye on that dog of yours.' And then because I must have looked so miserable, he seemed to relent because he added, 'We'll talk properly next time.' And he turned to say goodbye to Marianne and Gemma.

I looked at his back, at the slightly worn leather belt of his jeans, at the way he had one hand casually stuck in his pocket. He seemed so familiar, and yet utterly distant. He leant forward to kiss Marianne on the cheek in an oh-so-grown-up way. And he turned to Gemma and kissed her on the cheek too. He then headed back inside the house.

What I really wanted to do was sit down on the grass and burst into tears. But I somehow held it together, and turned round and led Albert back towards the garden gate.

Without looking back I went to Marianne's car and put Albert in the back. He was very subdued. Perhaps he had picked up on my mood.

The others came out and got in the car and we set off.

'Patricia's son is such an interesting boy, isn't he?' said Marianne to Gemma. 'Just from the way he talks, I rather imagine he's a good photographer.' She was looking at the traffic at a busy junction, so wouldn't have seen Gemma turn and look at me with an expression which – if I didn't know her better – might look a bit like pity.

'You didn't say much to Mark, did you, Chloe?' said Sally. 'Still, at least horrible Maggie wasn't there. That would have been awful, wouldn't it?'

I didn't even have the strength to want to strangle her, cheerfully or otherwise, I just looked out of the window, blinking very hard.

By the time we got to Friday, which was Day One of Mum's first treatment, I really was starting to look like 'the girl in the book'. The one that was all pale and interesting and wasting away.

The Falling-In-Love potion was working beautifully; I'd hardly eaten a thing, and I reckoned my thighs were on track to be properly thin in exactly twenty-four days.

But the worst thing was the tossing and turning at night. I just couldn't stop thinking about Mark – how lovely he looked, and was, and how I should have tried to have a proper conversation with him, tried to find out whether he really was seeing the school cow, whether he had ANY idea how much his not being in touch when he got back from America had hurt me. I went over and over and round and round, but the whole Falling-In-Love thing just seemed to get worse and worse.

'You're looking very pale, young lady,' said Gran that morning. (I hated being called 'young lady', but not so much that I had the energy to tell Gran that.) 'I hope you're not on a diet or in love with some boy or other.' She chuckled at her own hilarious joke, and didn't sound remotely sympathetic – even though either condition should deserve some sympathy.

'No, Gran,' I said, 'not on a diet, just tired from all the work I've got to do.' And with that half-truth, I left the kitchen to go and look for Mum. The night before she'd been even quieter than normal, and I knew she was dreading her visit to the hospital. Who wouldn't?

'Hope it goes OK, Mum,' I said as I came into her bedroom. She was all dressed and ready for the outdoors in her favourite brown coat with the sewn-up tear. Sitting at her dressing table, she was looking in the mirror and carefully brushing her hair.

In order to stop myself thinking that perhaps she wouldn't have any to brush quite soon, I went on, 'I've set the machine to record your favourite programme this afternoon. So you've got it to watch tonight and take your mind off it.'

'Thanks, love,' said Mum, smiling at me in the mirror. 'But I'm not sure how I'll feel about a hospital drama this evening. Might have had my own, mightn't I?!'

D'oh. What an idiot I am, I thought. Not being able to think of anything clever to say, I just went towards her and gave her an awkward hug. (We Bennets are very good at the awkward hug.)

'You get off to school, love,' said Mum, hugging me back more skilfully. 'I'll be here when you get back and I can help you pack for Paris and you can tell me all about your rehearsals.'

Friday was rehearsal day – the last one before we started rehearsing with the St Thomas's boys. Perhaps being a Wall would help me take my mind off things.

Miss Brewer bustled into class. 'Now, girls,' she said, 'we're going to focus on the play within a play. Take your places, and let's get on.' That Friday Miss Brewer was looking more than ever like Edna Mode in *The Incredibles*. Any moment now, I thought, she's going to adopt a German accent and announce flamboyantly, 'I never look back, dahling, it distracts from the now.' (One of my favourite lines in movie history. Apart from Scarlett O'Hara's never being hungry again, and the one about wearing pink on Wednesdays, but I digress.)

'Those of you reading the boys' parts, come forward now. Those of you who have a part in the final play will of course have learnt your words by now,' Miss Brewer said.

Horrors. I had been so busy getting annoyed at Gran for being Gran, God for letting Mum be ill, Mark for not apologising for something he didn't know he'd done, that I'd totally forgotten to learn my part.

At the other end of the room the QB had already started declaiming. She was reading in for Lysander's part, a boy part, so this time she didn't have to even pretend she could act. And she so couldn't. Although I was still frozen with horror at not having learned my part, I was fascinated by that whining, false-flirty voice, devoid of any expression. On the night, Maggie was going to be props manager. She had the perfect voice for the job.

'Gawd,' I managed to whisper to Sally and Gemma. 'Haven't learnt my lines. Miss B will kill me.'

Gemma didn't seem to recognise the true horror of this. But Sally, who was reading in for Pyramus, another boy part, took one look at my horrified expression and slowly but immediately started tearing out pages from her copy of the play. She held her book up with the pages with the Wall's part on facing me.

This girl is much, much cleverer than she is given credit for, I thought, as I realised I could see the words perfectly without it showing I was reading them.

'And this the cranny is right and sinister, through which the fearful lovers are to whisper,' I said in my best west-country burr. At least I think it was west country.

What with one thing and another, by the time I'd finished my Cornish clowning, I had scored a 'well done, Chloe' from Miss Brewer and at least three laughs from everyone else.

I was feeling really pleased that, thanks to Sally, I'd got away with it, and everyone thought I'd done well.

But as we were packing up and getting ready to go, I saw QB Maggie coming towards me. She had that mean-girl expression on her face. She looked right at me, deliberately pushed into me and walked out of the classroom.

'Jeez, Chloe,' said Amy, 'what on earth are you supposed to have done to Maggie? She looked meaner than mean.'

'I don't know,' I said, a bit shaken at seeing so much venom close up. Even though we should all have been used to the class beeyatch being a beeyatch, it still wasn't a pretty sight.

'Anyone'd think you'd stolen *her* boyfriend rather than the other way round,' said Sally, with an air of rather detached scientific curiosity. Which I would have found annoying if I hadn't had reason to be very grateful to her very recently.

'That's a point, isn't it?' said Amy. 'I mean, if she's cross with you, it might be because she thinks you're winning something, don't you think?'

I shrugged. 'You're brilliant at looking on the bright side, Amy,' I said. 'But it doesn't feel like I'm winning much right now.'

And yet...it would have been interesting to know why I qualified for an extra burst of hatred from the Queen B.

'See you at dawn tomorrow,' Sally said to me and Gemma. 'Don't be late!' The coach for Paris was set to leave from the school at 7.30. Hideous, hideous time of day to be dressed and ready for a coach. Or anything, come to that. But first I needed to find out how Mum had got on.

When I got back I found Mum was in my bedroom, where she'd put a big pile of things on my bed. 'Look, Chloe, I've found you my map of Paris!' She waved a blue dog-eared map triumphantly in the air.

I certainly wasn't going to be the one to tell her that the maps on my phone would be much easier to use and more up to date.

'Thanks, Mum,' I said. She'd also found her school French dictionary, a bottle of her favourite French body lotion, an umbrella with 'J'adore Paris' written across it, and a plastic mac that had pictures of French impressionist paintings on it.

'Now I know I've got a guidebook somewhere,'

Mum was saying, 'just can't remember what I did with it...'

I thought it was time to stop the pile of Old Person Holiday Packing getting any bigger or I wouldn't have room to put anything normal in my backpack.

'Don't worry, Mum, they'll have all that kind of stuff,' I said. 'But just tell me how it went today. Did it hurt, do you feel bad, or what happened?'

'Well, love,' said Mum sitting down on the bed. 'They gave me a blood test and then there was a lot of waiting around, and then they gave me a drip for a couple of hours or so. It didn't hurt or anything. And then I came home. So you see – nothing to worry about. They say I'm going to feel a bit sick for the next few hours, but that's all. Just got to take some pills, and then I don't have to think about it for another couple of weeks or so.'

I always knew Mum was going to make as little of it all as possible, that's the sort of mum she is. But I did think that even if she wasn't being completely truthful about how easy it was, that it didn't sound quite as bad as I'd imagined.

Pretty bad though.

I sat next to Mum and gave her one of my trademark awkward hugs. We sat there in silence for a little bit, and then she got up to cook some sausages for Ghastly Ralph (her work is never done. And his work never begins, it would seem), and I got up to try to pack some actual clothes.

French Frolics

Moments later – or that's what it felt like – it was 7.30 and I'd arrived at school.

A rather elderly-looking coach was parked in the middle of the playground, its engine idling and already half full of us. 'Happy Tours – Join the Fun Bus' it said in crumbly pink letters on its side.

Sally was waiting for me on the other side of the coach.

'Is it just me,' I said to her as we climbed up the steps, 'but doesn't being told to be Happy and have Fun make you instantly determined to be miserable and have a horrible time?'

'Yes,' said Sally, 'it *is* just you. I think most people just think they're going to Paris and they're probably going to have a nice time, and they don't feel they have to make a point about what it says on the bus.'

I thought it would actually be a bad start to the trip to have a quarrel with my BFF, so I quietly followed her to the back of the coach where I could see Gemma had saved us places.

'Can't believe you're here first,' I said to her. 'This turning over a new leaf thing is serious, isn't it?'

'Sure,' Gemma said. 'Obviously I don't really want to be expelled, but also obviously I didn't want to miss the bus, because we're going to meet Jack and the others in the Champs-Élysée this afternoon.'

So cool. It wasn't enough for her to be going to Paris, but she has to have an assignation with A Boy or Boys. I must have looked as amazed as I felt.

'Be good for your Boy Watching skills, won't it?' Gemma was saying. 'We'll have a bunch of British ones – Jack and Rob and Owen and Mark, that sort of thing – so all we've got to do is find some French ones and we can do a proper compare and contrast, can't we?'

Incredible. But I wasn't sure if I was more in awe of my cool friend, or very tense and nervous about seeing Mark again.

'Rob!' The loud pig-like squeal was coming from Sally on my left. 'But he said he'd be too busy with the rugby to meet up.'

'They've got an afternoon of nothing much before

the game, so I said they should come and meet us at two at the Arc de Triomphe.'

All this control over the opposite sex, AND she knew where things were in Paris.

At this point Madame de B and Mr Pampledousse got into the coach. They were smiling at each other a lot and generally looking much more cheerful than they were when we'd seen them at the shopping mall. Something must be going their way. In among all the other items on my List of Things to Do, finding out what *that* was all about went to quite near the top.

The coach's engine started to make a different noise, doors were banged and we began to roll out of the school gates.

My first ever trip to Abroad. If it wasn't a bit uncool to say so, I would have said that I was excited.

Apart from the passport checking at the entrance to the platform, the Eurostar train was really quite like the train to Cornwall – very long, and full of lots of people with lots of suitcases, most of which seemed to be blocking the gangways.

Our class had a whole coach booked and very soon

you could hear which end the Queen Beeyatch had made her own. She and her cohorts had colonised two tables and were laughing and squawking in that way that always meant that someone's reputation was being torn to shreds.

As we were settling down at a table at the other end of the carriage, one of the QBM cohorts walked back down the train towards us. Ignoring me and Sally, she looked at Gemma and said, 'Hey, Gem, aren't you going to come and sit with us? Maggie wants to talk about plans for this afternoon with Jack and Mark.'

I went cold. I could feel Sally staring at me; I could feel the amazed expression on her face.

Gemma, on the other hand, calmly got out her iPad and earphones and seemed to be ignoring the cohort. But just when it looked like she was being rude, she said, 'No, thanks, I'm OK here. I haven't got any plans for this afternoon with Maggie.'

The cohort looked at her, clearly amazed that anyone dared turn down an invitation from the Queen Beeyatch. She tried to adopt the classic mean-girl stare, and started to make her mouth into a sneer. But Gemma wasn't looking at her.

As well as being beyond impressed by my cool friend I found myself fascinated by the whole scene.

What do you do when you find that you're sneering into thin air? Well, you start to look a bit silly if the cohort was anything to go by. There were the very beginnings of a blush coming over her (as an expert on the subject, I know the signs very, very well), and she suddenly turned on her heel in a sort of flouncy way and walked quickly back up the carriage.

You could see that she was reporting back to the QB, because Maggie leaned out into the middle of the train to stare back at us. Then she leant into the middle of the table and seemed to be saying something in a low voice. All the cohorts burst into cackles and cackles of witch-like laughter, turned round and stared at us, carrying on cackling as they did so.

It was a master class in beeyatchery.

'Ignore them,' said Gemma, concentrating on her iPad. 'Maggie thinks the boys are only coming because they want to see her. I'm not so sure. And anyway, why on earth would I want to sit with that cow?'

I decided to think about something else and concentrated on following the progress of our journey on the map on my phone (another advantage of the electronic over the dog-eared paper). Soon the little green dot that was us disappeared and everything outside the train went black.

We were in the tunnel.

'Hey,' said Sally. 'Isn't that amazing – we're underwater. All that sea above us. What would happen if there was suddenly a hole in the tunnel and the sea came in? We wouldn't have a chance, would we?' And she laughed very slightly hysterically.

I started to feel a bit sick, and began to wonder in a scientifically curious kind of way, whether I was going to pass out. I suppose you have no way of knowing if you're claustrophobic until you're in a claustrophobic situation. Like in a tunnel under the sea.

Fortunately it wasn't long before everything went light and bright outside and the train manager welcomed us to France in French and English. Phew.

Outside in France looked very much like outside in England, except it seemed a bit flatter and the train was going much faster.

So fast that we seemed to arrive at the Gare du Nord almost immediately, and were outside the station, clutching our itineraries and our bags, moments after that.

It was pouring with rain, so I found myself strangely glad of Mum's 'J'adore Paris' umbrella, and put it up over Sally and me – even though I thought it made us look pathetically eager to please.

'Come, come, girls,' Madame de B said. 'We need to be quick, we have lunch and then we have free time, but we must be *à Louvre à quatre heures*.'

Somewhere between London and the Gare du Nord, 'Madame' seemed to have acquired a French accent. Which was, I suppose, very much entering into the spirit of things, but using the actual language might be a bit of a risk when it came to telling us what time to be where. I thought perhaps 'the Louvre at four o'clock' might have been safer.

We dumped our bags at the Hotel de Luxere, which, with its peeling walls, slight smell of drains and nearness to the back of a flyover didn't have very much 'lux' about it. But hey, it was Paris, and it had stopped raining and we were off for our first real French meal.

We walked for ages...past lots of inviting shops with beautiful boots and shoes in the windows, past groups of artists drawing people's portraits – who gestured wildly to us to let them draw us – and past lots of cafés with chairs outside and groups of handsome French boys in tight jeans standing around them.

Everywhere looked so inviting, so interesting, it was a miracle Mr Pampledousse – who was starting to look more and more stressed – and Madame didn't lose any of us.

Eventually we stopped at a street corner, and followed Madame and Mr P into a wooden doorway with the words 'Le Saumon Privé' written over it in curly pink letters next to a picture of a fish. Even I could work out what that meant, but clearly everyone must have thought that the 'salmon' was so 'private' that they weren't allowed in, because the restaurant was completely empty.

'*Asseyez-vous*, girls,' said Madame as our eyes got accustomed to the dark. 'We are going to *manger* the *déjeuner*, but very quickly because you will want the free time.'

Not so much us, as them, I thought, as the manager delivered dish after dish of smelly cheeses and odd-looking salads at high speed. Mostly everyone was too busy wondering what was in the salads to notice, but I could see our two leaders were having very heated discussions with the manager. The three of them were leaning forward rather intensely over two bottles of wine, gesturing at each other rather wildly and crossly.

'Look at them,' said Gemma, who was sitting opposite me. 'They're up to something with that manager. But they're not noticing us; let's go now or we'll be really late.'

It was nearly half past two, and everyone else was

getting up by now. Sally and I followed Gemma outside. Looking at the map on her phone – I guess she didn't necessarily know where everything was in Paris after all – Gemma walked quickly to the end of the street, right a bit, left a bit, and then we were in the most stunning road. Or Avenue, as I think it's called. Enormously wide, with huge houses, and all on a scale of oldness and bigness I'd never seen before in my life.

'Gosh,' said Sally. 'This is the *Change Elise*, isn't it?' She said it in a confident French accent, but I knew that's how she thought it was spelt. You could just tell.

'Something like that,' said Gemma, really hurrying now towards the giant arch at the top of the avenue.

I could see in the distance two groups of boys, standing around near the bottom of the right-hand foot of the Arc de Triomphe. As I strained to see if Mark was one of them, I found time to have a little bit of my own ohmigod moment in this amazing place.

'It's huge, isn't it, Chloe?' said Sally rather unimaginatively, and a bit breathlessly because she was running to keep up.

As we got nearer to the groups of boys, I was able to see that – yup – they were all there. Mark, looking particularly great in a denim jacket and a white scarf, was standing talking to Rob – who seemed to have acquired a biker jacket which made him look even shorter – and the lilty-hunky Owen.

In another group was Jack Harrington, looking it has to be said, very slightly godlike with his blond hair and black jacket.

Sally set off in the direction of Rob, and I followed Gemma as she headed towards the Jack group. 'Hey!' he shouted as we approached, and he broke away from the others and came towards Gemma. 'You're looking great, Gem, dig that red,' he said as he got closer.

I looked at Gemma and realised that yes, her dark red jacket did make her look extra good. Impressive that Handsome Jack should have an eye for colour, even if he did rather weirdly use the word 'dig' unironically.

I was just starting to think about how extra-good-looking people seem to extra-appreciate each other when my handbag started croaking. Amazing how loud the song of the frog ringtone can be, even in the roar of the Champs-Élysée traffic, but it made me jump out of my skin and feel slightly alarmed.

I was dead right to be alarmed. Yr mum fainted, back in hospital. Am going there now. When u back France? Ralph was the message from the ghastly one.

I stood on the edge of the pavement, buffeted by passing Japanese tourists taking endless selfies in front of the arch, gazing in horror at my phone. I pressed Call, but Ghastly Ralph's phone just went straight to voicemail.

Putting my hand over my mouth in the way that you do when you think you're going to cry, I pressed Call again and again.

'Hi there,' said a voice by my side. Mark. He was looking at me with a concerned expression on his face. In the midst of my horror and worry I felt a little burst of elation – surely you don't look concerned if you don't care about someone? 'You look a bit shell-shocked,' he said. 'Are you all right?'

At that moment a very large American tourist in a sickeningly psychedelic shirt and carrying a huge man-bag climbed onto the kerb behind us. Holding his phone up in the air he was yelling at three small (but also large) children in equally sickeningly psychedelic outfits.

'Chesney, Banjo, get over here. Kayleen, you stand in front,' he shouted. Trying to get all three in the photo he edged backwards. Mark, looking at me, couldn't see what was about to happen. With all the inevitability of a slow-motion film, Chesney, Banjo and Kayleen's father bumped backwards into Mark.

The considerable force of a lot of American fat (there is no other word) pushed Mark into me suddenly and hard. Instinctively we both put our hands out to stop ourselves falling, so for a very split second we had our arms round each other.

For that very split second I could feel his back under his jacket, I could smell a sort of warm soapy smell, and I could feel his breath on my hair. His hands were on my shoulders, and if I'd just looked up in that split second our lips would almost have touched.

'Oh gee whizz.' A rasping voice broke into the precious moment. 'Guess ah just din see you there. Aren't I the clumsy one?' And the fat (there is still no other word) American burst into peals of laughter. I could see the children edging away, quite understandably trying to pretend their father was nothing to do with them.

Mark barely acknowledged the fat one's comment, but just put an arm round mine and steered me towards the other side of the pavement.

'It's Mum,' I said, 'she's had this treatment thing,' for some reason I couldn't say the word 'chemo', 'and now she's passed out and they've taken her back into hospital. And I can't get through to my stepfather to hear what's going on.'

'Maybe he's in the hospital with her, and can't use his phone,' said Mark with a frown of concern. His hand was still on my arm. Even in the midst of being frightened for Mum, I somehow managed to concentrate on keeping my arm incredibly still so there was no chance of my accidentally brushing off his hand.

'You can't do anything about it for the moment,' he went on. 'Try and ring again in a couple of hours, but if she's in hospital she's safe. They've probably only taken her in as a precaution, you know.' He looked down at me, as he spoke, giving me what I think they call a reassuring smile. Except it actually was reassuring. Plus it was also a very beautiful smile.

'Hey, Marky!' This time the voice that interrupted the moment was female and English. The voice of someone who was a very bad actress and very short and very, very mean. 'Marky', indeed.

'Over here!' the QB yelled. 'We're bunking off the boring old Louvre and coming for coffee with you.'

Mark muttered something under his breath, which I wanted to think sounded like 'I don't think so', but as the others were all coming towards us now there was no chance of finding out.

'We're not.' Gemma's voice came from behind me.

'If you're going to skip the one thing we've got to do today, you're on your own, Maggie.' And she turned to Jack and said, 'See you tomorrow.'

Everyone went very still; some of the QB cohorts even looked a bit nervous. It was all shaping up into quite a power struggle. I had this vision of time suspended, like the moment before the bad guy draws his gun and points and shoots.

'Can't do that, Maggie,' said Mark. 'We've got to head off for the stadium in a minute.'

Even though we knew that wasn't strictly true, the moment was diffused. Everybody visibly relaxed and started to say goodbye to each other. I could see Rob give Sally a quick hug. Good, I thought as I turned to Mark. He was watching Gemma and Jack as they flirted with each other with their eyes. (They were doing it really well – a steamy stare that seemed to say 'I'm looking at you looking at me and you're gorgeous and I'm gorgeous and together we're really quite something so it's only fitting that we really fancy each other'.)

He looked back at me. 'I think your friend's got a plan for us all to meet up tomorrow, Chloe. So I'll see you then. Let me know what happens with your mum, won't you?'

I nodded. I longed to ask him what he really thought

of Maggie. What he really thought of me. Was he being nice to me because he just felt sorry for me?

I set off after the others, down the *Change Elise*, towards the Louvre. It started to rain again. As I put 'J'adore Paris' back to work, I hoped that some Serious Art would take my mind off it all.

Culture is exhausting.

Official.

The Louvre turned out to be *enormous*, and very full of people as well as pictures – the one stopping you seeing the other. Mr Pampledousse was in his element, which I suppose shouldn't be surprising in an Art teacher, but what with the noise of the crowds and his thick Greek accent it was quite hard to understand very much of what he was telling us.

'I think,' said Gemma at one point, 'that if I have to look at one more little baby Jesus I am going to scream.'

I was pretty sure you shouldn't say stuff like that in a world-famous art gallery. A bit like you shouldn't swear in a cathedral. But she had a point. Baby Jesuses and saints, I thought, as I looked up at a picture of

Saint Sebastian, who had an arrow sticking into every available bit of flesh. There seemed to be no end to the horrible things people did to saints, but why so many artists had to paint a picture of them was beyond me.

'And now you must follow for piece of resistance!' Mr P was bouncing around in excitement as he signalled to us all to gather round. It must have been infectious, because Madame de B/Bracegirdle was smiling and nodding behind him in a way that made her look a little bit half-witted.

'I reckon Doris has been at the bottle,' said someone just behind me.

I turned. Incredibly, it was the QB herself. She was looking up at me; she was actually speaking to me. She put on a sort of sneery, giggly expression, but now she was directing it at Madame de B. Double incredible. She was being a Beeyatch to someone and expecting me to join in on her side.

I could see some of the cohorts watching us with puzzled expressions on their faces. It was as if I were being publicly invited to join the gang. Curiouser and curiouser.

But before I could think about this properly we were being herded into the Mona Lisa room. Hundreds of people in this one. Hundreds. All pushing towards the famous picture at the end of the room, cameras held high.

Mr P was saying something about 'illusion' and 'light and shadow' which I couldn't understand. Greek Artspeak was too much of a challenge this late in the day.

Plus I'd just remembered the only thing I knew about the Mona Lisa smile: if you look at her eyes she appears to be smiling, but if you look down to her mouth she doesn't. This turned out to be such a good game – seeing if she smiled or not – that it kept me occupied for ages. When I looked round everyone else had gone.

Feeling the onset of panic, I headed towards the most likely-looking exit. I had no signal on my phone, couldn't understand the French signs, and had completely lost my sense of direction. All the strange people milling about who'd seemed just annoying a moment before, now seemed vaguely threatening.

I headed out of the Mona Lisa gallery into more crowds and turned left.

It was either that or turn right.

I marched on past the entrances to other galleries and found my way blocked by a large group listening to a bearded mad-professor type gesticulating wildly by a bright white sculpture of two-thirds of a man's body.

The people listening were all aged about sixteen or seventeen, all obviously French and nearly all boys. In the interests of pursuing our science of Boy Watching, I thought I'd just stop for a moment and have a bit of a practice.

They were all carrying folders of notes, which they looked at constantly and interestedly, and they all looked neat and smartly dressed. Plus you could bet your bottom dollar – or euro – that they had had a shower more than once in the last year. They listened respectfully to the mad professor, and they had that indefinable *Frenchness* about them. They looked as if they'd be romantic on a date – take you to dinner rather than the football.

I decided to get a bit closer for a better look. And I realised that they all had phones hidden in their notes, that some of them were quite smelly, and that their bags all had 'Sidgwick School, London', written on them.

It just goes to show, I thought. But then I wasn't quite sure what it went to show, and decided to focus on trying to find the way out.

I was in the large entrance hall, just about despairing

of ever being found again, when I suddenly caught sight of everyone standing by a large sign saying 'Exit'.

Mr P and Doris were looking tired and cross, the QB and her merry gang were obviously giggling at someone else's expense (very probably the marble naked young man they were standing next to), and Sally was gazing rapturously at her phone.

At any other time I could have been irritated with any one of them. But this time they all looked adorable, and safely familiar.

'Lovely' in Paris

I had woken up the next day in the Hotel de not-at-all Lux feeling quite cheerful, despite having been kept awake a lot of the night by the merry noise of the flyover and Sally's snoring.

My conversation with the ghastly stepdad had been short but reassuring. Mum was OK and had fainted mostly because she hadn't eaten anything much for days. (I guess Fear-of-Hospital potion must be right up there with Falling-in-Love potion for putting you off food; at this rate, both Mum and I are on track for super-thin thighs any minute now.)

Plus I was cheerful because I was going to see Notre Dame in the morning, and Mark in the afternoon. (I'd texted him to say Mum was OK; I was sure he meant it when he said he wanted to know. Or fairly sure...)

The thought of the Notre Dame bit was rather overshadowed, though, by the thought of the Mark bit. I expect it's a sign of deep shallowness to be more excited by the thought of seeing a boy than of seeing a famous cathedral, but I think there's plenty of time to be deep when I grow up.

We arrived at the Pompidou Centre, our meeting place with The Boys, about half an hour early. The cathedral experience had featured two interesting and unexpected elements. The first was a climb up the tower (great views, horrible vertigo) and the second was a church service – a service in a cathedral? On a Sunday? Who knew?

At a distance, The Boys looked very lively. There was a lot of dancing around, pretend kick-boxing, and the sort of mutual shoving that only boys know how to do.

As we got closer there also seemed to be quite a lot of noise coming from their bit of the square.

'I think there's been a lot of celebrating,' said Gemma. 'Wales won, which I gather was a surprise. So I expect your friend Owen, Chloe, will be all happy today.'

It was true. Even at a distance I could see that Owen's buzz-cut was buzzing about the group as he bounced and banged into them. You could almost imagine that he'd had a beer or three.

'Hiya!' called out Rob as we approached. He came up to Sally. 'Hey, girl, how was Notre Dame?' He pronounced it as if he were American, but I was impressed that he asked Sally a question about her day as soon as he saw her.

Rob is definitely one of the good guys, and asking a girl a question first (a nice one, obvs) was high up on the list of things to score for (also in a nice way, obvs) on our Boy Watching list.

I smiled my best friendly smile at him, even though he wasn't looking and probably didn't care whether he scored Boy Watching points or not.

'It was amazing,' said Sally. 'Whole place was filled with smoke! What do you think about that? I thought it was illegal to smoke indoors.'

'Not if you're a priest,' said Owen, who'd calmed down and had come over to us. 'Reckon they could put all sorts of dodgy things in their incense, and they'd be happy, and we'd never know.'

He turned to me, 'Hello, lovely,' he said in his lilty-Welsh way. 'Is Paris being nice to you?'

I liked the way 'lovely' came out in lilty-speak, and was thinking how no one had ever called me that before. So it took me a bit longer to answer his question. 'Yes, thank you,' I said, 'very nice.' There. That was worth waiting for, wasn't it? Here I am being talked to by a handsome (well, quite handsome) boy and I come up with one of my classic middle-aged tea party responses.

'Great place, Paris,' said Owen, seemingly not too bothered by my inability to say anything interesting. 'Don't suppose you've seen much of it so far, have you? Not the real Paris?'

'Well, no,' I said. 'I suppose not, really.' Another cracker.

'Let me show you something, then,' said Owen smiling. 'Just over here, behind the square. It's a bit of absolutely classic Paris. Come on, this way.'

And smiling, he put his arm round me and led me off to the corner of the square. It was a huge square so it took a long time to get to the edge, and when we did we went down a narrow street, and then another one, and eventually we ended up in a street that backed on to a building site. It was covered with corrugated iron, and on it someone had painted in huge red letters 'make love – often'. In between the letters there were loads of heart signs and names and graphic instructions – some in French and incomprehensible, some in

English and only too comprehensible.

All around the site were couples snogging.

Okaaaaay, I thought to myself, feeling distinctly unnerved. I suppose this is 'real' Paris, but what's it got to do with me? For real Paris, I definitely preferred an incomprehensible service in French in a smoky cathedral.

I looked up at Owen, half hoping this was all just a joke. He was looking down at me grinning, but not in quite such a nice way.

'Sort of thing that puts ideas into your head, isn't it?' he said still grinning. And he put his arm round me and pulled me towards him. 'City of love, Paris is. Let's put a bit of love in it.' And he pulled me closer and started trying to kiss me.

I tried to push him off, but he was so strong and was holding me so close I could hardly move.

Panic surged up in me as his grip got tighter and tighter, I twisted and turned, and tried to kick him on the shins but nothing seemed to have any effect.

And then suddenly it all stopped. Owen let go of me and stood back.

Still dazed I opened my eyes and realised that Owen's right arm was being held in an iron grip. It was Mark – looking at Owen with an expression of fury and disgust that I never thought I'd ever see in real life. If I hadn't been so weak with relief, I might almost have been frightened of him myself.

'What the *hell* do you think you're doing, you creep,' said Mark, anger making his voice shake. 'Get out of here before I smash your teeth in, you *pathetic* piece of crap.'

Owen looked shaken. Huge though he was, he seemed like a little boy, deflated, shamefaced.

He looked at me. 'I'm sorry, lovely,' he said. 'Got carried away.'

'Like hell you got carried away,' said Mark, still shaking. 'You brought her here deliberately. Now disappear. *Now*.'

Owen turned and started to walk back the way we'd come.

I felt so happy, so relieved, so shocked that not even I could overthink what I did next.

I fell into Mark's arms and started to cry into his shirt.

'Hey,' said Mark softly, as he stroked my hair. 'All right now. He's a tit, but he's gone, and it'll never happen again.'

I looked up at him. It was so wonderful to be in his arms that already I was forgetting the fear and horribleness of what had just happened. I smiled a bit. Mark smiled back. We gazed into each other's eyes, and then Mark gently kissed me on the forehead.

I felt so protected as he put his arm round me and we started to walk back towards the square.

'All right, now?' he said.

'Yes, thank you,' I said. And then, because that seemed so very much more than usually inadequate: 'Actually, thank you doesn't even come close.'

As we approached the square, arms round each other, I could see that it was full of strangers, and there was no sign of any of the others.

For a second I felt the same sense of abandonment that I'd felt in the Louvre. And then I felt an unfamiliar sense of security. I was with Mark. Everything would be all right.

'Where are you meant to be now, Chloe?' said my knight in shining armour. 'What's next on the Queen Mary's agenda?'

I looked at my itinerary. The Eiffel Tower. 'OK,' said Mark, looking at the directions over my shoulder. 'Let's go there together, shall we? I've got an hour till I need to be at the station.'

So we walked together. Not arm in arm this time, but still together. We didn't really say much; I think I was still in shock. And anyway, I couldn't think of anything to say that wouldn't sound dull, humble, or goofy.

Mark was concentrating on his map. Oddly, it was made of paper and was blue and a bit dog-eared. If only Mum could see us now, I thought.

When we got to the Eiffel Tower, Team Queen Mary's was still milling around the bottom. Safely delivered and still at a distance from them, I said goodbye to Mark.

He gave me a hug, and set off for the station and I went towards the entrance of the tower.

Despite my horrible, horrible experience, I actually felt like a million dollars. Or euros.

The rest of the Paris trip went by in a little bit of a haze, but in a good way. The view from the top of the Eiffel Tower didn't make me feel sick at all, the two-hour tour of the Sacre Coeur seemed to go by in a flash, and Sally's quest for the perfect cheese joke didn't irritate me nearly as much as it should have done. (We do know, Sally, what you use to lure a bear out of his cave... But if only we hadn't been given *camembert*

that first night, you'd never have asked us. Twice a day. Every day.)

I was still no nearer knowing what was going on in QBM's mind. She hadn't addressed a word to me for the rest of the trip, but then nor had she gone out of her way to make my life in some way unpleasant. With Maggie, no attention is good attention.

By the time we arrived at the Gare du Nord, we were tired and laden down with shopping. Or, at least, some of us were. I didn't feel the need for a T-shirt with 'J'adore Paris' written on it, or for a pair of French boots when I probably couldn't afford some English ones.

Madame de B and Mr P, though, were the most laden of all. They arrived at the station in a taxi from which they took out box after box of something heavy. We knew it was heavy because there was an awful lot of grunting and groaning – and shouting at each other with thicker and thicker accents. Mr P was becoming more and more Greek, and Doris had now become more French than the French.

'He needs to be lift YOUR end!' shouted Mr P as he struggled with a red box.

'Is not helpful to carry zem all at once!' shouted back Madame de B.

Curious, Sally, Gemma and I started to follow them to the back of the train where they were getting their boxes checked into the luggage compartment. As we got nearer we could see that written on all the boxes were the words 'Le Saumon Privé'. And they were making a very loud clanking noise.

'Ha,' said Gemma. 'Thought so. *That's* why Doris and Pimplemouse were so keen on a trip to Paris, and that's why we ended up in that dodgy empty restaurant. It's all about their little wine-importing business. Interesting.'

'Great,' said Sally. 'Have we caught them out? Does that mean we can blackmail them now?' There we were again. In amongst the knitting and the baskets, looking out for trouble and bad stuff.

'Nope,' said Gemma, 'but it's just useful to know. Always good to have something on the other person.'

Blimey, I thought. Who knew my friends had such a thirst for criminal activity? I followed them back to our carriage thinking maybe a foreign country brings out people's true colours. Whether it was blackmail, dodgy wine importing – or rescuing damsels in distress.

Which brought me neatly back to thinking about what I'd been thinking about before anyway. Him. And thinking about him kept me fully occupied all the way to London.

Three days in Paris had felt like twenty. So many things had happened, most of them good, some of them even quite educational. But by the time we arrived at St Pancras, I think I speak for us all when I say we were properly tired and happy to be home.

As we emerged from the station I could see a ring of people waiting for our train. Ghastly Ralph was easy to spot (the fat one in the outsize football shirt reading a football magazine), and so were Liv (the slim one in a tracksuit and full make-up, holding the hands of two small boys who were shouting at each other) and Merv (the one in black denim, baseball cap over his long grey hair and completely unnecessary sunglasses).

I emerged just behind the QB and Madame de B. Reluctant to greet Ralph before I absolutely had to, I walked deliberately slowly.

QB Maggie had separated herself from the cohorts and was walking quickly on ahead. Which I reckon had all the signs of her being ashamed of something. And when I saw the woman whose face lit up when she saw the QB, I thought I understood why. Maggie's mother was short (perhaps no surprise there), and also mousy and rather timid-looking. She looked rather nice but a bit frightened. The QB went quickly up to her, allowed herself to be hugged briefly and then immediately led her mother away in the direction of the car parks.

There wasn't enough time to be fascinated by the thought of a perfectly nice woman producing the class cow (and probably having a horrid time being her mother), because just ahead of me was a remarkably handsome man in army uniform. He had a thick black moustache which made him – amazingly – look very macho, tall leather boots and a cape with epaulettes on it. You would put him top of the list to play the hero in any costume drama, not least because it looked like he could provide his own costume.

'*Cheri!*' called out Madame de B/Bracegirdle just in front of me. '*Te voilà!*' And she hurried towards him, suitcases banging at her legs.

Handsome Army Officer looked down at her, and said in a broad Yorkshire accent, 'No need for any of that now, D, you're back in England.' And together they headed off to wherever you go to pick up case after case of Private Salmon wine.

Life's very curious sometimes, and people are endlessly fascinating, I thought, as I went up to the ghastly one.

Although, I thought, as Ralph looked up at me and grunted, some are a lot less fascinating than others.

Back to Earth...with a Bump

When I got home that evening, Mum was sitting in her favourite Sudoku chair in the kitchen, pencil hovering over the empty squares, a cup of tea and a plate of biscuits by her side. So all should have been well in Mum-land.

She greeted me with one of her best Chloe-smiles, which was nice to see, but less nice was how pale and tense she looked. But I suppose living with Gran and Ghastly Ralph and having twenty-six hospital appointments hanging over your head was enough to make anyone pale and tense.

I got out the box of special French chocolate biscuits I'd bought her in Paris (which I had, now I came to look at them, a sneaking suspicion she could get at her local supermarket) and sat down at the table opposite her, ready to talk about all my adventures. I'd worked out a way of telling her about Mark's Great Rescue of me without going into too much detail about the horrible thing with Owen.

I'd finished on the Louvre and the Eiffel Tower and had just started on a rather dramatic description of Notre Dame full of smoke, when in came Gran, tapping the floor suspiciously with her stick as if to check it was still solid and hadn't gone all spongey while she wasn't looking.

Amazing how there are some people who can just spoil the moment. And I could see from the way Mum's face fell that she thought the same.

'So you're back,' said her mother, my grandmother, predictably and irritatingly. 'I hope you made the most of it and learnt a few lessons about French culture and art. No shopping and being silly. You're very lucky to go on a trip to Paris, my girl. We never had anything like that in my day.'

Right at the top of all the things to be annoyed about in this little speech (and there were many) was being called 'my girl'. I could hardly believe I was thinking it, but 'young lady' seemed positively loving by comparison.

'It sounds like Chloe's seen nothing but paintings and churches, Gran,' said Mum loyally. 'I was enjoying hearing all about it,' she added in a tone that was the nearest she was going to get to criticising her mother, my grandmother.

'Well, I'll leave you to it, then,' said Gran, slightly huffily. 'But don't forget, We Need to Talk about Albert.' And with that she turned on her stick and left the room.

We both breathed out and smiled at each other perhaps a bit disloyally.

After a moment, Mum said, 'So go on, did you and Sally and Gemma see any of those boys while you were there?'

'Yes, we did,' I said, 'but that's a long story – first what's all this about Albert? Has he been bad?'

'No, not really,' said Mum. 'But he had a little go at nipping Gran on the ankle the other day. Just a friendly nip, I think it was. But anyway, she wants him put down.'

Oh dear. I was quite sure that there couldn't have been anything friendly about Albert's nip, but actually killing him was a little extreme even by Gran standards.

'Gawd,' I said. 'We'll just have to keep him out of her way. Imagine telling crabby old Mr U that we want to have his dog put down?'

'Exactly,' said Mum. 'Now go on then, tell me about the boys – and the shopping and being silly.'

By the time I'd answered that one in full – without being at all graphic about the Owen moment – it was late and Mum was getting tired. I'd noticed a quiet satisfaction in her when I told her about Mark and how he'd reassured me about her fainting, and then how he'd seen off what she decided to call 'an unwanted admirer'. And by the time she heard that he had the same map of Paris as she did, she was well on the way to liking him almost as much as I did.

'But you still haven't talked to him about the football match and seeing him with that girl?' she said as she got up to put the kettle on for her hot-water bottle.

'No, Mum,' I said. 'I don't know what to think about all that. Don't really know what to think about anything for the moment. Bit tired though. Might have an early night too.'

Later, as I closed my eyes, I wondered what my subconscious would make of all my recent adventures. Surely I was due for a surreal dream about Owen and Albert running into the Louvre with Mark and Mme Bracegirdle chasing them with giant chocolate biscuits and bottles of wine?

But perhaps real life was enough for my fevered imagination, because I slept deeply and dreamlessly until it was time to get up for yet more education.

It felt rather odd going to school on a normal bus with a normal bag of normal stuff. It was going to be a morning of English (Mr Fanshawe, more psychos from *Lord of the Flies*), Maths (hideous Miss Grunbar), various scientific horrors, topped off with Swimming (which for those of us who can't really swim brings its own sort of horror).

But within the first few minutes of being back behind the school gates it was as if we'd never been away. Blinking Mr Carson was as nervous as ever, Mr Fanshawe's nose as blocked as ever, and Miss Grunbar's need to make us feel stupid and inadequate was as strong as ever.

'Chloe,' said a small voice as I came out of the changing rooms, ready for the hell that is called Swimming. Sally. 'Are you going to come round on Saturday? Mum says something exciting is going to happen, but you never know with Mum, she was a bit slurry when she said it, and anyway I thought we could just, you know, hang.'

Sally said all this a bit humbly, almost as if she were frightened of something, so I didn't – as I usually would – ask her exactly what she meant by 'hang'. I could see that would have been quite irritating of me.

'Yes, sure, OK,' I said. 'But what sort of exciting? Good exciting or bad exciting? I mean, did she seem happy in between the slurs?'

'I dunno,' said Sally, struggling with the key to her locker. 'She wouldn't say, she just said it was a surprise.'

'Fine. Well, I'll be there, course I will,' I said as I took Sally's key and put it in the lock the right way up. 'What are friends for, anyway?'

It looked like it was going to be a busy old Saturday. That morning, Mum had announced that Steve was coming home for a lightning visit (with or without Ethan the EM Forster scholar, we didn't know), and Amy had told us she was running in some really important race in the local stadium which she wanted us all to watch.

Plus Gran had her exhibition to go to. Usually reluctant to leave the flat, she was going to make the supreme effort to actually go out because she wanted to see this particular exhibition of china dolls in the town hall. I know. But china dolls were Gran's Great Obsession. Personally I thought the mad eyes staring at you out of bright white faces were the stuff of nightmares.

As I say, people are endlessly fascinating.

It was a slow start to the day that Saturday. Mum was starting to feel quite a bit better ('Shame you're only going to be feeling rubbish again when you have the next dose,' Ralph had said, rather unhelpfully) and had got up early to make scones for Steve. That age-old need a mother has to bake things for her menfolk was alive and kicking *chez* Bennet.

'If he doesn't come soon, Mum,' I said at about eleven o'clock, 'I'm going to have to go. Sally said lunchtime and don't be late, though I don't know why.'

The ghastly one looked up from his paper. 'I think you can wait to say hello to your brother, missy. It's just all about you and your friends with you, isn't it? Never a thought for other people.' And he turned back to his sports section.

I felt a wave of fury wash over me. Revolting, selfish man who made everyone's life unpleasant and difficult because he was so unpleasant and difficult. I couldn't do self-control any more, and took a deep breath. For once I was going to tell him exactly what I thought of him.

'Of *course* she thinks about other people,' Mum said in the nick of time. I breathed out. And as if Fate were determined to save my from myself, the bell rang at that moment. 'Off you go and let your brother in,' said Mum calmly.

Brother Steve had a different sort of army uniform on this time. Dark green, with lots of buttoned-down pockets and a beret stuck under the strap on his shoulder. He looked taller, and neater, and less acnified.

'Hi, Chlow,' he said, when I opened the door. He smiled a smile that made the 'Chlow' slightly less annoying. 'How's Mum?'

'Not too bad. You'll see,' I said. 'What about Ethan? Isn't he with you this time?'

'Nah,' said Steve as we came into the kitchen. 'Ethan's given it all up. Decided he's not cut out for the military. Going to try to get into drama school. I reckon he'll be good at that. I'm sure we'll still be friends, though.'

'One of those, wasn't he?' said Ghastly Ralph. 'Army's no place for him. Not for his sort.'

Steve looked so scornfully at his stepfather that for a minute I thought he was going to hit him. Instead he approached Mum and gave her a proper hug – not at all awkward Bennet.

Perhaps it was the army, or perhaps it was just the passing of time, but my brother seemed to be starting to do the growing-up thing. I felt a rush of affection for him. I could almost have given him a hug too.

But instead I left him to it – to Mum, and his scones, and his trying not to beat up his revolting stepfather – and headed off for the familiar bus to Sally's.

When Liv opened the door to me, I had to stagger back for a minute from the overpowering smell of her perfume. And I'd never seen her with so much make-up on before, ever – and Liv was no stranger to heavy make-up. Clearly she was trying to impress.

'Come in, come in,' she said. 'We're all here.' I wondered who 'we all' were.

I followed her into the kitchen and saw a strange and unexpected sight. Harris and Jock were sitting at the table (that was a first for a start), Sally was at the cooker stirring something that might have smelt quite nice if you could smell anything apart from Liv's perfume, and there at the head of the table was a man I'd never seen before in my life.

'This,' said Liv, looking rather intently at him, as if she wasn't quite sure if he was real, 'is James. My husband. Last seen departing on a secret mission to

315

Afghanistan. He flew in undercover. And maintained radio silence ever since. I think that's the right technical term... But the short of it is, that he's decided to come back to us. That's about it, isn't it, James?'

'James', who had orange hair like his daughter and a craggy, and rather tough-looking lined and handsome face, nodded wryly and took a long drag from the bottle of beer in front of him.

Extraordinary. I looked at Sally, who was looking at the stranger with a fascinated but puzzled expression on her face. I looked at Harris and Jock, who were completely and uncharacteristically silent as they stared at this strange man in their midst.

'Hello, Chloe,' said James, putting the beer down. 'I'm pleased to meet Sally's friend. It's true what Liv says about the radio silence. I *was* undercover and it was difficult getting messages out.' He caught Liv's eye at this and immediately seemed to look away with a guilty air. 'But I'm back now. And this is it. Me and the family. This is for good.' He looked back at Liv, who by now had a large glass of Mr PG in her hand, and he said again, 'Really is. For good.'

Everyone nodded, still seeming a bit bemused. I guess not surprisingly. For all that Liv knew he was out there somewhere, Harris and Jock didn't, and even

Sally had started to think her father might not exist. Liv got up and began to bustle about getting something out of the oven.

'Sally says you're going to be a prize-winning writer when you grow up,' said her new dad, pulling out the chair next to his for me. 'That's great, but it's tough being a writer these days. What's your fallback position?'

I realised I didn't have one, not a trace of one. And no one had ever asked me a question like that before. It was as if Sally's new dad was a proper dad and asked proper interested questions. I still didn't have the answer, though, and began to feel that old familiar feeling of a blush coming on.

'Chloe and I have a band. It's called OTTO,' said Sally from the other end of the kitchen. 'That's what she's going to do when she's not writing. She's going to sing and play keyboard.'

'Well, just in case none of that works,' said James, 'best if you get those exams under your belt, eh? My fallback position is teaching flying. Whatever else happens I've got that qualification. Not being boring or anything, but they do help.'

Liv and Sally dished out the dishes. Roast something and hundreds of vegetables. It was all a bit tense, but basically rather lovely – like being in a real family, eating real food.

Looking at Sally, carefully picking out the broccoli to stop it contaminating the vegetables she liked, I thought how lucky she was to have her father magically back in her life, even if things were going to be awkward for a bit. And then I had a moment feeling sorry for myself because I would never get *my* father back.

We were just starting on the strawberries, and Harris's explanation of why he was better at computer games than his brother, when a whole pondful of frogs erupted from my bag. 'Sorry,' I said as I grabbed my phone and got up from the table.

It was the hideous stepfather calling. 'It's your gran this time,' he said in his grumpiest voice. 'She hasn't come back from the town hall. We've gone to look for her.'

I went back to the table and explained that I had a missing gran. And one whose hatred of mobile phones meant that she was not just missing but positively untraceable.

Sally came with me to the door. 'Isn't it amazing?' she said. 'There you were saying he'd come back, but it just sounded like the plot for a film. I can't believe he's really him and he's here. And Mum seems pleased, even though I think she's quite cross with him. And the twins. They've never been so well behaved.' She looked thoughtfully at the ceiling. 'It's amazing,' she said again.

I set off for the bus stop telling myself I was very happy for them all. Really happy for them all. But I couldn't help being a little bit sorry for myself.

Mum was on her own in the kitchen when I got back. She had a sad expression on her face, and an empty Sudoku puzzle in front of her. Typical that Gran had spoilt Mum's day with Steve, I thought, but didn't say. Mum looked sad enough already.

'Steve and your stepfather have gone to the park to look for her,' said Mum. 'The exhibition's closed so she can't be there.'

'Shall I stay and keep you company, Mum? Make you a cup of tea?' I said, starting to do battle with the horrible Bennet kettle and its vicious lead. It was all getting much too late to go and see Amy run her race. I felt a bit guilty about that, but not too sad because I reckoned there would probably be years of watching Amy run races, what with her being so very good at it.

'No point in all of us getting lost, is there?' I went on. 'And anyway, got to tell you what's happened to Sally.'

'Well, that's extraordinary,' said Mum when I'd finished telling all about the Mystery of the Reappearing Dad. 'The last I heard, Liv was living with her gardener. What an exciting life she leads.'

'I think Patrick was her revenge on James,' I said, as if I knew what I was talking about. 'I think James had left her to go and be dramatic and romantic, doing that undercover stuff abroad. Plus he probably had loads of affairs, so she tried to forget him and convinced herself she'd moved on, which meant taking up with someone young and hot.'

I was quite pleased with this analysis. And still thought it had the makings of a novel. Perhaps I could use it in my Creative Writing Prize essay. Perhaps the man looking through his wife's things could be a woman, and she could find out he was an undercover spy...

This burst of creativity was interrupted by a burst of barking downstairs. Albert was back from wherever he'd been. I got up to go and say hello, as I hadn't seen him for days and days, and I expected he'd been pining for me.

I went down and opened our front door. And found

myself face to face with Gran, leaning heavily on her stick. Albert was bouncing and barking at her feet, and behind him was a grumpy-looking Mr Underwood.

'Hello, dear,' said Gran rather feebly, the hand on her stick shaking.

'She had a fall,' said Mr Underwood, since there wasn't any sign of Gran saying anything more. 'Tripped up in that path that goes through the bushes,' he went on. 'Albert found her. She couldn't get up.'

'Gosh,' I said. That was all I could come up with, because I was a bit shocked by how pale and wobbly Gran looked. Otherwise, I think I might well have shouted, 'this dog saved your life, this dog that you wanted to KILL', or words to that effect.

Instead I thanked Mr U in my best polite-schoolgirl voice and bent down and gave Albert a lot of fuss and a hug. I promised him (Albert) that I would bring an extra big bag of treats next time I saw him, and take him on his favourite walk past all the smelliest lampposts.

Gran looked on at this with a complicated expression on her face. A large part of her no doubt thought it very silly to have such a long conversation with a dog, especially one who was prone to nipping people on the ankle, but then another large part of her (there were plenty of large parts to go round with Gran) must have felt very, very grateful that she'd been rescued by this canine creature (even though he *was* probably riddled with fleas).

Mr U soon had enough of all the fuss, and took Albert back into his flat. I gave Gran my arm and we went slowly upstairs.

'I think I'd like some tea, dear,' said Gran, still a bit shaky.

I set to work on the kettle again, put out the tea things, texted the brother and Ralph to say that it was safe to come back, and then went off to my room to have a think.

Families. Can't do with 'em (especially not when you have a gran like mine), but also can't do without 'em (not even if you've been abroad for years having lots of adventures, as James the Reappearing Dad had).

I decided to try to work it all out some other time. First I had a pressing engagement with the St Thomas's website.

As I looked at all the pictures of him, art appreciation took on a whole new meaning.

22

The Play's the Thing

After her brush with mortality – AKA fall in the bushes – Gran became quite subdued. She behaved more and more like a proper old person and took to calling me 'dear' more often than 'my girl'.

I wish I could say that I regretted this loss of spirit in my mother's mother, but it just made me think that perhaps every not-very-nice person should have a character-forming nasty fall.

For instance, the QB. Maggie was now back in full-on mean-girl mode. I was pretty sure she'd seen me and Mark walking to the Eiffel Tower together, because ever since then she'd ignored me with a venom and intensity that could make one feel a bit sick.

You wouldn't think you could ignore someone viciously, but Maggie could do anything viciously. It was the way she looked through you, excluded you from a conversation with someone while you were actually having it, pushed ahead of you as if you didn't physically exist, talked to everyone about you as if you weren't there when you were standing right next to her.

No one can do these things as well as Maggie. No one.

And the fact is that when I wasn't dreaming about other ways in which Mark could rescue me (ways which always involved him having to put his arms round me), I was still having nightmares about what on earth it was that made him put his arm round Maggie that terrible day in the summer.

This particular Thursday was the day of the dress rehearsal with the boys of St Thomas's. Everyone involved was supposed to gather in the school hall at four o'clock for a complete run-through.

It was amazing how many people had developed a passion for Shakespeare that term. Those who didn't have actual parts queued up to be reserve fairies or handmaidens to the queen, or they volunteered to be assistant extra stand-by stage managers, or deputy junior costume assistants. A cynical person might think that the passion was not so much for Shakespeare as for the after-play party...

Amy was the only one of us not involved because

she was training for another big race. She had been annoyed that none of us had gone to see her run in the stadium, but being Amy and being super nice, her annoyance just took the form of her looking a little bit reproachfully at us. We all promised her that from then on we'd go and watch her run in all her important races. I think we really meant it.

But even Gemma had succumbed to Shakespeare at the last minute and offered her services as attendant to the fairy queen. (Perfect for her. Swan around onstage looking cool, but no need to learn any lines.) And Sally was – rather appropriately given how helpful she'd been to me – assistant prompter.

When we arrived at the school hall it looked weird. Not just because of all the props lying about, but because it was full of Boys. They looked so big and out of place, and they sounded so shouty and deep-voiced.

There were lots of them I didn't know, but one I did. As Gemma went off to say hello to a group of boys dressed in togas, and Sally went off to collect her script, I went to the back of the stage where Mark was talking to Miss Brewer.

He was wearing a rather grand red cloak over a black shirt and trousers. It made him look like a surreally modern Roman emperor. It also made him look particularly handsome. And even more handsome when he saw me and gave me one of his dimply smiles.

'Hi, Chloe,' he said. 'All bricked-up and ready for your big moment?' Miss Brewer, who I could see had been looking at Mark like a fond aunt at a favourite nephew, smiled at us.

Before I could answer, who should come and interrupt us but the props manager, AKA the Evil One. She was followed by two of her cohorts who were carrying various odd garments and objects.

'Marky!' she said in her best little-whiny-girl voice, almost elbowing Miss Brewer out of the way in her haste to get to him. 'I've got your special crown! Here, look! I think you could say it's fit for a king!' She said this in an extra-special flirty voice, as she looked up at him like a sickly adoring subject. Ugh.

She handed him a dark gold crown with lots of pointy bits and some pieces of red and blue plastic that on a dark night might almost be mistaken for bits of plastic made to look like jewels.

'Thanks, Maggie,' said Mark, and I regret to say that he smiled at her. Absolutely not a dimply smile. I'm sure it wasn't a dimply smile. But it definitely looked like a smile.

Then the QB turned to me. And another smile, this

time of pure malice came over her face. She glanced at her cohorts to make sure they were listening. 'And now for the wallflower,' she said, starting to cackle. 'See what I did there? Wallflower?' she said to them, starting to cackle even harder. They started to cackle too. As of course they had to.

And the next moment she'd thrust a brick into my hand and a sack. 'There!' she said with a giggle of glee. 'There's your costume. Enjoy!'

Even if I could think of something smart to say, which of course I couldn't, there wasn't time because Miss Brewer was summoning us to our starting places. I had to go off and join the other 'peasants', but not without noticing that Maggie had briefly stroked Mark's hand and said, 'Good luck, Your Majesty,' in a stomach-churningly coy tone.

And then we all had to concentrate. Mark as Theseus opened the proceedings and was, of course, commanding and wonderful. Plus he spoke the words so well that you could almost understand what they meant.

Most of the boys and all of the girls had actually learned their lines, and some of them even knew where to stand and how they were supposed to act. Which meant everything was proceeding so smoothly that we quickly got nearer and nearer to my cue.

I picked up the sack and started to put it over my head. And it was at that point that I realised that the sack must have been carefully and repeatedly dipped in dung. And not just any old dung, but the smelliest oldest pile of dung available. Although where dung would be available in an inner-city school I absolutely dreaded to think. But whatever it was, it was a terrible smell and I knew I smelt terrible all over once I'd put it on.

But it was too late to do anything about it. All had been going smoothly with the rehearsal, and I mustn't be the one to hold us up. I picked up my brick and went onstage...

I put the brick down and stood on it.

Ouch. There was something sharp sticking out of the brick. I looked down and saw a gigantic rusty nail. It had badly scratched the side of my foot, but seemed to have been designed to do even greater damage.

As I gasped at the pain, I still found time to wonder that it must have taken a helluva lot of admin to find a brick with a nail sticking out of it (how do you DO that unless you get someone to glue it on to a bit of concrete?).

You had to hand it to the QB: she was the best at her job.

But under the pretence of being a very clumsy stupid sort of Wall, I adjusted my brick, tripped a bit, and manage to stand on the brick with my other foot without touching the nail.

With a heroic effort (really heroic, in the truest sense) I gave my speech. And I was so heroic, that I even got the laughs.

And then of course Theseus/Mark has to say, 'Would you desire lime and hair to speak better?' I looked him in the eye as he said this. He was smiling, but he had a slightly concerned look beneath the smile.

The play went on. I hobbled offstage – entirely in character to be hobbling – and went in search of a chair backstage.

'That was good, Chloe,' said Gemma, who was backstage, taking her duties as handmaiden to the queen very lightly indeed. Then she looked properly at me. 'Hey, you all right? You like white as a sheet. Also you smell unbelievably disgusting.'

'I know,' I said, struggling to get the sack off me, 'and my foot is killing me. Maggie is SUCH a piece of work. Goddamn.'

Sally came backstage at that point. 'That was a

waste of time,' she said. 'Everyone knew their words. How boring is that?'

And then she looked at me with a curious expression on her face. 'WHAT,' she said, 'is that REVOLTING smell?'

'It's Chloe,' said Gemma. 'Maggie has cunningly managed to make her smell like a lavatory. Get a load of that piece of sacking.'

'Ugh, and double ugh,' said Sally, lifting it up to her nose in disgust.

'Plus my foot,' I said taking my shoe off and investigating the damage.

'You might need a tetanus injection, Chloe,' said Gemma. 'Rusty nail. God, the girl is trying to kill you!'

The rehearsal had finished by now and everyone was taking their costumes off and putting away the props.

I could see Mark disentangling himself from his red robe and crown and heading over towards me. I was in a quiet corner, so I took some finding. As he approached, the others tactfully disappeared.

'Chloe,' Mark said. 'Are you all right? It looked like you were really hobbling.' He started to sit down next to me and put his arm round me, but suddenly recoiled. 'Yeurch, Chloe,' he said, standing up again. 'What's going on? You smell very, very fruity. Is it that sack?'

'Yes,' I said looking up at him, already feeling better about it all because he was near me. Although not too near me, I couldn't help noticing. 'Maggie. Queen of props. Sabotage. Horrible smell, horrible nail in that brick. I don't know how I got through it.'

Mark took a deep breath and sat down next to me. 'God, I don't believe that girl. What a cow. Why ever would she do such a vile thing?'

'Because she hates me, I suppose,' I said. 'I think she can only be jealous. I mean,' I went on hastily because I didn't want him to think – well, I didn't know what I wanted him to think, 'I think she doesn't like you noticing anyone else, because she thinks that you're her boyfriend.' I looked him in the eye when I said this. It seemed that now was the time to finally get all this out in the open.

'I think,' I said, 'that she really does. And maybe you are. I mean why else would you come home early from holiday and go out with her secretly?' There. I'd said it.

'Go out with her?' said Mark, looking very puzzled. Or maybe it was just the brilliant actor in him. 'What do you mean go out with her? I can see what she is. I've always been able to see what she is. Why on earth would I want to go out with her?'

'I saw you,' I said, looking down at the floor. Which was covered in fluff as floors always seem to be in moments like this. 'I saw you on that Tuesday at the end of the holidays. You weren't supposed to be back, but I saw you at the football match. With Maggie.'

'Oh lord,' he said. 'Is THAT what all this is about? Oh, dear Chloe. I wish you'd said something at the time. And I'm sorry. I'm so sorry. I'm an idiot, but I can explain. I really can explain.' He looked thoughtfully at me.

'I dunno how you can explain,' I said slightly hysterically, as the pain in my foot was getting worse. 'You were out with my worst enemy. Secretly. And at a *football* match.'

'Exactly,' he said. 'It was Dad's treat to us all to get tickets for that match. It was a big deal. And he also got tickets for his clerk of chambers. And his clerk's got a niece called Maggie. I only discovered later that she'd bullied him into giving her the ticket that was meant for his wife. So, yes, she was there, she was part of our big party. And I was polite to her, but I can't stand her. How can I put it more plainly, Chloe? I. Can. Not. Bear. That. Girl.'

It was all such music to my ears, and I was within nanoseconds of forgiving all and falling into his arms (if he could bear the smell), but I couldn't let it go quite yet: 'But you had your arm round her. As you went into the ground, you did...' It felt all wrong to be saying this now, spoiling the moment, but I had to say it.

'So *that* was when you saw me,' said Mark. 'I *see*... Well, Maggie was dithering and dawdling and being so slow. She needed a push through the turnstiles. I remember that. She's such a piece of work, I think she was trying to separate us from the others. Oh dear, Chloe. What a positively Shakespearean misunderstanding!'

He put his arm round me. 'Now, how can I persuade you of all this? I am an idiot for not telling you that I was coming back early for the match, but I knew you'd hate the idea of going to football, so I just thought I'd quietly get on with it and see you properly two days later. But then you disappeared. Cut me off. And now I understand why.'

My foot by now was really beginning to hurt a great deal. But I was strangely able to bear it. I looked into Mark's eyes and I thought how could I have doubted the boy behind those eyes?

I leaned closer to him. He took my hand. 'Chloe,' he said, 'I really want to give you a big hug. At least a big hug...' He looked deep into my eyes. 'But the fact is you really do smell quite horrible, and I think we should get your foot looked at.' His dimply smile took the sting out of this unromantic comment.

'Come on,' he said, helping me to my feet. 'Let's get you to the nurse and then home and a shower.'

Together we hobbled – or I hobbled, Mark just held me helpfully but distantly – to the school First Aid. This was run by Nurse Watkins, a rather fearsome woman with buck teeth and a way of looking at you as if it were your fault there was anything wrong with you. As well as being deeply unsympathetic, she also had a harsh hand with the antiseptic. As she gave my foot a hard rub she told me to go to the doctor the following day if there were the slightest sign of infection.

She also told me that I had a severe hygiene problem and I'd best get the doctor to look at that too.

'Right then,' said Mark as we left the First Aid office. 'I'll come with you on the bus. That way I can make sure you don't get into any more scrapes, and I can say hello to your mum.'

He put his arm round me – wonderful, wonderful feeling, I could never tire of it – and guided me out of the main entrance.

Just at that very moment the QB came up the stairs from the side door.

The look on her face as she watched the two of us head out towards the bus stop was rather wonderful too.

Party Time

Mum and Gran had been dozing in their rooms when we'd got home, so we decided to save the reunion for another time.

I knew Mum would have been horrified to have a handsome, charming boy see her all dishevelled and sleepy, and besides I was in urgent need of painkillers and a shower.

So Mark said goodbye to me at the door. It was a gentle goodbye, an arms-round-me goodbye. With a slow, soft kiss at the end. It was such a perfect beautiful kiss I think I could easily have fainted from the ecstasy of it had my foot not hurt so much.

Mark smiled at me, wrinkling his nose, but not at all in a hurtful way. 'Get yourself cleaned up. We can finish this next time. See you on Saturday.'

I went with him to the street front door and watched

him walk down the road, with his quick confident step. When he turned round and waved I thought I just wanted to bottle the moment and keep it with me for ever. 'See you on Saturday' – what lovely words, what promise of togetherness.

Mum was looking out of her bedroom door when I got back in the flat.

'You look happy, love,' she said. 'You've straightened things out with Mark, haven't you? I'm so glad.'

'Me too,' I said, aware that I was grinning like a fool. 'But I've got to have a shower now, Mum. Long story, but don't get too near. You going to be all right to come to the play?'

'Yes, I think so, love. Not feeling too bad. But I've got a surprise for you. Come in,' and she opened the door a bit wider.

Her bedroom was dark and smelt of sleep, but when Mum turned the bedside light on, I could see a package in the corner of the room.

'It's your early Christmas present, love,' said Mum. 'I checked with Sally and I think they're the right ones.'

I went over to the package, trying hard to disguise my hobbling.

Dear Mum, I thought, as I threw off the paper and opened the box, even when she's in the middle of being ill she thinks about me. For there, glinting away as only the best black boots in the world can glint, were my chosen ones.

Oh, the irony of having the perfect fashion item for the foot when the foot has been scratched and scraped. But as I hugged Mum my thanks (a really good professional hug this time, and Mum was extra-heroic not to recoil at the smell of me), I thought that however swollen my foot, it is jolly well going to be jammed into my new boots for the after-play party.

The morning of the great Play Day had a good start from a completely unexpected quarter. Ghastly Ralph turned out to have a friend (that was unexpected in itself) in the building business. Which meant he had access to a clean sack – or as clean as things like sacks could get – and a large smooth brick.

As I arrived at the school with my new costume all wrapped up in a bag, I felt things were definitely on the up, and we'd be a theatrical triumph. Our *A Midsummer Night's Dream* was in the first half of the evening's programme; the second half was a performance by the Year Elevens of something from *The Merchant of*

Venice. Having checked out the plot of *The M of V*, I was quietly confident that we'd get a lot more laughs.

Sally was already in the hall when I arrived, sitting on the edge of the stage, staring even more intently than usual at her phone. She looked up when I went over to her.

'So here's the thing,' she said immediately without any sort of 'hellos' or 'how are you?' and 'how's the foot?' (Thanks to some of Mum's painkillers, it felt heaps better.) 'Rob says I can do the second set with Shedz at the party tonight. But I don't think I'm good enough but I can't admit it because I've told him how much I've been practising and I haven't really so what do you think I should do, Chloe?'

'I think,' I said, 'that you should say you're really nervous and he should sit right next to you just in case you get too nervous so he can take over. That way you can be all loving over the drums, and he can be all manly and save the day. And then you can be all grateful, and then you can dance off into the sunset when the DJ starts.'

Sally looked gratifyingly pleased with this, and more or less instantly started tapping away at her phone at high speed.

So she didn't see Gemma come up, looking rather

339

pale and a bit preoccupied.

'Hi, Gemma,' I said. 'What's up?' I reckoned I was on a roll with my problem-solving skills, and Gemma looked like she needed my help.

'Bit awkward that Jack and Jezza are both coming to the party tonight, and neither knows the other's going to be there,' said Gemma. This was a tricky one, and might be above my skill set. 'Plus Merv's been trapped all week with tax inspectors, and he's saying it's looking a bit difficult in a bit-difficult-going-to-prison sense.' Right. Well, that one was definitely above my skill set.

'Gawd,' I said helpfully.

'Gawd is about it,' Gemma said. 'But maybe it's time I made a decision about Jack. And maybe Mum can get Merv disentangled from the taxmen. She's supposed to be arriving there any minute.'

So it looked like Gemma didn't really need my help. Plus, so long as you had Marianne on your side, I was sure that anything was possible. Even getting Merv out of trouble with the Inland Revenue.

All the boys were starting to arrive for the afternoon dress rehearsal, so we were soon distracted and in our costumes.

Mark was late. This was because he had had to help

his mother with a puppy crisis. Apparently one of them had got trapped in the garden shed and would only respond to Mark's voice. I thought this was such a fine reason for being late for something, but Miss Brewer didn't seem to agree. As we stood around waiting for Theseus, she looked extremely testy. I think she was suffering first-night nerves.

But once we got started, everything went pretty much as it should do. The QB lurked about backstage, rather in the shadows. There was no attempt to chat up Mark, and no sign of her when I was putting on my nice new sack and gathering up my nice new brick.

Apart from Lysander tripping up on his toga and Titania forgetting her lines (Sally's big moment) Miss Brewer had every reason to be proud of her troop. And I think we were all in good heart when we went off to the canteen to get lots of sugar and salty things to keep our strength up for the big performance.

Lights. Camera. Action.

The darkness outside, the big signs in front of the school's main entrance, and the sound of people starting to arrive could almost make one feel nervous.

Members of staff and Year Twelves handed out programmes and ushered the audience to their seats, and as the rows and rows of chairs gradually filled up with lots and lots of grown-ups I realised that I actually *was* nervous.

'Look, Chloe,' said Sally as the noise of the audience got louder and louder as more and more people came in, 'what a lot of people. I'm glad I'm not in the play or I'd be feeling really nervous now.' And she looked at me expectantly, as if she wanted to see a shaking, sweating wreck. It's Sally and the baskets and the knitting thing again, I thought, sweating slightly. And then I noticed that the programme in my right hand was shaking.

'I'm going backstage,' I said. 'Going to find Mark.'

I went along the passage to the classrooms behind the stage which were our equivalent of 'backstage', and went over to Mark, who was standing in a corner, all red-robed up and looking at his copy of the play.

'Hi there,' he said as I came up to him. 'You feeling nervous?'

'Yup,' I said. 'I know I haven't got anything like as much as you to say, but I can't believe this sick feeling I've got.'

'Me too,' he said. 'Don't know why I'm looking at my

342

part, I either know it by now or I don't. Just nerves, I guess.' He put the papers down, and put his arm round me. 'Soon be over though,' he said with a grin.

I suddenly felt much better. Much, much better. AND my foot didn't hurt.

Seconds later, or that's what it felt like, all the lights went out, and the audience went quiet.

Then the stage lights came on, and Action...

As we got nearer and nearer to my bit, so far so good. Theseus was beautiful and brilliant, no one had fallen over or forgotten their lines, and the audience were paying attention – or at least from what I could hear backstage they weren't making any noise.

All was going according to Miss Brewer's plan.

I could hear the Prologue to my bit, and I picked up my brick and made my way to the steps of the stage. I climbed up to the top, and could feel everyone looking at me, onstage and off-, as I hobbled (no acting required there) my way to the centre of the stage.

With lots of fuss I put my brick down, and then stood on it. I looked up and out to the audience. In that second I could see Mum in the front row smiling and looking proud, next to Ralph, who was actually awake; behind them I could see Liv and her new ex-husband, next to her Patricia Anderson, and behind her I could see Marianne and Juliet, and at the end of the row Madame de B and her soldier husband, next to Jack Harrington and Amy and Charlie.

For a moment I felt utterly unnerved by the realisation that the audience was full of actual individual people. And then I pulled myself together, got out my best West-Country accent and started.

'In this same interlude, it doth befall,' and I was off.

As the audience gave a proper laugh at my wobbly brick routine, everything seemed to fall into place. And as I went off the stage – with my now-perfect Peasant Hobble – I even started to imagine myself at drama school with Spindly Ethan. And then, watching Mark's final speech from the wings and listening to him tell us about the 'iron tongue of midnight' I went all tingly all over again. Such authority, such elegance, such a beautiful voice. Plus he DID look great in that red cloak.

The clapping and stamping and bravos that greeted the end of our play were wonderful and exciting and exhilarating. We'd done it! But mostly I was so relieved it was over and that it had gone all right, and here I was lining up with the rest of the cast and taking a bow. Incredibly, and whether it was my doing or his I didn't know, I'd ended up standing next to Mark, so we were actually holding hands as we bowed.

It was lovely.

And it was also lovely in the interval. Lovely to be surrounded by all the people who mattered most to me, and to be told we'd done well. Not just Mum ('It was wonderful, love, you were the star of the show') and Amy and Charlie, who you could always rely on, but also Liv ('That was good, Chloe, surprisingly funny') and the awe-inspiring Marianne and her other half, Juliet.

At one point I was standing next to Marianne (who, according to Gemma, had gone through all Merv's paperwork and told him where he'd gone wrong. She'd left him with two days' solid work, but less chance of actually going to prison) and Juliet, when up came Patricia Anderson and Georgie.

'Chloe,' said Patricia. 'That was great fun. Difficult to pull off a Shakespeare "clown" part. Well done.'

'And didn't you think, Mum,' said Georgie, 'that brother dear did well? Looking very handsome in that red cloak, eh, Chloe?' And she looked me full in the eye, and smiled the smile of a co-conspirator. It gave me an extra inner glow, this approval from his amazing and wonderful family.

If only Albert – now in danger of being ousted from his role of most-reliable-male-in-my-life – had been there to give me an approving bark, the moment would have been perfect.

Two hours later and it was hard to believe we were in the same hall. Instead of Shakespeare, the air was filled with the sound of Shedz. And I do mean filled. It was impossible to hear yourself think or anyone else speak. It reminded me a tiny bit of the disastrous school dance the year before last.

But only a tiny bit. Because this time, instead of standing alone in an island of despair, watching my friends have a horrible time in their different ways, this time I was standing in the corner holding hands with the Duke of Athens.

I could have stood there all night. Noisy or not. Foot poundingly painful in my lovely boots or not. Nothing really mattered compared to the feel of his hand in mine.

I might almost have been thinking all this out loud, because as I looked up at him, probably with some kind of stupid smile on my face, he looked down at me, and gave me a quick kiss.

I smiled even more stupidly and then reached up

and said in his ear, 'Sally on the drums for this next bit. Could go either way.'

We threaded our way through the crowd in order to get nearer to Shedz, who were on the stage.

On the way, we bumped into Gemma. She was looking amazing. Whoever said 'less is more' when it comes to make-up, had never seen Gemma in full rig-out. She was dancing with Jack, who also looked pretty amazing.

She smiled at us and jerked her head over towards the door. Following her glance I could see a despondent-looking Jezza leaning against a pillar. He looked angry but so miserable that I really did find it in my heart to feel sorry for him.

As I watched him, I saw the QB go up to him, obviously in full-flirt mode. She, too, was in full make-up, but it didn't seem to be having the desired effect on the Scottish one. Jezza was looking down at her with an expression of – well, if not actual disgust then at least disdain.

Still holding Mark's hand we were pushed forward so I couldn't see the end of the story, but it really did look like the QB might have to dance with herself. As we strained to see what was going on in the drum section of Shedz, I found it very, very hard to find the slightest bit of me that felt even slightly sorry for Maggie. The Queen Beeyatch.

There was a pause in the music, during which we managed to make our way to the front so we could see the band. It started up again just as we could see what was happening. Sally was sitting at the drums, but Rob was sitting so close to her, practically holding her hands as she hit the drums and cymbals. As we watched he gradually and gently took over. And Sally moved out of his way, smiling at him in a rather goofy fashion, I thought.

And then I thought: I know that smile. It's exactly the same as the one on my own face. I looked up at Mark. He was smiling down at me. And I think I have to say that his smile was a little bit goofy too.

He bent down and put his lips on mine.

If it weren't for the fact that it makes no sense, I would say that at that moment we were the only two people in the hall, and the moment would last for ever.

Acknowledgements

As always and ever, I owe a great debt to my agent Caroline Sheldon. She is simply the best.

I'm also hugely indebted to the lovely people at Orchard Books, especially Megan Larkin, and my editor, Anna Solemani, whose professionalism and editorial sensitivity have made this fussy author very happy.

Particular thanks, too, to my American friends – Patty, Catharine, Emily, Avery and Abby – for their hospitality and help, and to all my British ones who have cajoled, encouraged, entertained and generally made my life as Chloe a joy. Couldn't do it without you all!

About the author

Chloe Bennet is the pen name of Val Hudson, a former publisher and editor responsible for a number of famous bestsellers over the years. She used to love spending her time helping other people write. Now, through writing the *Boywatching* series, she has discovered that it's more fun to do it herself.

Coming soon:

BOYWATCHING...SEASON THREE

Christmas is over, and with Mark away on a French exchange for half of the spring term, Chloe must find something else to take her mind off Boy Watching.

Enter Oscar, Mark's handsome but awkward cousin. Can Chloe succeed in transforming him into a suave, girlfriended gent – in time for Mark's return?

Can the Bennets keep it together in the face of Mum's treatment and Gran's hideous china doll collection?

Will the girls' friendships survive amidst all the broken hearts, promises and toes?

And finally...with Mr Underwood announcing he wants to leave the country, what will happen to Albert...?

Boywatching...Season Three –
the hilarious and heartwarming sequel.